MALICE

CORALEE JUNE

CORALEE JUNE

Copyright © 2021 by June Publishing
All rights reserved.
No part of this book may be reproduced in any form or by any electronic or mechanical means, including information storage and retrieval systems, without written permission from the author, except for the use of brief quotations in a book review.

MALICE

Dedication:
For Ruth.

CORALEE JUNE

chapter one

The night I killed a man, it was blistering hot outside. It felt like hell was bubbling up and drowning the grimy Kansas City streets with fire.

The air-conditioning at Dick's Diner was broken, so it smelled like body odor and breakfast. My boss was a cheap bastard who didn't care if we were sweating our asses off. We had every window in the place open and prayed for a midnight breeze.

"This coffee tastes like shit, Juliet!" Rick, one of our regulars, shouted at me as I passed by.

My annoyance erupted into a loud huff. "You order

the same shitty coffee every night, Rick. If you hate it so much, stop ordering it," I snapped back. These customers didn't come here for the service or the shitty food. They came here because they had nowhere else to go. We were a diner poised in the hearts of those who lived, breathed, and died in this town. We were a poor man's paradise with scratched vinyl booths and burnt food.

Rick took a sip of said shitty coffee and rolled his eyes at me. My spine was slickened with sweat, making my work uniform cling to me. I almost didn't show up for my shift, but Grams's meds needed refilling, and they weren't cheap. Sinemet sure was an expensive ass drug, and the side effects were a bitch: nausea, dizziness, confusion, and hallucinations, to name a few. It often made me wonder if the treatment for Parkinson's was worse than the disease itself.

"It's hot as hell in here," another customer complained while fanning themselves. I grimaced. A busted AC meant pissy customers, and pissy customers meant no tips. No tips meant my trip to our local pharmacy this week would be fraught with tears, anxiety, and begging.

A sticky tiled floor held the bottoms of my stained, black tennis shoes as I clutched the carafe full of coffee. My short black skirt was riding up, and the top of my tank was stained with tomato sauce. Every muscle in my body ached from being on my feet all day. I was fairly athletic and curvy, but by the end of my shift, I was ready to get off my feet. Salty sweat kept dripping into my brown eyes, and my long brown hair was soaked. I needed a shower and a vacation.

A strong, stoic guy sat crammed in the middle booth. His muscular body was almost too big for the seat. The red vinyl he sat on was faded and ripped, a striking contradiction to his crisp Armani suit. He had a large skull tattoo on his neck, and bulging veins that pulsed. That rigid spine of his was like steel. He seemed frustrated tonight. Rogue huffs of annoyance escaped his lips every three minutes, making everyone within earshot aware of how mad he was. His arms were crossed over his chest, and he had shades on his hard face, despite it being eleven o'clock at night. He wore those Gucci sunglasses like a mask.

"You sure are huffing and puffing up a storm tonight," I observed, knowing damn well he wouldn't respond. He never responded. "Is it the AC? You know, you could take off that suit jacket you're wearing. It's miserably hot in here, and that added layer is probably making it worse. I'd strip naked, but it's not that kind of place. I'd probably get better tips that way, though."

He grumbled and shifted in his seat.

"Or not," I quickly added. He watched as I poured him a cup. "How was your day?" I asked playfully. No response. I paused, pretending like he was actually speaking and not just silently willing me to leave him alone. "You don't say?" He was like a silent wall. Nothing amused him. Nothing intrigued him. "I swear, Stranger. You sure are chatty tonight."

The man had sweeping, light brown hair, a jaw sharp as a blade, and a scabbed cut just above his brow. He looked just a bit older than me, but carried this incredible weight of experience that made him seem timeless. He was handsome, in a devious kind of way.

Dangerous and observant, he sat in the same spot in the same booth every Thursday night. Despite the terrifying familiarity, I didn't know his name. I didn't know who he was. I just knew that he had a job to do. His nose flared in annoyance.

He wasn't here for the mediocre food or to breathe in the Americana air and get grease splatters on his button-up shirt, he was here to protect my best friend: Vicky.

I rarely spoke to him but was feeling bold tonight. "Enjoy your coffee," I said with a bright smile. He licked his lips and hunched over the cup like my attention made him uncomfortable. It was one of our unwritten rules: I ignored Vicky's bodyguard, and she ignored the dark circles under my eyes.

"Are you done taunting my shadow?" Vicky asked in a brief tone. "I don't know why you bother giving him coffee, he is such a snob. Prefers the finest Australian roast." Across the table sat my best friend. She was picking at a plate of french fries with her fork and had a blank expression on her face. She wore all black. She had a black choker necklace with a single diamond in the middle on her long, slender neck. Flared black jeans ripped at the knees. A black T-shirt. Black eyeliner. And a black watch wrapped around her wrist. Her pale blond hair was tied up in a classic bun—with a black elastic band, of course—and her glossy lips were pressed into a thin line.

I couldn't imagine my silent stranger being a coffee snob, but now that I thought of it, he never did touch the food or coffee I put in front of him.

"I'm just trying to stay awake. I'm dead on my feet tonight," I replied with a lengthy sigh. I needed a full night's sleep and some hard-core self-care. Maybe even a self-induced orgasm or two.

It was my best friend's nature to be arrogant and destructive. Her nails were always perfectly manicured, and her porcelain skin never was marked up from work. The makeup on her eyes was always smeared, as if she put it on in the morning with the intention of feeling fierce but had cried it off by midday. Tonight, she looked tired and bored. I was supposed to get off work an hour ago so we could chat, but Candy, one of the other waitresses here, had to go home early to take care of her sick kid. I was covering her shift until midnight.

"You know you don't have to stay here," I said in a low voice. It was embarrassing that my extravagant friend had to meet me at this dump once a week. "I'm sorry I have to work later. I tried to text you, but—"

Vicky rolled her eyes and stole her silent companion's untouched mug of coffee. "I don't mind waiting here. It's better than going home," she replied in a soft, faraway voice. It was on the tip of my tongue to ask her what was wrong, but I swallowed my concern and let it boil in the acid of my stomach. There were three rules for being best friends with a Mafia princess.

1. Don't ask any personal questions.

2. Don't show up at her house unannounced.

3. Don't ever, ever let anyone know you're friends.

"I get off at midnight. I need to get home and check on Grams, so I probably won't be able to talk for too long."

Vicky waved her hand. "It's okay. I'm used to watching you work your cute little butt off all hours of the night in this poor excuse of a diner. It's painfully normal, and I love it. Shut up and go give that creeper in the corner some coffee before he stabs you in the parking lot. Actually, that might be kind of cool. You could feature him on your podcast." She nodded in the direction of the man she mentioned, and I followed her gaze. He had a seventies mustache and wore a stained shirt.

"I could interview him mid stab," I replied while

wagging my eyebrows. "Brilliant." Not a lot of people got our dark humor, but then again, not a lot of people grew up surrounded by death and danger.

Vicky was intrusive. She was the type of person to bulldoze her way into anything. Our becoming BFFs started because she decided that we were friends. There was nothing organic about our bond. It was forced. It was all-encompassing. It was perfect.

We met at a cemetery three years ago, a grim start to a beautiful friendship. I was doing research on a cold case and wanted to take some photos of a victim's tombstone for my true crime podcast. I stumbled upon her crying at her mother's grave. I might not have had a tombstone to weep at, but we found common ground regardless. She decided we were friends right on the spot, and I just kind of went along with it because Vicky intimidated me. I vividly remember my first impression of her. Vicky seemed strong and gorgeous and outgoing. She simply grabbed my hand, waltzed us out of the cemetery, and informed me that we would meet there again the following Thursday. We'd been meeting every Thursday ever since.

I checked on the two occupied tables in the diner, making sure they didn't need anything, before wiping down the counter and heading back to Vicky and her bodyguard.

"Sit down," she said while patting the seat next to her. "We have fifteen minutes before your shift ends, and I want to soak up as much time as possible with you."

I slid into the booth and ignored the grumpy guy sitting across from us. I learned early on that I just had to get used to talking about my life while someone blatantly listened in. It wasn't so bad. He was stone cold, an emotionless statue that never responded. Even when I told Vicky about the time I lost my virginity, he never said a word. He never reacted. He knew just as much about me as Vick did. Sometimes I wondered what he thought about me.

"So, how was your last podcast?" Vicky asked with a grin.

"The podcast did great," I beamed. "I'm up to fifty subscribers."

Vicky pinched her lips together, trying desperately not to laugh. "A whole fifty, huh?"

"Your best friend is a celebrity, Vick," I teased. I ran a very small passion project podcast where I talked about true crime. What started as a coping mechanism turned into an obsession. I might not know what happened to my own mother, but I found closure by researching and discussing other victims. "I got an email about it, actually. A legit fan email."

Vicky curled her fist and rested it under her chin. "What did they want?" She leaned in excitedly.

"Well, you know how this week was about the 1946 Phantom Killer?" I asked.

"Of course," Vicky lied. "I listen to all your super, hella creepy-as-fuck podcasts right before bed so I can have awesome nightmares." She gave me a broad grin to accentuate her point.

Her bodyguard cleared his throat.

I replied with a smile, placing my hand over my chest. "Thank you for your dedication to my passion project. Anyway. I got an email from Clownboner78@gmail.com asking me if I wanted to suck his phantom cock."

Vicky tipped back her head and laughed. "What does that even mean?" she choked out through bursts of bright laughter.

"I think he has a ghost dick," I deadpanned. "I kind of want to see it."

"You should absolutely marry this man. Then you can have little ghost babies."

I grabbed her hands and giggled. "You'll be my maid of honor, right?"

The conversation turned serious when Vicky replied, "I'd be offended if you didn't ask, and then I'd kill whoever you picked instead of me." I forced a smile and giggled, not sure if she was joking or not.

"Oh my Hemsworth!" she exclaimed. "I wouldn't actually do that!"

"That's what all the murderers say. Maybe I'll pick someone else for my phantom cock wedding just so you'll kill them, and I'll have an epic story for my podcast," I replied jokingly.

"Then you'll have fifty-one subscribers!" she replied with a wink.

We both laughed once more, and I felt the weight of my stressful week melt from my body. Vicky and I only spent one day per week together, but it was very precious to me. Our time together meant a great deal to me.

I didn't let very many people in. Most of the time, it was Grams and I against the world. I'd just graduated high school a few weeks ago and couldn't tell you anything personal about my peers. Don't get me wrong, I could force a smile and make small talk with the best of them, but at the end of the day, I kept my circle small. It was easier that way. The fewer people you had in your heart, the fewer opportunities you had for loss.

"How's your Grams?" Vicky then asked. My good humor slipped, and her bodyguard tilted his head to listen to my answer. Always listening, my stranger.

"Her Parkinson's is getting bad. She dropped a pot of water the other day, and I was so freaked out. Thank fuck she hadn't started cooking yet. What if it was boiling? I can't ever tell if it's her medicine making her sick or her actual Parkinson's. And her doctor is a piece of shit. It's hard getting an appointment, and then he sits with her for two minutes. Barely asks her any questions, then writes a prescription and sends us a bill."

Vicky reached out and patted my arm. She had a vacant look in her eyes, but her mouth was twisted into a pitied frown. "I can't imagine how hard that is."

I cleared my throat. "I'm just constantly worried about her falling. She has more good days than bad, but I get anxious. I started making all her meals for the day in the morning."

"Have you considered that place we talked about? You're going to have to find something before you go to college," Vicky asked. She'd brought me a brochure for an assisted living place for Grams a few weeks ago. Eventually, my grandmother would need a lot more help. Parkinson's was a nasty disease that affected her nervous system. She trembled constantly and was already struggling to speak.

The brochure was nice, and I even took the bus there to look around last week. But the truth was, even if I could afford a place like that, I didn't feel like I could leave her. Grams took me in after Mom...disappeared. She held me the night Mom didn't show up after her shift at the grocery store. She dragged me to the police department when we couldn't get a hold of her the next morning. She called the news stations when the police didn't prioritize Mom's missing persons case. She helped me research. Grams never gave up on Mom. She was my greatest advocate and protector. I didn't want to abandon her now.

"They have a spa and a twenty-four-hour nurse. She'd have her own apartment, and the food apparently is amazing," Vicky added, proud of herself for researching.

The home was also seven thousand dollars a month. I didn't have that kind of money. I refused to tell Vicky that I was already planning on attending college part-time online so I could stay home and take care of Grams. My best friend was so determined for me to go out and make something of myself. I wanted the full college experience, but it just wasn't an option for me. "I went to look at it," I replied.

"And you loved it, right?" she asked with bright eyes.

The bodyguard shifted in his seat and grumbled something under his breath.

"I'm really thankful you took the time to research that," I evaded. Vicky liked being helpful, she just sometimes lived in her own dream world of opportunity. We were from opposite sides of town. Money wasn't really a problem for her.

"I love you, girl! It's what I'm here for."

"So...Diamond? Was that his name?" I asked, changing the subject. Vicky devoured boyfriends like I devoured true crime stories. She attended a private school downtown and always had stories about parties in empty mansions with stupid teens fucking on every surface. It was something I wished I could do. I graduated from the high school by my house where we had metal detectors on all the doors and bomb threats on Fridays.

"He wanted to hang out too much," she replied with a wave of her hand and a huff. "We were having fun, but then he wanted...more."

That seemed to be a common theme with Vicky. She could never let people get too close. Never let them into the fold. Although we were best friends in all the ways that mattered, there was still a lot I didn't know about her personal life. Part of that was because she grew up in the mob. For my safety, she didn't talk about her family or where she lived. She didn't want anything to come back to me. We didn't text or call often. We just had these brief moments of surface-level love. I guess, unlike the guys she dated, I was okay with the scraps. It was better than having nothing.

It was better than being completely alone.

"So who is your next victim?" I asked.

Her bodyguard grumbled once more and tapped the Rolex on his wrist. "It's time, Vicky." I snapped my attention to him with wide eyes. It was the first time I'd ever heard him speak.

And oh, man, his voice was deep but smooth. It was the kind of voice that melted panties clear off a woman. "You can talk?" I asked incredulously. He pulled off his sunglasses and stared at me for a lingering moment, his brown eyes piercing into mine. I swallowed. Having his full attention on me made my stomach do a flip.

Vicky cleared her throat and looked down at the table. I tore my eyes from her nameless bodyguard and stared at her with concern. "I'm not going to be dating for a while, Juliet."

Well, that was a surprise. "Oh? Taking a break from dick appointments?"

She frowned. "I'm taking a break from a lot of things. I...I have to do something for my family. I actually wanted to talk to you about it today..."

She wouldn't look me in the eye, but I sensed she was about to drop something big. "What's going on? Are you okay?"

"I can't meet up on Thursdays anymore, Juliet," she whispered.

I flinched. Surely I had misinterpreted what she said. "What? Why? What? You can't go a week without seeing my face. Stop fooling around." I nudged her wryly.

She shook her head. "I'm not joking. I can't tell you what's going on. It's just...it's not safe right now."

Her bodyguard slapped some money on the counter for their food, a sign that they were about to leave. "Are you in danger? Wait. When will I see you again?"

Vicky scooted out of the booth and wiped her eyes. "I promise to text you when it's safe. I didn't want to upset you, but I wanted to tell you in person."

"You haven't told me anything, Vick," I replied with a scowl. "Come on. It's me. Are you ending our friendship?" Panic rushed through my body. She was leaving me? Would she really do that?

She grabbed her purse and looked at me with glossy eyes. "I'll text you when it's safe again." What in the ever-loving whiplash?

Vicky and her bodyguard started walking out the door, and I followed after them. I started to cry while calling at her back. "Are you even going to hug me goodbye? We're best friends, Vicky. I've followed your rules. I never pressured you. I kept your secrets."

She paused and spun on her heel, hot tears streaming down her cheeks. I stood there dumbfounded as she wordlessly approached me. "I love you," she whispered before wrapping me up in a huge hug. I squeezed her tightly, a billion questions burning on my tongue.

"Just tell me what's going on, Vicky," I whispered.

She squeezed me tighter before pulling away. "Thank you for making me feel normal, Juliet."

I looked at her bodyguard, a man I'd seen weekly for the last three years but barely knew. He had a sad expression on his face that I didn't understand.

"Don't do this," I pleaded. He averted his eyes, a surprising flash of pain flickering across his expression.

Vicky was about to leave me crying there on the hot asphalt when a convoy of Mercedes-Benzes came peeling into Dick's parking lot.

"Shit," Vicky cursed before standing in front of me, like a human shield.

"Shit," her bodyguard echoed.

chapter two

"Shit," I muttered under my breath as the car doors jerked open and throngs of men in suits poured out.

I tried to count how many people there were, but they faded in and out of the night air like shadows. There could have been twelve or a hundred. Their presence was massive and intimidating, and not being able to see clearly added to the complete terror of it all.

"Go inside, Juliet," Vicky whispered urgently.

Yeah, no. Like hell I was going to go inside; I had a very strong sense that running would draw even more attention to me. I'd be like a fish in a barrel. Not to mention, I wasn't a total coward. I might not have known this world, but I wasn't about to let my best friend face whatever this was alone.

I would not abandon my friend.

I watched in awe at the dangerous synchronicity of them. Their suits were all in varying shades of black and charcoal gray. Their leather shoes were polished and pristine. I only saw a couple of women in the bunch, but they wore outfits similar to the other men, as if the expensively tailored designer suit was some sort of work uniform.

"You have to go, Juliet," she whispered.

Sensing that Vicky's life was in danger, I planted my feet firmly on the asphalt, waiting. I wasn't ignorant about the Kansas City mob and what they were capable of. I didn't exactly know her family's rank in the system, but the fact that she had a bodyguard following her around was enough to assume that she was important in their organization—or important to somebody.

Despite the hot night, a chill slithered down my spine, and I fought that instinctual, overwhelming sense to flee. It wasn't until one of the middle cars opened and a tall man stepped out of the idling vehicle that my breath caught in my chest.

He was...beautiful. Terrifyingly so.

Blond hair swept to the side. Plush lips. Broad shoulders and a muscular build. He towered over everyone and had the sort of presence to make you sit up and take notice. "Fuck," Vicky cursed. "There's no escaping this now."

"What do you mean?" I murmured as she pressed closer to me, her back colliding with my chest. She wrapped her arms back and around me while tilting her chin up defiantly. Her bodyguard stood his ground and was on alert, but for the first time in my life, I noted a submissive slump in his shoulders, as if he too feared what was coming for us.

It was easy to tell that the man stalking toward us was in charge. It was like an energy shift. Everyone turned to stare at him. They moved when he moved, breathed when he breathed. I found the entire experience to be very... ethereal since they were so perfectly in tune with each other. It was like the entire world spun at his command.

"William," the blond man greeted. His voice was rough and rugged. Polite, controlled. He didn't raise his voice over the night air, he spoke like a man used to the world bending closer to hear what he had to say. Every syllable dripping from his lips was a luxury.

"Nicholas," Vicky's bodyguard replied before walking forward. The two men embraced. The hug looked forced but still comfortable, as if they'd practiced the move at political events to prove something.

William? William?! Vicky's bodyguard's name was William?

I blinked a couple times while rolling the name around in my mind. My secret stranger, my fly on the wall, the man who knew everything about me by association had a name. Knowing this and hearing his voice all in one night made him feel more real.

I couldn't really bask in the realization of this, because they started mumbling something to one another, then turned to look at me. Waves of terror hit me like a thunderbolt.

"Vicky. You sure do know how to stir up trouble," the blond man—Nicholas—said. My best friend cleared her throat at his words.

She replied wryly, "Nicholas, you sure know how to be a giant pain in my ass." He looked amused for a split second, but his expression morphed into controlled anger. Vicky then looked around at the line of cars parked around us and sighed. "Did you seriously need to bring the entire caravan for this?"

Her question was met with an annoyed huff. "I just wanted to make sure you weren't running away from your responsibilities," he replied coolly. "Show me who you have hiding behind your back."

"No." Vicky's response was swift, forceful, and full of venom. "Not happening, Nicholas."

He bit the inside of his cheek and glared. Apparently, this blond man was not used to being defied. I peeked at him from behind Vicky, and his unnaturally bright eyes flamed with anger. "I think you forget who is in charge here," he said, punctuating each word with fierce power.

"I think you forget that you're my brother and not some prison warden." Brother? They were related? After spending the last three years in this odd friendship limbo where I wasn't allowed to know anything about Vicky's private life, it was such a strange sensation to now be meeting her brother. Staring at him, I saw hints of their similar traits. Their sharp nose. His fierce eyes and long legs. But if they were family, why was Vicky trembling? She turned to look at her bodyguard—William—and shook her head. "And you? Sometimes, I think you care about me. Other times, I wonder how on earth we're related. I thought you cared too, William. Don't lie and tell me you don't."

I was so confused but too frightened to do or say anything. I chewed on my lip as they exchanged a silent standoff. I wanted to see if the people in the diner were watching or if they'd turned their attention elsewhere. Everyone knew not to mess with the mob. Even if I'd never interacted with them outside of my visits with Vicky, I knew to keep to myself. If you see something, say nothing. I didn't survive in the bad part of town by putting my nose in other people's business. It's why Vicky trusted me so much.

My cheap phone started to ring. The shrill sound broke

through the ominous silence, and I cursed. There was only one person who would be calling me right now. Grams.

I felt everyone's attention on me, and Nicholas grinned. "Are you going to answer that?"

I swallowed. I had a brief moment to think over my options. As bravely as I could, I quipped, "I didn't want to offend you."

William's eye twitched. Vicky wrapped her body tighter against mine. My phone continued to scream into the night air. "Please, be my guest," Nicholas replied maliciously. This felt like a trick that I wanted no part of.

But still...

Perhaps it was because of my mother's disappearance that I struggled to ignore my grandmother's phone calls. I never wanted my Grams to wonder or worry if I was okay. Not knowing what happened to Mom meant that we were forced to perpetually worry about her for the rest of our lives. I needed to work on it, but it made me anxious to not answer. Besides, if I was about to die, then I wanted to talk to my Grams first. I pulled my cell with the cracked screen out of my bra and quickly answered it.

"Hey, Grams. You okay?"

"Juliet, is that you?"

"Yes, Grams, it's me. Are you okay?" I stared at the pavement but heard footsteps walking toward me.

"I-I can't remember when...you're coming home. I was

worried."

Grams's voice was worn and full of concern. She was the type of woman to call before a thunderstorm to make sure you stayed inside. And if you didn't call her to let her know that you arrived at your destination, she'd give you a stern talking-to.

"I'm okay, Grams. Just working late. You didn't have to stay awake. Why don't you go to sleep, and I'll…"

Nicholas looked menacing as he marched closer to Vicky and me. I instinctively knew my call would be cut short the moment he got to his destination.

"I'm going to make us breakfast. I know waffles are your favorite. But I can't find the syrup. And someone took all the knobs off my stovetop," Grams complained, oblivious to the chaos I was smack dab in the middle of. I wanted to tell not to worry about me.

My mouth cracked into a manic smile. What the fuck was happening? "I'll cook you waffles as soon as I get home, okay? I've got a customer. Call you later. Love you."

"L-love you too."

I hung up and let out a shaky exhale. "Sorry," I said softly before bracing myself for what was to come.

"Who are you?" Nicholas asked.

"None of your motherfucking business," Vicky snapped before letting go of me to get in her brother's face. "Why do you have to fucking ruin everything? You come here with your army of thugs and try to scare my friends. Not everyone is the enemy, Nick!" she screamed. I went rigid from the tension.

Nicholas cracked his knuckles slowly. One by one—crack, crack, crack. The sound made me tremble. It was so meticulous and calm, with a frightening edge to every movement. Then, with a move so swift I almost missed it, he quickly backhanded my best friend. Neither of us had time to even process what just happened. It was brutal and quick. She fell down and hit her forehead against the hard concrete.

"What the fuck?" I hissed in a whisper before crouching beside her to make sure she was alright. In an instant, Vicky shot up to a sitting position, and like a seasoned badass, she wiped at the blood on her face and glared at him.

Hands threaded through my hair, and I was yanked off the ground before I could even check on Vicky. My scalp burned, and I was pulled tight against Nicholas's body. "Who is this?" Nicholas asked William.

"Just a waitress," William lied.

"Just a waitress? Oh, well, in that case." With his free hand, Nicholas pulled a glock that was strapped to his side and pressed the barrel against my cheek. The cool metal of the gun bruised my skin, and I cried out. The grip he had on my hair didn't waiver. I squeezed my eyes shut and whimpered, too frozen from fear to do anything. "You don't care if I kill the bitch then, right?"

"Please stop, Nicholas," Vicky choked out. I opened my eyes and stared at the three of them, not sure what to say or what even was the problem. I always thought Vicky was keeping me a secret because of her enemies, but I had no idea she was related to a monster. "She's my friend, Nick," she admitted, this time her tone soft and familiar.

William took a step closer to us. Nicholas's grip on my hair loosened just a little bit, but it was enough to feel a semblance of relief. "A friend, huh? Civellas don't have friends. We have enemies and business partners. I should blow her fucking brains out just to teach you a lesson."

"I didn't tell her anything about our family," Vicky promised. "Ask William, he's been with me every time we meet up."

"Every time, huh?" Nicholas asked before moving the barrel of the gun to my bottom lip. He pressed it hard and stared at my face. "Tell me, William. Why have you been keeping this hot little secret from me?" My mouth was so dry that my tongue involuntarily darted out to lick my lips, but instead I brushed it along the metal of the gun. It tasted like copper and smoke. Nicholas stared at my mouth, and I watched his Adam's apple bob up and down.

"Vicky needed a friend after Mom died," William explained calmly. "You remember how bad it was."

"That was three goddamn years ago. She got a

prescription for Prozac and was fine."

"She wasn't fine, Nicholas. You know that. When they became friends, I noticed that Vicky was doing better. I started tagging along to make sure Vick didn't say something she shouldn't. It was harmless."

"If it was harmless, then you wouldn't be keeping it a secret from me. You know we have a rat. I just didn't realize you were feeding it cheese right under my nose."

"She's not the rat!" Vicky yelled.

"And you're not trustworthy!" he yelled back.

"Fuck you. It's not like you usually pay attention to what I do, Nicholas," Vicky replied. "Apparently, you only care what I'm up to when it affects your profits."

"You're supposed to be on a plane to Italy in four hours. Forgive me for making sure you did what you're supposed to. You have this nasty, selfish habit of doing whatever the fuck you want, consequences be damned."

"Italy?" I asked before immediately slamming my lips together. I didn't mean to speak. I wasn't exactly sure how to get out of this. My friendship with Vicky was supposed to be this carefree thing, an escape from both of our lives.

Nicholas looked at me, anger written across his expression. "Do you know Cora, little waitress?" he asked, his voice dark and threatening.

I shook my head. "I don't know anyone by that name."

"Liar!" he boldly exclaimed before pulling my hair

harder. "You thought you could just sneak right in and tell all my secrets? Cora is going to learn not to fuck with me."

Tears started streaming down my face. "I don't know Cora. I don't know what you're talking about," I cried out.

"Hale!" Nicholas called before spinning me to face him. Both his hands wrapped around my arms, and he squeezed tight. Up close, I could breathe his whiskey breath. Hear each exhale. The stubble on his sharp chin was so close I could run my tongue along his jaw. It was like staring at the sun for too long. I couldn't blink, could barely breathe. I was both in awe and completely terrified all at once. We stared at one another as a large man approached. I gasped when Nicholas pressed his body against mine. Hard planes of muscle collided with every soft curve of my flesh. Goose bumps broke out on my skin.

"Yes, boss?"

"Take her to the dead basement. Call Anthony and tell him I'll have a new body for him soon. This diner looks like a family establishment, and I don't want to stain their parking lot with blood. I'm nice like that, aren't I, Vick?"

"No," my best friend cried out. A stunned scream traveled up my throat but was stunted by the force of a gun slamming into my right temple. I blinked twice, I cried out, and I collapsed into the arms of Satan himself.

CORALEE JUNE

chapter three

Dried blood stuck to my chilled skin. It was so cold that my teeth chattered, a stark difference to the heat outside. The air-conditioning overhead was on full blast, sending an icy breeze over my exposed flesh. My shirt was gone, but luckily I still had on my miniskirt, a bra, and underwear. Tight ropes that bound my wrists together behind my back were rough, rubbing my skin raw. I was on the hard concrete floor but couldn't see much of anything. Everything about this room felt designed to humiliate me and draw out some sort of psychological torture. Heavy chains weighed me down and kept me tethered to the floor. I didn't know how long I'd been here. My bladder felt impossibly full, and pretty soon I'd have to piss myself.

My approach to trauma was clinical in nature. I didn't scream when I woke up bound and alone. I didn't cry. I didn't hyperventilate. I analyzed the situation in such a detached way that my dormant terror clawed at my soul, aching to get out. Perhaps it was a lifetime of seeing the world through the eyes of a pessimist. Maybe I'd expected this to one day happen to me. Since my mother's disappearance, I'd been preparing for the evil of the world to snatch me, too.

My mind raced over trivial things to cope. For some reason, I couldn't stop thinking about my lunch shift. Had I already missed it? As more time passed, I worried about Vicky. I worried about my Grams. I worried that I wouldn't make it out of this goddamn place alive.

She'd never know what happened to me. She'd never know if I was alive or dead. She'd never know if I was safe. If I'd run away. It would be like my mother's disappearance all over again.

The room smelled like rust. It had a chilling energy, like death was around every corner. Though my mind was fuzzy from the hard hit my skull took back in the parking lot of Dick's Diner, I still pieced together that I was in a basement somewhere.

I'd spent most of my life reading cold cases and researching true crime, but being in the middle of it wasn't some hobby. It wasn't like my carefully cultivated podcast. It was terrifying.

The metal door opened, bathing me in bright fluorescent light. I held my breath and squeezed my eyes shut. My head was throbbing from the hit. My lips were cracked.

In an ominous tone, a deep voice cursed. I heard movement and blinked half a dozen times to clear my vision so that I could see who was approaching.

As the man crouched in front of me, heat rose off of his body and caressed my skin. I felt a shiver travel down my spine, and I saw my stranger. It took me a moment to remember his name. What had they called him?

"William?" my voice cracked. "Please let me out of here."

He reached out and stroked my cheek with his soft fingers. I flinched away from his touch. It was so odd to feel so familiar yet distant from him. The touch was far too intimate for what we were, and despite the comfort it briefly gave me, it also doused me in fear. For so long, my stranger was a fly on the wall. An obligation we had to meet. A price to pay for my friendship with Vicky. I teased him. I normalized him. But now, he was the enemy.

"I never wanted this to happen," he whispered in a soft voice. "I wanted to keep you as far away from Nicholas as possible."

I licked my dry lips and shuffled as far away from him as I could. But my stranger didn't let up. He leaned closer. Closer. "What are they gonna do to me?" I asked.

He cleared his throat and brought his forehead close to mine. Every time he blinked, the flutter of his eyelashes brushed my skin. What was he doing? "Do you want the truth?"

"I think you owe me that much," I growled. There was still some fight in me despite my aching body and throbbing head. I worried about Vicky about as much as I was angry with her. How could she let this happen? I always thought the risk was worth the reward, but now...

"I owe you a lot more than the truth," he replied ominously, a sense of admiration in his words that made me frown. "You have to do everything in your power to convince Nicholas that you aren't the rat."

I sobbed. "But I'm not. I don't know anything."

"I know that," William assured me. "But shit has hit the fan lately, and Nicholas isn't fucking around. He'll kill you, Juliet."

A sob tore through my dry throat. Kill me? "I didn't ask for this. I don't know anything," I cried out.

William gave me a look drowning with pity. "He'll test you. He'll break you. He'll burn you. You have to do everything you can to prove your loyalty," he said. "My brother doesn't value human life. He cares about our family name and the empire he's built. Everyone else is just in the way." That bitter admission sounded like verbal venom. William obviously hated his brother.

Swallowing, I felt stuck, trapped in a hopeless situation I couldn't escape. "How long is he gonna keep me here?"

William pulled away slightly and bit his lip. "Vicky just got on a plane to Italy, so I'm guessing his interrogation will start soon."

Pain rocked through me as well as relief. I didn't understand why Vicky had to go to Italy, but at least she was away from her monster of a brother.

"Who is he?"

"Nicholas is the boss and our oldest brother. He inherited this gangster kingdom."

My hope dwindled. "And who are you?" I asked. "All this time I thought you were her bodyguard."

His lips formed a tight smile, and he responded, "I guess in many ways I am. She's my baby sister. I just...I wanted to make sure she was okay. When you came along, I saw an easy way to help my sister deal with her grief."

He stood up and wiped his palms on his thighs before shoving both hands in his pockets. "Why does Nicholas think I'm a rat?" I asked. Maybe if I knew more, I could find a way out of this. Maybe I could prove to them that I was nobody. I didn't have any friends. I didn't talk to anyone outside of Grams.

A second person opened the door and walked through the threshold. The already chilled room seemed to drop another twenty degrees the moment Nicholas's icy stare landed on me. "That's exactly the kind of question a rat would ask. And for the record, while we're here, you will call me Malice."

An icy chill struck me at that name.

Malice.

Malice.

Malice.

He fit his namesake perfectly.

Behind him, two strong men carried a prone body into the cold basement. I recognized one of the suited guards as Hale, the man who hit me in the head with a pistol. The man grunted and coughed, like every single one of his ribs was broken. Malice nodded beside me, and the two guards dropped the strange, broken man right at my feet. The crunch of bones made me nauseous. He cried out, and I looked to William. What was I supposed to do with this?

"Your Grams is a nice lady," Malice said while popping his knuckles. "Such a shame she's sick. I suppose her medicine isn't cheap. Cora pays her rats nicely."

I wanted to be strong, I really did, but more tears streamed down my cheeks. He'd seen my Grams? "Please don't hurt her. She's innocent."

Malice checked his watch. "I didn't want the poor woman to worry, so I told her that you spent the night with Vicky. Strange thing, though. She didn't even know who Vicky was."

I let out a shaky breath. "Vicky made me promise never to talk about her to anyone. She had rules."

"I see," Nicholas—Malice—said. "Tell me about these rules."

I steadied my voice. It was a mantra I knew by heart. "Don't ask any personal questions. Don't show up unannounced. Don't ever, ever let anyone know we're friends."

"I'm surprised. Usually my sister is careless. She must actually give a shit about you," he mused while rubbing his sharp jaw. "So you never met up outside of the diner?"

"We met at the cemetery a few times," I replied. "But every other time was at the diner."

"And William was always there?" he asked.

I looked at my secret stranger and swallowed. "I didn't know his name, but yes. He was always there, watching, listening." William shifted his weight.

"Interesting."

Malice walked over to his brother and tapped him on the cheek with his open palm; it didn't create a smacking sound, but it still looked hard. "Three years you've gone behind my back. We will discuss this."

William nodded slightly, though his lip curled.

"You see, Miss Cross, I have some rules of my own. I keep a tight leash on my family because our enemies are creative bastards that like to tear us down. I'm not completely convinced that you don't work for Cora—"

"I don't even know Cora!" I sobbed, interrupting him.

He ignored my outburst and continued. "I'm going to need some leverage to make sure that moving forward, your loyalty is to the Civella name and my organization."

I sobbed harder. "I'll do anything."

Malice nodded at the body before me. I'd almost forgotten the wheezing, broken man before me. I was still chained to the ground, kneeling like a woman stuck in perpetual prayer. "You want to prove you aren't a rat? Kill him," Malice said before crossing his arms over his chest.

"What?" I gasped. "I don't know this guy. I'm not capable of…"

"It's you or him. He's been working with Cora behind my back. Actually, he's the reason you aren't dead right now. The fact that he didn't know you probably saved your pathetic life," Malice said before undoing the buttons on both his wrists and rolling up his crisp white sleeves. "If you want to prove yourself worthy, kill him."

"No. I-I can't just…" I looked at the man. His eyes were bruised and swollen shut. His shirt was stained red with blood. His leg was bent at an awkward angle. From the looks of it, he was already half dead. But I wasn't a murderer. Did this man have a family? Was he an innocent bystander sucked into the deadly world of the Kansas City mob? "I can't..."

"Fine," Nicholas said with a shrug before pulling out his gun and aiming it directly at my head. I cried out. William flinched.

"I'm not a murderer," I sobbed. "I can't."

Malice walked over to me and crouched down until we were eye level, his head cocked to the side. He had the most beautiful emerald eyes. "You're a pretty little thing, you know that?" He reached out and tucked my hair behind my ears, and the moment his skin brushed across mine, I started peeing myself out of pure, unadulterated fear. He looked down at the puddle forming around me but didn't move to save his designer shoes from getting wet. Shame filled my body, and he laughed. "I'm not afraid of piss, Juliet Cross." He reached out and grabbed my throat and squeezed. "I'd fuck you in a puddle made up of your urine and that man's blood without a second's hesitation. Your existence is what disgusts me. Your fear just turns me on."

"Nicholas," William interrupted, but the crazy man beside me ignored his brother.

"Kill him, and all of this will be over."

I started sobbing, and Malice leaned in to lick my tears. I gasped and heaved. My heart felt like it was about to beat through my chest. A sluggish line of thoughts crawled through my mind. "Does he have a family?" I asked. How could I even consider this?

"Does that even matter? If you want to live, I'm your family. I'm your law. I'm your everything."

"How would I even…" More sobs cracked me open and swallowed me whole. Was I willing to give him my humanity in exchange for my life? I couldn't imagine…

I heard the chains binding me to the ground move, and soon, I was free. I still felt weighed down, though. Heavy with a choice I didn't want to make. The man started crying out. "No! No, don't do this." His voice was garbled and broken. "My wife…"

He had a wife?

"Get creative," Nicholas suggested with a malicious grin. He was enjoying this. "You have two minutes before I lodge a bullet into your skull."

My wrists were still bound behind my back. My legs were weak. My entire body trembled. "I can't," I cried out.

"I don't care what you can and can't do. Figure it out."

I shuffled over to the man and stared down at him. He had no discernable features that I could tell. I wondered how many times I'd seen him around town. Did he have life aspirations? How old was he? Hot tears streamed down my cheeks as he begged for his life with garbled, slurred words. Time moved too quickly. I didn't have the luxury of hating myself for what I was considering.

"One minute," Malice said.

His guard, Hale, laughed. William stared at me encouragingly.

I knew from studying various crime cases that it was really difficult to suffocate someone. It took a lot of strength I didn't quite have at the moment but was a humane option.

The time clock kept ticking. A deep dark part of my mind had already made the decision, though. It felt primal. It was him or me. It was my life, my future, or his end. It was Grams or... I leaned forward and whispered in his ear, "I'm so sorry." At the end of the day, I'd survive. I wouldn't leave anyone behind, wondering what happened, not like what happened to me.

I refused to die today. I refused to be intimidated by murder. I let the darkest parts of me take the wheel, and I did what I was told, like a soldier at war.

Malice grinned when I pulled back. He laughed when I slowly stood on shaky legs. He crossed his arms over his chest when I raised my bare foot up and slammed it down on his skull. I repeated the action. Again. Again. The sound of crunching bones filled my ears. With all my weight bared down, I stomped on his skull until blood poured from every orifice. His concave bones cut through brain and veins and my humanity. He didn't struggle, but wheezes escaped his lips as I crushed him again.

And again.

And again.

Despite the adrenaline, my foot ached from the brute force of it. It was stomping on concrete. I prayed his sharp, cracked bones didn't stab me.

Whatever Malice's men had done to him leading up to this point had broken him far past repair, or at least, that's what I told myself. I hugged the reality where I didn't have a choice, where he was dead regardless. Where when given the option to kill or be killed, I made the selfish sacrifice. I'd forever be haunted by this decision. I closed my eyes and let my roaring pulse drown out the disgusting sound of his groans and gurgles. His cracking bones. His pain.

Then, he went still. Too still. No pulse. No shuddering breaths. Nothing.

And when it was done, I felt a wave of rolling nausea travel up my throat. "Good job." Malice creeped up on me. Slowly, slowly, he moved until his lips were hovering over the shell of my ear. Awe littered his tone. I looked for William, who stared at me with a mixture of kindness and disgust.

I removed my foot and put as much distance between myself and the dead body as possible. Blood covered my skin, it dug into the cracks in my heel. I stared at my crimson toes with disgust. My back-tied arms and back crashed into the concrete wall, and a wave of dizziness washed over me. I nearly crumbled from the realization of what I'd done.

I killed a man.

I killed a man.

"For the record," Malice began, "I was never going to actually shoot you. I didn't think you had it in you."

I could barely see from the tears. Shadows moved around the room as his guards left. "What?" I choked out.

"He was dying anyway. Probably wasn't going to last much longer. I punctured his lung before we got here. But you finished the job." Malice pulled out his cell, and the glow from his screen illuminated his cruel, beautiful face.

"You're a fucking monster," I whispered.

"Says the woman who just crushed a man's skull with her bare foot," he snapped back distractedly while typing away. I felt my chest tighten. I could barely breathe. What had I done? "It was beautiful. I've seen grown men cower at a request like that."

More hollow tears fell down my cheeks, and I stared at him in disbelief. "You're insane."

"Tell me," Malice demanded. "When you cry, is it because you genuinely feel a sense of sorrow? Or do you cry because you feel like you're supposed to, because the world watches how you respond and you don't want anyone to know how much of a monster you really are?"

I choked on the shock. It was a question that completely stunned me.

"Your Grams has a doctor's appointment tomorrow. You should probably hurry up and get rid of the body so you can get home in time for dinner. She's making meatloaf. She likes cooking, Juliet. Let the woman cook."

I shook my head, feeling sluggish and confused. "What?"

He huffed, rolled his eyes, and pocketed his cell. "Get rid of the body, go home, and make sure your Grams gets to Dr. Hoffstead's office on time tomorrow, Juliet. I don't make a habit of repeating myself."

"Dr. Hoffstead?" I asked in a cracked voice. I recognized that name. He was one of the leading neuroscientists in the state. I'd been wanting to take Grams to him ever since we'd gotten a diagnosis, but the wait list was too long, and I couldn't even afford a consultation, let alone the treatments he offered.

"Welcome to the family, Juliet. There are perks for selling your soul to the devil," he said with a grin.

chapter four

The scalding water turned my skin an angry red color. My gaze was downturned to the tiled floor, where crimson-stained water swirled over the drain. I still wasn't sure where I was. The basement had a hidden door that led to a bathroom with a compact walk-in shower. Steam quickly filled the room from the hot water, and I tried to pretend that I was in a normal space, taking a normal shower, and not washing off the blood from my victim. I was acutely aware of the man standing just outside the door.

I was in numb shock. Hollow emotions scratched at the

surface of my mind, but I could only stare at my foot. It was too easy to stomp on his skull. I didn't even question it. I was in survival mode. It was do or die, and I did.

"I was never going to kill you..."

I couldn't tell if Malice was testing me or grooming me. My body was enveloped in a sense of shame that wouldn't let go. There was a strange disconnect between my mind and my ability to express what happened. I knew it was wrong. I knew that I was now a murderer. I connected the dots and made sense of the brutal thing I'd just done. But it felt like this gory out-of-body experience.

"Hurry," Hale, the guard standing outside the bathroom door, instructed. I'd gathered that he was Malice's right-hand man. He was always first to be given a job, and right now he was in charge of watching me. I turned off the water, wondering when they would let me leave. Malice's comments about Grams had me itching to make sure she was okay.

But there was something else he wanted me to do first. He wanted me to get rid of the body.

I found a threadbare towel and wrapped it around my shaky torso. It barely covered me. The clothes I was wearing were sitting in a pile on the floor, covered in blood and piss. There was no way I would wear that again. I wanted to burn the evidence of what happened here today—I had to burn the evidence.

I was a murderer.

I cracked open the door and stared at the man standing guard. "I don't have any clothes."

He rolled his eyes and huffed. "Not my problem. Anthony is waiting."

He wrapped his beefy hand around the door handle and yanked it open with a single jerky movement, pulling me with him. I nearly face-planted on the concrete floor. My towel, which was already hanging open, fell to the ground, giving Hale an eyeful.

"Another show, eh?" he asked while looking at my exposed breasts. "It's my lucky day."

He grabbed my arm and helped me right myself, and I felt his heavy stare on my naked, shivery body. I'd already endured enough trauma for the day and felt my skin turn to ice at the feel of his stare on my breasts.

"Back off," I growled before tugging my arm free and quickly picking up the towel to wrap around myself. The basement was still dark, but the light from the bathroom brightened it some. From the corner of my eye, I could still see the abandoned body of the stranger I'd murdered.

My throat closed up. Panic went up my spine.

"I suggest keeping your eyes to yourself, Hale. You know how Nicholas gets with his pets." A strange, bright voice cut through the dim basement, making me snap my attention to the source.

"Yes, boss," Hale—my babysitter—said. Boss? I was still trying to figure out the dynamic of this terror squad, and knowing that there were multiple men of varying ranks in my presence made me nervous.

"You can leave now," the voice said.

I heard a light switch turn on before the flickering fluorescents attacked my vision. In the room's corner was a long metal table with various tools on it. Beside it stood a man in a rubber suit with gloves up to his elbows and a beanie on his head. Strands of brown hair peeked through his cap, and he licked his lips appreciatively at the sight of me. He had Malice's cruel eyes and William's broody mouth. But most importantly, I noted a tattoo on his neck that looked oddly familiar. It was a pair of angel wings identical to ink on my best friend. With one glance, I knew that they were related somehow.

Hale excused himself and exited the basement torture room.

"Want some clothes? I had to get rid of a druggie last week, and she was about your size. Poor prostitute died of an overdose at the club. Bad for business, you know?" he said with a smile before grabbing a box from under the table and sliding it across the floor to me. It bumped into the dead body I was desperately trying to ignore.

"You have a box of dead people's clothes just lying around?" I asked incredulously. Of everything he had said to me, that was the most ridiculous of it. Didn't he know how to get rid of evidence properly? That was enough to send someone to prison. I sure as hell wasn't about to wear a jail sentence.

He grabbed a saw and slammed it on the table, making a loud boom echo around me. "Is that weird?" he asked.

"It's stupid. You should bleach them and then burn them. Make sure there isn't a trace of your DNA on it. What if the cops got a warrant for this place?"

The beautiful man cocked his brow at me. "Why do you sound so experienced with this? Wait, wait, wait. You're Juliet, yeah? You have that true crime podcast that Vicky made me subscribe to," he said, as if it somehow explained everything. "My sister said it could help me up my game. I'm still on episode seven. That serial killer Joe Ball makes me want to start an alligator farm. Could you imagine? You'd get an epic pet and a free cleanup service. He's a genius, honestly."

"You listen to my podcast?" I stuttered.

"Whatever Vicky wants, she gets," he said with a delightful smirk. "I'm a sucker for my baby sister."

"You're her brother?" I was just a revolving line of questions. There was so much I wanted to know. Three brothers. My best friend had three brothers, and I didn't know any of them.

"Her favorite brother. And you're her secret bestie," he

replied before shimmying his shoulders playfully. "It really pissed Nicholas off that everyone knew about you but him. Can't blame Vick for wanting to keep you to herself, though. Nick likes to take over, yeah?"

I nodded, like I understood. Like this wasn't crazy. Like there wasn't a dead, bloated body beside me.

"Speaking of," he continued, "mind getting dressed? You can stay naked if you'd like, but we have a body to get rid of. A fucking messy one, too. Gravity is such a bitch. He's already got postmortem lividity, and I'm guessing that once we move him, there will be some nasty skin slippage. Just another day in paradise."

With one hand, I clutched my towel, and I held the other to my mouth to stop a scream from escaping. I might have been numb before, but the feeling of terror was bursting from me.

"Ah, don't get squeamish now. We haven't even started yet. I'm Anthony, by the way. It's a pleasure to meet you."

"Started what?" I choked out, ignoring his greeting.

Anthony rolled his eyes and walked up to me. I had to tip my head up to look at him, and the closer he got, the softer his features became. His face was exotic and beautiful. Despite his insane career, he looked delicate up close. Beautiful. He had Vicky's energy, and even though I didn't know him, I was comforted by their similarities.

Ignoring my nakedness, he placed both hands on my

shoulders. "We're gonna get rid of this body, babe," he said in a low voice while looking down at me. I shook my head, but he was unfettered. "Yep," he insisted. "We're going to get rid of it."

"Why? Why do I have to?" I asked in horror.

"Nicholas's rules. If you've got the balls to kill someone, then it's your job to make sure it's cleaned up properly. Keeps his men from getting trigger-happy."

I looked down at the ground where the stranger was lying and let out a gasp. "Oh, God. No. I can't."

"Sure you can," he replied with an encouraging smile. "It's just a body. And as soon as you're done with this, Nicholas said you can go home to your Grams."

Getting the fuck out of here motivated me some. I wanted to get as far away from this mess and these men as possible. "I can leave once we're done?" I asked. It felt like there was some sort of catch.

"I'll be honest here, Killer. You never really leave. But yes, clean up your mess and you can go home."

I let out a shaky exhale. My mind was like a giant puzzle. I just needed to remove the part of me that was freaking the fuck out about murdering someone. "Okay, fine. What do we do?"

Anthony smiled and dropped his hands from my shoulders and hung them at his side. "Killer's choice," he replied.

Killer. I was a killer.

"I don't even know where to start. Do you not have a mass grave you use? Certainly a gang has protocols for shit like this," I countered.

"You're the true crime expert. What would you do if you were a serial killer?"

I let out an exhale, my mind suddenly running through a range of scenarios. There were so many variables. It was impossible to narrow it down.

"Where'd they pick him up from?" I asked in a shaky voice.

"River Boat Casino," Anthony replied easily, a hint of curiosity in his tone.

"Shit. You might as well have waved an enormous flag with your home address on it," I cursed. "Casinos have the most sophisticated facial recognition software in the world. Once word gets out that he was last seen there, it's only a matter of time before they trace him here. Did you at least get into an unmarked car?"

"Of course. We're not complete idiots," Anthony replied with a grin. "And the casino won't be a problem."

"You can't be cocky about this. The casino is an enormous problem."

"We own the casino," Anthony replied before digging in his pocket for a toothpick and putting it between his teeth. "All footage has been deleted. He was never there."

"What about his family?" I asked.

"His wife showed up at a PTA meeting with two black eyes three days ago. She won't be looking for her asshole husband. If any cops come snooping, which they won't, she'll inform them of his very extensive affair with a call girl from Vegas. Nicholas already paid her for her troubles and cooperation."

My brows raised. "Where's his car?" I asked.

"Chop shop. Bastard drove a BMW." He shifted his weight between his two feet. "Can I just say, the fact that you're thinking through all of this makes me hot?"

"What was his name?" I croaked. This was the personal part. I needed to know who he was. Even if he was a shitty human, knowing who he was painted a picture of guilt that I needed to hold on to so I could at least maintain a semblance of my humanity.

"I'm not going to tell you," Anthony replied. "It'll do you no good. Don't learn their backstory. Don't personalize them. Don't remember them. Take what you did today and shove it into a tiny box, then put that box in a bigger box. Then chain that box shut and drop it in the bottom of the ocean and pretend that it never existed."

Yeah. That didn't exactly sound like a healthy coping mechanism. Anthony looked at me for a lingering moment. "Is that what you do?" I asked.

Vulnerability flashed through his expression, a softness

that reminded me of Vicky. "No. I thrive in the darkness, babe. You could tell me to chop off his arm and then jack off with his hand, and I would."

"That's a really specific example, and I really don't want you to elaborate," I interjected, making him laugh.

"You weren't born in this world, so I'm going to go easy on you. Nicholas will coach you. William will save you. I'll just accept you where you are. And right now? You're in no place to hear this asshole's name or know his backstory. It wouldn't make any difference anyway. So drop it and tell me how we're going to get rid of his body."

I let out a shaky breath. I didn't want to be coached. I didn't want to be saved. At this point, I wanted to be left alone. This felt like the start to something inescapable. Anthony had a point, though. I wasn't sure I could get through the rest of today if I was obsessing over the consequences of what I'd done. I needed to be a robot. Emotionless. "Do you have access to a crematorium?" I asked. Burning him seemed like the best course of action.

"Nope," he replied, popping the p. Shit, I was really hoping they had one. I thought about episode thirty-four of my podcast and grimaced.

"I suppose we could do what the drug cartels do," I murmured speculatively. "Do you have any sodium hydroxide? Or lye. If we heat it up to three hundred degrees, we can liquify the body in about three hours," I offered before shivering. "Some bones might survive the process, but we can always grind them up into a fine powder. Then we can just...pour the liquid down the drain once it cools." Anthony's brows raised in shock as I continued. "We'll need like a fifty-five-gallon drum? Lye is really cheap. It's $15 at a farm supply store. Eight pounds of it can dissolve at least three bodies. It's almost economical." A hysterical giggle burst past my lips. Was this real?

Anthony held his hands up. "Okay. So, like, you're full on psycho. Cool, cool. I was joking about the crematorium thing. We actually have a funeral home on our bank roll. We just gotta get him into the hearse and drop him off. But, like, cool for having a Plan B—a terrifying Plan B. That just feels like a lot of work, man."

So this was the line? I observed Anthony for a moment. He was completely at ease next to the dead body. Was he desensitized, or was it something else? He didn't have the same authoritative energy as the others, but he still had a powerful presence. He was contradictory, quirky, and unique.

"You asshole," I finally replied before stomping my foot. My body jiggled from the movement, and his eyes zeroed in on my barely contained tits. My cheeks flushed as his teeth sunk into his bottom lip, and his sweeping eyes looked me up and down.

"Please put the dead prostitute's clothes on. I'm about

to pop a boner in the torture room, and I was told I wasn't allowed to be sexually aroused around dead bodies anymore."

The fact that Anthony had to be told this was fucking terrifying. Yeah. Okay. Dead prostitute's clothes it was.

chapter five

Standing outside our tiny house, I spent a long time watching the world go by. My bare feet clung to the hard concrete as I stared at the living room window where Grams had left the light on for me. It was late at night, the moon hung high overhead, cradled by a blanket of clouds and stars. It would have been a nice night, and I might have enjoyed the serene moment, had the last twenty-four hours not been so traumatic.

I smelled like death, the stench permeating my skin and the clothes I wore. It clung to my hair, which was a tangled curtain over my right eye. I was drenched in evidence that could lock me away for the rest of my life.

Disposing of my nameless victim was a lot easier than I imagined. Years of researching true crime conditioned me to believe that murder was this complex thing that was grim and terrifying, but when you had the network the Kansas City mob had, it was easy. They simply flashed a stack of cash, and the entire world bent to their whims. The hardest part was wrapping his sloshing body up in the tarp and lifting it onto a cart. We used a shovel to scoop up parts of his brain and skull. If my stomach wasn't completely empty, I would have vomited everywhere. My only saving grace was that I hadn't eaten anything since lunch yesterday. We rolled up to the funeral home, slid the body into the furnace, locked the door, and walked away.

Throughout the entire journey, Anthony kept his chaotic mind to himself, mumbling under his breath occasionally. I could sense that something was on his mind, but when he wasn't coordinating with the funeral home, he was watching me with an inquisitive stare, as if I was some complex problem he wanted to figure out. The ease with which he conducted himself made it all feel so ordinary. I was shocked and calmed at the same time. It made me sick.

Grams would know something was wrong the minute I walked through those doors. I honestly didn't know what to say. She was probably worried as hell and not sure what to do. They'd taken my cell phone away, so it wasn't like I could call to let her know that I was okay. Not to mention Malice had been at my house. He was in my space, near my grandmother. She was probably scared out of her mind. I needed to face the music. Every second I prolonged the inevitable was torture.

I walked up the steps, noting the lavender roses she'd planted a few years ago. I knew exactly where to step on the dilapidated front porch so that I wouldn't break through the rotted wood. The front door was scuffed, showing off the many layers of paint that had been slathered on it. Some homes you merely stayed in, but we lived in ours. We boldly used up every square inch this place had to offer.

I opened the door and walked inside, my eyes immediately scanning the room for my grandmother. I needed to change and scrub my skin raw, but it would have to wait. To the right of the entryway was our tiny living room, and in the old leather recliner we owned, Grams was sitting. "There you are," she exclaimed while touching her chest. "Where have you been? Why..." Grams paused while slowly standing up. Her hand shook at her side, and she squeezed her eyes shut, as if frustrated with her words for not spilling from her mouth. "Why are you wearing that?"

I marched up to her and gave her an enormous hug. The second I was in her arms, a sigh of relief escaped my lips. Grams was my safe space, my home. Reunited with her after such a tragic night, I was so relieved that I cried tears of relief. "I'm okay," I whispered. I pulled away, assessing every inch of her appearance. Her short, brown curly hair with wisps of gray seasoned in. Her kind, but concerned, brown eyes. The deep-set lines in her face. She wore a tank top with a bright red strawberry pattern and loose trousers. She was barefoot—she was always barefoot—but her toes were painted a bright shade of red. "I had to borrow a friend's clothes today. Are you okay?"

"I'm fine now that you're home. I'm sorry your cell phone broke. I've got some money saved up in the cookie jar to get a new one. I didn't like not being able to get a hold of you all day. Nicholas gave me his number, but he seemed real busy-like."

I shook my head in confusion. "My cell phone?"

Grams arched her brow. "Nicholas told me how it broke when he came to grab your work uniform. Such a gentleman. He said you ended up having to work overnight and just stayed with your friend, Vicky. Was so sweet when he stopped by..." she whispered. "He was real polite...but unsettling. Kind of a strange boy, isn't he?"

Nicholas.

I held her hands and guided her to our thrift store couch. "Did he ask you anything?" I asked. Anger burned in my chest. How dare he come here? How dare he invade my space and trick my Grams like that? I was so furious with him for showing up here that I could hardly think straight.

"Not really. He just said he was excited to finally meet me. I was so ashamed that I didn't even know your friend's name. Are..." She huffed and sat down, pausing for a lingering moment to calm herself. "Are you embarrassed of me, baby? Is that why I haven't met your friend?"

"Of course not, Grams," I immediately replied, though she didn't look convinced. I looked around our tiny house, trying to see what Nicholas saw. Our home was small and run-down. We got everything we needed second- or sometimes third-hand. It wasn't extravagant. I had a few things I wanted to fix up, but we lived well. Grandpa's life insurance paid off the mortgage, so we only had to come up with taxes. "Vicky is just really private. She prefers for us to go to her house."

She nodded nervously at the scratched coffee table before speaking again. "Oh! He left you something." Grams then nodded at a crisp box with a bow wrapped around it on our coffee table. Grams grinned. "I think he has a crush on you. Was real excited to see your baby pictures. I handed him the whole album!" she teased.

I swallowed while standing up. I trusted my Grams with my life. I could tell her about what I'd done today, and it wouldn't change the way she looked at me. She loved me so fiercely she probably would have helped me bury the body. But...

But I refused to incriminate the only family I had.

Parkinson's was triggered by stress. The knowledge of what I'd done today would wreak havoc on her body, and I couldn't allow that.

The box started vibrating on the coffee table, and I slowly went to pick it up. Grams watched in silence as I opened the box and stared at the brand new phone waiting for me. "Oh! Did he get you a new phone?" she asked. "He definitely likes you. I'll go get some stationery so you can write him a proper thank-you note. How kind."

The name on the caller ID said Malice. I debated answering it, but my sense of self-preservation won out in the end.

"Hello," Malice greeted.

I let out a shaky exhale and stared at Grams. I was slightly emboldened by her expression of concern. "Hello, Nick."

"Only the people I like may call me Nick. My business associates call me boss. And my toys?" He paused for dramatic effect. "My toys call me Malice." I swallowed and remained silent. I didn't know what more he wanted with me.

I considered Malice to be a suitable name for him. Malice was the desire to cause pain, injury, or distress to another. He made it perfectly clear today that this was his primary goal.

"How was your afternoon with Anthony?" he asked

conversationally.

"We did what you asked," I snapped back. If he wanted an update on the job, couldn't he have asked his brother?

"That's not what I asked. Did you enjoy your time with him?" Nicholas—Malice—asked.

Grams was shuffling around her bedroom, searching for stationery for the man who forced me to kill someone. I walked to my bedroom and quietly shut the door.

"Are you still there?" Malice asked.

"I had to go to my bedroom. I didn't want Grams to hear," I replied quietly. "I want to keep her out of this as much as possible."

"Such a predictable weakness, you have," Malice replied. "Not only did you show your cards the first moment we met, but you made her so incredibly accessible. I walked right into your house and learned everything I needed to know about you in a matter of minutes. It was almost refreshing how open she was."

There was something chilling about the way he threatened me without actually threatening me. Malice wanted me to know that he was in my space, near my grandmother, and capable of hurting us both. "What is the point of all of this?" I asked.

"I don't owe you an explanation. I believe I asked you a question first, Juliet."

I rolled my eyes. Being out of the torture room gave

me a false sense of bravery. "My afternoon with him was fine. He's a little quirky but reminds me a lot of Vicky," I admitted. "Speaking of Vicky, is she okay?" I could only worry about one thing at a time. I spent my day in survival mode, but now, I finally had the mental capacity to question whether or not my best friend was in danger. All in all, I had a strong impression that Vicky's brothers were all deeply concerned about her. I couldn't quite piece together what had them worried, though. This Cora lady had their nuts all in a twist. I wanted to know why.

"She's fine. Anthony and Vicky have always been close. They're more like friends than siblings. He doesn't feel the amount of responsibility that William and I do for protecting our baby sister, so he's not burdened by what needs to be done in order to keep her safe. It worried me that Anthony would be critical of my decision to send Vicky to our family in Italy. But it seems you provided quite the distraction for my brother."

"Why are you telling me this?" I asked. "What do you want with me?"

"I haven't quite decided what I want with you. At first, I wanted to kill you for being a rat. Then, I wanted to punish William for keeping you a secret. I like to know everyone involved in my family's business. It was a slap in the face to know that you've been sniffing around for the past three years right under my nose." His voice dripped with venom, and I imagined his cruel face twisted in anger. He continued as I used my free hand to clutch my chest. "Today, I saw how useful you can be. It's obvious William wants you, and I like having leverage. You want to take care of your grandmother, and I can help you with that. You're in deep. If I wanted to blackmail you, I could simply use the murder you committed today, but I don't think it hits as hard as I'd like it to. You'd help me out of obligation but not because you want to. I like my toys to be motivated. I'm going to provide your grandmother the best care money can buy, and in exchange, you're going to be whatever I need you to be."

I sat down on my lumpy mattress, then let the numbness slip away and mold into helplessness. "What exactly do you need from me?" I asked, shocked that once again I was considering an ultimatum from Nicholas, or Malice as he wanted me to call him.

"I need lots of things. One day, I could call and say I need you to burn down a building. The next, I could need you in an evening gown and on my arm at an event. I could need you to keep Vicky obedient. I could need you to hurt my brother. Sometimes, you'll know why you're somewhere. Sometimes you won't. You'll be my little pet, showing up whenever and however I need you to."

I gulped. I didn't want to be under Nicholas's control. I didn't trust him, and the more he pulled me into his web, the harder it would be to escape alive. But I was already trapped. I'd killed a man today. I'd disposed of his body. I'd done something unbelievably horrific—something that would stick with me until I took my last breath. "And if I don't?"

Then he let out an exhale, and I could hear him lean back in his chair as he considered all the ways he could ruin me if I did not cooperate. "Juliet, please don't make me insult your intelligence by spelling out how you have no other choice. If you go against me, you'll end up in prison for murder. If you cooperate, every single problem you've ever had will disappear." He was lying. Nicholas Civella would become my problem. He'd create a storm of issues for me. "I put the information for your grandmother's doctor's appointment in your phone. Go to it tomorrow. See what he has to offer. I think you'll like him. Afterward, I want you to come to the address I just sent you. You only saw Anthony's death dungeon, but you might like the mansion." My phone pinged, and I shivered. "I've got a job for you."

He knew he had me in his clutches.

I swallowed down my anxiety and tried to stay calm. But my throat had closed up. My anxiety was so bad I couldn't force my words past my teeth. Everything that had happened finally hit that sweet crescendo of terror, and I was helpless to stop it. "See you tomorrow, Juliet," he whispered before hanging up the phone.

chapter six

Grams and I enjoyed going to Penn Valley Park together. A small park with a great view of downtown, it was a special place for the two of us. We used to walk laps here all the time when I was a kid. Penn Valley had a small pond and an overpopulation of aggressive ducks. Grams and I would save up our stale bread and feed them from her favorite bench.

It was a warm summer day. My eyes itched from the pollen in the air, and I rolled my shoulders, reveling in the heat of the sun beating down on my bare skin. Grams was wearing a pair of jeans and her favorite shirt—with a picture that said "My Grandkid Thinks I'm Cool."

She held my arm as we went along the trail, the hot air wrapping itself around us. The doctor we'd met with earlier today said that regular exercise can help slow down the Parkinson's destroying her nervous system. He recommended getting a stationary bike because the motion can help ease the motor complications she was experiencing. I made a mental note to check my local Goodwill to see if they had one for sale. Buying one new right now wasn't an option.

"Is this really necessary?" Grams asked while looking down at our linked arms. I didn't want her to fall on the hard concrete.

"What? Do I stink or something?" I teased, knowing that she was a strong, independent woman, and feeling frail was a shot to her sensitive ego. I couldn't help it. Grams was all I had, and I was the equivalent of a helicopter mom where she was concerned.

"I just think it's a bit much. I'm more than capable of walking this trail. Back when you were a toddler, I used to carry your ass to the car when you were too tired to walk, you know. I could probably jog circles around you." She used her free hand to wave in frustration. She wasn't wrong, back in the day, Grams would jog circles around me. She was fit and healthy. I remember almost laughing at the doctor when we got the diagnosis. It seemed impossible that such a strong woman would have this happen to her. It wasn't fair. "I can also still swat your ass for being a brat," she added.

Grams started laughing at her own joke, but I rolled my eyes. She was having a good day, and it was such a pleasure to see her in good humor.

Our doctor's appointment went as Malice demanded. I had to lie every step of the way. I explained that Grams qualified for a charity study I applied for. It was hard to come up with an explanation on the spot, but I told her a last-minute spot opened up and it was too good of an opportunity to pass up. She wanted more details but was stunned into silence when we arrived at the luxurious office. We didn't have to sit by someone coughing and sneezing. We didn't have to wait to see the doctor. They even offered us lemonade. Lemonade! It was a wonderful experience, and I learned about some different treatment options available to improve Grams's quality of life.

In addition, I was given a six-month supply of an experimental drug. I couldn't imagine how much it actually cost, and the three large pill bottles weighed my purse down. Dr. Hoffstead insisted that I take it with me, and as I was leaving, he pulled me aside and begged me to tell Nicholas Civella that I was well provided for.

"Anything you want, I'll give you. Here's my cell. Call anytime. Just please tell him I'm doing what he asked.

Please."

Seeing the fear on this grown man's face made me wildly uncomfortable. Malice and his crew were capable of committing some of the foulest acts imaginable, and I was familiar with the terror Dr. Hoffstead felt deep in his soul.

"I can't believe how long the trail is." Grams sighed as we walked down the path. I looked down and noticed that she was dragging her right foot. Pretending to be tired, I led us to a wooden bench overlooking the park's water fountain. "I need a break," I lied when she arched her brow at me.

"Can we talk again about the strange doctor's visit we had today?" Grams asked as we both sat down. My bare thighs scorched against the bench, which had been baking in the sun all day. "Baby, I know you're lying to me."

"I'm not lying," I insisted.

"Dammit! I kn-know you are!"

She stopped talking and paused to collect herself. Anxiety was a common non-motor symptom of Parkinson's disease, and unfortunately, stress and anxiety made her motor symptoms worse. I knew she was trying to keep calm for my sake, but hearing her struggle to speak just reaffirmed my decision to only give her the bare minimum of information.

I cleared my throat. "Why do you say that?"

"You're working all hours of the night, taking double

shifts and spending your hard earned money on my medicine."

"Grams, you've done the same for me. Hell, you worked seasonal jobs every Christmas so that I had presents under the tree," I said as she let out a sharp exhale. I hated lying to her, but I needed her to take this medicine. "This doctor is really good, Grams."

"But at what cost?" Grams slowly reached out and squeezed my hand. "Baby, you're already working yourself to death. Don't think I didn't see those college applications in the trash either."

"I told you. We qualified for—"

"Free help?" Grams finished for me. "Ain't nothing in this life is free. I don't want you selling your soul for my benefit," Grams replied while shaking her head. "I-I know how these things work. I'm going to take this medicine, and then they'll pull the rug out from under me…"

She turned pale and rubbed her neck with trembling hands. Grams was a pessimist. Maybe it was Mom's disappearance that made her this way. We'd gotten our hopes up about finding Mom one too many times. Now, she didn't trust anything that seemed too good to be true. "Can you at least try taking the medicine?" I asked.

"And become dependent on them? No thank you. I don't want to become stuck in a situation that has me paying later."

I rolled my eyes. "Grams, what if it helps for just six months?" I replied, hope bleeding through my tone. "What if you end up having the best six months of your life? You feel normal again. This medicine doesn't have the side effects your other pills do."

"And what if you end up thousands of dollars in debt for a lost cause?" she snapped back. "I'm not going to let you get buried in my responsibilities. This is my life."

It was on the tip of my tongue to let Grams know that I was already in too deep, I was already stuck in a situation I couldn't get out of even if I wanted to. I stared at the pills, wondering if I could put the medicine in Grams's morning cup of coffee without her knowing.

"I just think we should take every opportunity you can. It is your life, but you only get one life to live," I insisted.

"That's enough," Grams replied with a sigh before patting my thigh. "Let's walk again. That fancy doctor wants me to exercise, so let's fucking ex-exercise," she huffed. I was used to her avoiding shit. I had a grandmother who was extremely stubborn.

We both stood up and slowly made our way down the path. "I think I want to visit my sister in Palm Springs," Grams said unexpectedly.

"Great Aunt Agnes?" I asked. "Is she okay?"

Grams smiled and nodded. "Yes. I just think you're right."

I cocked a brow. "I'm right?"

"Life is short. I should take every opportunity I can. I'm just not sure how many more chances I'll have to visit her. I'd like to maybe go stay with her for a month. Soak up the sun by the pool and maybe go to one of the casinos there. Would you be okay if I went?" she asked. "She's been offering to fly me out for a while, but with you working so hard, I never felt right accepting her offer. But you're right, life is short. She's willing to pay for my ticket, and I miss her. It's been almost a decade since I've even been on an airplane."

It hurt my soul on a visceral level to think that Grams truly believed that her opportunities to visit Aunt Agnes were dwindling. Of course I wanted her to visit her. In my selfishness, I was trying to savor each second and minute with her like it was a prized possession. But she deserved a nice trip with her sister.

"Of course, Grams. I think that would be great. I can hold down the fort. You should never feel guilty about my job, Grams. I learned from you that family is about stepping up whenever you can for the people you love."

With a little pep to her step, she smiled and walked a bit faster. "Thank you, baby. I'll call Agnes tomorrow. She'll be so excited," she said.

An idea struck me... "But only if you try this experimental drug. Look. We have six months of it. What could it hurt to try? What if it makes your trip to see Aunt Agnes that much better?"

She huffed. "That's a low blow," she grumbled.

"I learned how to bargain from the best," I teased.

"Is it really that important to you, baby?"

I quickly nodded. "Yes. Please? For me?"

She slowed her steps some. "Okay. I'll take it. As long as there aren't any withdrawals for when I stop taking it once we run out. And as long as you aren't paying more money to that doctor."

"Deal," I snapped, eager to take this opportunity when I could.

"Deal," she replied with a wide, toothy smile.

chapter seven

The Civella Mansion was imposing and impressive. I stood at the base of their empire in awe, staring up at the large iron gate circling their property. A large letter C was positioned prominently in the middle. They lived on the outskirts of town, and I had to take three city buses just to get here. The last time I was here, I was chained up in the basement and crushing a man's skull with my bare foot. I didn't really get the opportunity to see the home, because we left through a back entrance in a hearse. I didn't really have a chance to take in my surroundings outside of the death dungeon, because I was too busy disassociating from the entire experience.

My work uniform made me feel less than impressive. I wore a pink tank with the word Dick stretched across my tits. I'd decided to wear this so Grams didn't ask questions about where I was.

I was racking my brain, trying to figure out how I was going to get out of this while still reaping the benefits of Malice's connection with Dr. Hoffstead. I'd sell my soul to give my Grams a better quality of life. Consequences be damned. Taking Grams to the doctor was a huge motivator—the kind that Malice thrived on.

He had me right where he wanted me.

There was also a nagging thought in the deepest, darkest corner of my mind. It was shameful in every way.

I was curious.

I wanted to learn more about their organization and about Vicky. I wanted to know who these men were that my best friend had been keeping from me. I hated to admit it, but knowing about her secret life and living it were two different things. She felt like a stranger now.

I also wanted to get in touch with her. Whenever I tried calling, the line went dead. I wasn't necessarily sure I could trust them to be honest about her safety. I wanted to hear her voice and make sure she was actually alive. And, I kind of wanted to yell at her too. She was the reason I was caught up in this mess, and if she'd just explained to me what was going on, maybe we could have escaped all of this.

After obsessing over what to do all morning, I came to the conclusion that there was no way out. I was stuck. Although I knew I was being blackmailed and my grandmother's well-being was hanging in the balance, I still felt ashamed. The draw that I felt to Malice was not necessarily deterring me. I was not dragging my feet on the walk over here. Even though I was overwhelmed with what I had to do yesterday, the murder I committed wasn't tearing apart my psyche. I did what Anthony suggested. I wrapped up what happened in a tight little box and dropped it off the edge of my subconscious. Of course, intrusive thoughts still attacked me when I wasn't actively forcing away the image of me crushing his skull. But mostly, it wasn't as difficult as I thought it would be. And that thought both thrilled and terrified me.

Was I a psychopath? Was I just as bad as the murderers I researched? Or was I just a girl who was given a painful ultimatum? I did what I felt I had to do to survive, and it was difficult to feel guilty about that. I'd do it again. Was it so wrong to want to live?

Hale walked up to the gate and opened it. "Boss has been waiting for you. You're late."

I let out a sigh. "I had to walk Grams home. She was tired," I explained.

Hale gave me a once over. His eyes were beady. His lips

cracked and bloodied. He shoved his hands deep into his pockets, but I could see him stroking his dick with his meaty fingers through the thin material of his pants. I squirmed in disgust as he examined me closely. Aside from the obvious pervy behavior, there was something about him that made me really uncomfortable. I could feel it in my gut. Like he was the type of man to hurt a woman for sport. Malice was evil, but I got the sense that he was calculative, and every decision he made had a purpose. He researched and found my weakness with Grams, then exploited me for it. Hale? Hale seemed like the impulsive kind of bad. This kind of man did things on a whim and wrapped his hands around your neck because it made him feel good. He just had bad energy.

"Hurry up," he grunted at me as I walked through the gate and up the path toward the main house. The Civella home was a stunning three-story mansion in the heart of Kansas City's wealthiest neighborhood: Sunset Hill West. I felt like I should have to empty my pockets just to walk on the sidewalk here. Naturally, there were guards covering the perimeter and a line of armored cars in his driveway. I wondered how that could affect a person's psyche, to never be alone. To always fear for your life. To have an entire armory at your disposal.

The house was a Georgian Colonial-style home, proudly standing like a gangster landmark in the breastbone of what looked like two acres of land. It was shocking to see the amount of wealth on the inside. The elegant decor was subtle and soothing, completely different from the harsh masculine man who owned the property. There were high ceilings, deep moldings, and marble flooring. The entryway was large and open, and when I looked down the hall, I saw French doors leading into various portions of the home. "Follow me," Hale instructed.

Hale guided me through the home. We passed a formal living room, a dining room, a family room, and a walnut-paneled library with a fireplace. We made our way toward the back of the house where a dimly lit office was nestled in the corner. A large oak desk was in the middle of the room with two oversized leather chairs in front of it. I saw Malice almost immediately. Standing at a wet bar in an expensive suit, he greeted me while pouring himself a glass of bourbon. "You're late," he said, his back still turned to me.

"I had to take my grandmother home," I explained. Malice turned around to face me, his green eyes appearing almost bored by my excuse. His blond hair was swept to the side, and his soft lips were pulled tight. I fought the urge to apologize to this man. Something told me he didn't appreciate sorries. He wanted his world to run on his schedule, and anyone who didn't comply was punished.

"How is Grams?" Malice asked conversationally before

going to his desk and picking up a switchblade. His skilled hands started spinning it around, making the veins in his hand bulge. I stared at the way he rolled the knife over his knuckles with ease.

"She's well," I croaked out.

"Good. Did Hoffstead treat you like family?" Malice asked before sitting down at his seat. "Family is very important to me, you know."

"He was great," I whispered.

"Send Hoffstead a fruit basket," Malice said to Hale with a wink. Something told me that a fruit basket was code for something else. With a simple nod, Hale pulled his phone from his pocket, typed something, and exited the office. "Have a seat, Juliet," Malice said while nodding in the direction of the leather chair in front of him.

Malice still had that switchblade in his palm and was spinning it around threateningly. I half expected him to throw it and treat me like his own personal dart board. I slowly moved to the open chair and sat down in it. "Why am I here?" I asked.

Malice stopped playing with his switchblade to bring it to his lips. Pressing the flat edge of it against his pout, he contemplated my question for a lingering moment before dragging his lip along the sharp blade. I watched in sick fascination, and when he finally decided to answer my question, I gasped at the stark sound of his rough voice in the silent room.

"Let me tell you something, Juliet," he began while circling his desk and walking toward me. Every hair on my body stood on edge. "Instead of asking why you are here, I suggest you ask what I need. We've already established why you're here. We already know the lengths you're willing to go to keep yourself and your grandmother safe. Don't ask why anymore. I don't have the patience for questions like that. I don't have the patience for ignorance, either. Now try again."

Malice leaned against his desk, one arm crossed over his chest. His switchblade still in hand, he dragged it along his piercing jaw with a featherlight brush. I swallowed.

"Fine," I grumbled. "What can I do for you?" I voiced my words with a bite. In response to my small voice of rebellion, Malice glanced up at the ceiling and smiled, releasing a short laugh. I wondered if people ever treated him with snark.

Malice pushed himself off the edge of the desk and leaned closer to me. Then, he braced one hand on the armrest of my chair and tipped in so close that our eyes were only an inch apart. His hot breath flowed over my face, smelling like mint and bourbon. I felt him slowly, slowly, slowly ease his switchblade to my lips. "Open your mouth," he directed in a soft sensual tone that was both frightening and intriguing. I obeyed. Partly because I was held at the end of the blade and partly because I was curious about what he was going to do to me.

Malice then slipped the knife into my dry mouth. My chest tightened when he placed the knife on my tongue ever so carefully. The flat edge rested there for a moment, and he used his thumb to press against my bottom lip. He breathed me in while taunting me with the danger on my tongue. "You're so feisty. So full of life. Do you know what I do to people who don't speak to me with respect?" he asked. I couldn't even respond to him. Couldn't shake my head. He continued, not bothering to wait for my response. "I cut off their tongues."

He pulled the switchblade out of my mouth but, while doing so, made sure to nick my lip, forcing a fresh bead of blood to pebble up and spill from the small wound. He swiped the crimson stain from my lips with his thumb and then licked it. It was both erotic and terrifying. My heart raced at the sight of him.

"You're lucky that I have better plans for your tongue," he whispered before straightening. Standing tall, I was now level with his waist. I could see his hard cock pressing against the expensive material of his perfectly tailored pants. It looked almost painful, how hard it was straining against his clothes.

Malice set down his knife before curling his finger at me, beckoning me closer. I slowly stood up, my legs trembling from fear and an emotion I wasn't willing to even feel let alone say out loud. He reached out and wrapped his hands around my throat, applying the slightest bit of pressure while staring me in the eye. I caught him glancing occasionally over my head. What was he waiting for? Who was he looking for? This was a purposeful man. I felt like an animal caught in his trap. But I wanted to catch him off his guard.

"How is Vicky?" I asked. He tightened his hold around my neck, and I reached up to grab at his wrist.

"She's none of your concern," he snapped before letting me go.

"I'm worried about her," I admitted. "You know, it's so strange. Vicky always vaguely warned me about her second life, but it never felt real. Vicky wanted to protect me. I don't think she would have kept me away from you all otherwise. Which says a lot about what she thinks of you."

Malice scoffed. "Stop talking. And my sister only cares about herself. She wouldn't know loyalty if it slapped her across the cheek. She's safe and with extended family, which is more than I can say for you."

Something about his siblings made Malice crack. It was his one weakness. Somehow, I had to use that to my advantage to get out of this twisted spiral of blackmail. "I would just like to speak to Vicky," I pressed on.

"Maybe if you do your job correctly today, I'll let you

call her, hmm?" Malice said. "Though I don't honestly know why you would want to. She's a shitty sister and an even worse friend. You're better off."

My brows rose. I wasn't done challenging him yet. "Are you a good brother, Nick?" I asked, boldly using his first name.

He bit his bottom lip for a moment, anger burning through his expression. "I'm a good killer. I lead a good empire. I protect my own. Everything else is just bullshit, and I suggest you shut your pretty little mouth before I shove something in it, and this time I won't be as careful."

I heard footsteps down the hall and moved to see who was walking into the office, but Malice grabbed me by the chin and slammed his lips to mine.

chapter eight

I tried heroin once. The moment the drugs hit my veins, a thrill like nothing I'd ever experienced before washed over me. It was like a mental orgasm. I felt powerful, confident, and free. For ten hours, I didn't think about my grandmother's diagnosis. I didn't think about grief or all the shit I needed to do. I enjoyed a weightless feeling in my body. My limbs were swaying from the heroine's charm and the discordance in my surroundings. The high released me from all the burdens of living and left behind this hollow sense of euphoria.

I wish I could tell you that kissing Malice was like taking

a shot of the best heroin money could buy, but it wasn't. It was like lying on the ground as everyone piled heavy bricks on top of my body. It was this hard, damning experience that weighed me down in ways that felt unnatural.

He was demanding with his mouth. He sunk his teeth into my bottom lip like I was his possession, and his hot, sweeping tongue rolled across mine with punishing waves. I couldn't escape him. His hands had me tightly confined in his grasp. He locked himself on my mouth.

So fucking good.

So fucking painful.

Malice growled as he devoured me. It was intrusive and thrilling but oh so heavy. It wasn't an out-of-body experience. It was like dying. He delivered the kiss of death to the last bit of good left inside of me, and I wanted more. I let him weigh me down with his kiss, and worst of all, I kissed him back.

When he pulled away, there was a thrilled and beguiled expression on his beautiful and sharp face. A long moment passed as he stared at me. The kiss shared between us softened him in some way. He caressed the back of my neck, easing his hands beneath my chin to tuck a dark brown strand of hair behind my ear. He dropped his hands after that, as if touching me burned him. He murmured, "I may keep you."

That kiss made him want to keep me, but it made me

want to run away as fast as I could. Because if I didn't get away, that darkness hidden inside of me would want to kiss him again.

At my back, William spoke in a bored tone, "Did you need something from me?" In my red-hot shame, I turned around to greet him. I didn't owe William anything, least of all an explanation. But it felt wrong. William saw what Malice made me do, and now I was kissing him. What did this say about me? Did Malice plan on this? Was he hoping William would see it?

William wore a steely face as he kept his expression free of any protest or disappointment. He barely glanced at me before focusing all his attention on Malice. Although I couldn't tell if resentment was present in the way he looked at his older brother, there was definitely some tension in the air. I just wanted to leave. Why on earth did I let that happen? And more so, why did I enjoy it?

"I need your help with a project," Malice said, jerking me from my shameful thoughts. William nodded in response, silently encouraging him to continue. "Juliet is going to start working at Eden's Place."

Well, that was news to me.

"What's Eden's Place?" I asked. However, no one immediately answered.

Instead of a straight response, I was instantly given insight to what kind of establishment Eden's Place was by

William's immediate look of disgust. The protest quickly fell from his lips. "No. Absolutely not. A girl like Juliet doesn't belong in a place like that."

I paused. What kind of girl did William think I was? He did know me well. Everything I'd ever told Vicky, he was eavesdropping on. He knew about Grams and my struggles with school. My jobs. My love life. He was the unsuspecting fly on the wall, and now I found myself curious how he felt about everything he'd learned.

Malice wrapped his arm around my waist and pulled me flush with his chest. He was warm and hard, and I should've pulled out of his grasp, but instead, I let him touch me. Fucked up. I was seriously fucked up. "I think you'd be surprised with what Juliet is capable of. And last I checked, you don't make the rules or the decisions. If I want Juliet to work in the yard, that's where she'll work. If I want her at Eden's Place, then that's where she'll be. And tomorrow, if I decide that she's going to be chopping up bodies in Anthony's little death dungeon, then she'll be there." My stomach sank. The grip Malice had on me turned foreboding. He dug his fingers into my flesh, and it took everything I had not to cower away from him. Malice fed on weakness, and I didn't want to show him that I feared him.

"As if I could forget that you're in charge. Would you like to take your dick out and measure it, Nick? Maybe go piss on a few bushes to mark your territory?" William offered, visibly pissed off. "You're the oldest. You make the rules. Dad loved you the most. We get it already. What the fuck ever. Juliet is my responsibility. She has been for three years now, so if I want to better understand your plans for her, then I'll do whatever the fuck I need to, got it?"

"I should have let you die all those years ago," Malice replied in a cool, calculated tone.

"Would have made everyone's life a hell of a lot easier," William agreed. "But I'm here. What will you have Juliet do?" William asked.

Their back-and-forth had me swiveling my head to watch the verbal pissing match. There was so much anger and pain shared between them that I could barely keep up. I didn't want to be stuck between two rival brothers who I honestly barely knew. I wanted to make my own decisions.

"I'm more than capable of handling our own arrangements," I said before confidently shifting out of his grasp. My heart was racing in my chest, and I worried about the consequences of defying him. But I couldn't continue to let this man walk all over me. I needed to show at least a semblance of strength if I wanted to survive. I didn't want to be a pawn in his game. I wanted to be a business associate.

The truth was, Malice had something of value to me. Grams needed this medicine, and I needed more cash flow.

I was already elbow deep in this world. The only way out was through it. I killed a man. I was in charge of my own destiny.

"That you are," Malice replied with a sly grin. William shuffled from one foot to the other, as if taken aback by my confidence. "Eden's Place is the club I own. It's just a place for my business associates to wind down after a hard day. A few local officials like to use it as well, as a home for their business dealings. We offer pretty women, a fun time, and every illicit fantasy you could ever imagine."

My stomach sank. Maybe I was out of my depth. William huffed. "So what, you're gonna have her dance on stage? Or do you want to have her book private rooms with your men?" he snarled.

"No," Malice replied quickly with more force than I was expecting. I was glad that he wasn't going to make me do that, but still confused about the nature of this. "I need a new hostess. Someone to coordinate our girls and make sure my clients are happy. She'll greet people at the door and set them up where they need to be. Miss Cross can be the face of the place. I want her to get close to my clients but also seem unavailable. Men are quick to open up to women they want but can't have. She's going to help me find my rat."

I couldn't tell if this job was worse or better. At least he wasn't making me kill any more people. "So you just want me to spy?" I asked.

William stroked his chin, thinking over everything Malice had said. "It's pretty smart. Juliet is good with people. I've seen her at the diner, and it's like she can connect with just about anyone. But there are some shady people that walk through our doors. I don't want her to be unprotected."

My heart softened at his concern for me. Was it because he felt some sort of connection? Or was it out of duty to Vicky? "Yes. I know how much you care about everyone's safety," Malice replied with teeth clenched. "I'll put Hale on guard duty."

William nodded as if that were enough. But something in my chest bloomed with anxiety. Hale still made me nervous, and I didn't want to spend more time with him than necessary. This conversation was tense enough as it was, and I wanted to talk to Malice about money. Maybe I was unfairly judging Hale because of his gruff exterior. I could try to give him a chance.

"And how much are you paying me?" I asked. I tipped my chin up and stared Malice down. My not-so-subtle confidence brought a grin to his stoic face.

"Juliet," he began, "I truly think you've found your calling here." He picked up his glass of whiskey and took a slow drink. I got the sense that he was doing that to draw out the time and make me squirm. I kept my spine straight and proud. I wouldn't be backed into a corner by this man. It sounded like he needed me. Even if I only would play a small role in his organization, I'd use every drop of this opportunity to my advantage. We might've been locked together by fate, but I wasn't going to be his pet. I was capable and strong, and even though I felt a lot of apprehension about this job and what exactly it entailed, I was determined.

"Are you avoiding my question, Malice?" I asked. His games were not going to work on me. I wasn't sure where my confidence was coming from, but I held on to it with two hands.

"How much do you want?" he asked.

This was the hard part. I was determined to be clear in my needs. "Well, obviously I want my grandmother to keep seeing Dr. Hoffstead." I didn't mention that I would somehow have to convince my grandmother that I could afford her visits, but that was an issue for another day. "I think fifty thousand a year with full benefits is reasonable." I barely made twenty thousand a year at the diner—and that was including tips. With this, I could afford a few online classes at the local community college and get my degree.

William shook his head. Malice bit the inside of his cheek and looked me up and down. Was it too much?

"I'm open to negotiation," I quickly added. I knew that

my grandmother's doctors' appointments were ridiculously expensive, but I was hoping since I was doing some spy work on top of the hostess job, he would—

"I'm going to teach you a lesson today, Juliet," Malice said. William pulled out his phone to read a text message, seemingly distracted.

"Oh?" I asked, eyebrows raised in speculation. I could handle this. I could barter with a badass Mafia boss.

"Always know your worth, then double it. My employees at the club easily make six figures. You're dealing with very powerful, very private men. They pay a premium for good service and sealed lips."

Shit. So I lowballed myself?

"Okay," I replied. "Then I want—"

Malice interrupted me. "No. You'll get your fifty thousand a year. And I'll pay for your grandmother to go to the doctor and get her medicine. We can revisit your salary if you prove to be useful. But in the future, Juliet, if I give you an option to name your price, I suggest you aim high."

I flushed with embarrassment.

This world felt like a giant game board. I feigned confidence even though I was embarrassed. "Fair enough," I growled. "When do I start?" I had a shift tomorrow at the diner, and I would need to give them my two weeks' notice. I also had to figure out how I was going to keep this a secret from Grams.

"You start tonight. William is going to take you to get some outfits. Something tells me you don't have anything hanging in your closet that's on-brand for Eden's Place," Malice said while looking me up and down. I wasn't sure whether or not I should be insulted.

I wasn't exactly sure that I needed a shopping buddy, but I was willing to do just about everything and anything to get out of Malice's office. I nodded and started to walk out when he reached out and wrapped his hand around my wrist. "One more thing," he said in a gravelly voice.

I swallowed and looked up at him. William was on alert. "Yes?" I asked.

"Nobody touches you. They can look all they want, but you are not one of their toys. You're my toy." His teeth sunk into his bottom lip, and I felt a sickening wave of arousal wash over me. There was something about the possessiveness in his tone that made every single one of my muscles curl up like a cat. I was preening and desperate. Why was I so determined to be claimed by this man? Did I have Stockholm syndrome?

William cleared his throat, and Malice looked over my head at his brother. "Is there something you'd like to say?" Malice asked.

"I'm just curious how long you'll play with her before you decide that you are bored again."

Malice finally let go of me, and I fought the urge to rub the spot where he had gripped me so hard. "Oh, William," Malice began. "You know as well as anyone that I play with my toys until they break. And then, I play with them harder."

And with that ominous statement, William and I left.

CORALEE JUNE

chapter nine

After Malice sent us off to collect my work uniform, I couldn't help but think of his army of bodyguards and the way they dressed, spoke, and moved as one unit. I pictured his men, all dressed in their suits, with guns and knives strapped to their chests and a deadly expression on their faces.

"What are we doing here?" I asked. The storefront was painted all black, as if it were an escape or a devious secret hidden on the corner of Gwendolyn Drive and Mulberry Street. It was called Bloom Apothecary. There were no shop windows. The main logo was minimalistic and gold.

William had been silent the entire car ride here, which was unsurprising for me. If anything, I was thankful for the quiet. It felt surprisingly normal for my secret stranger, and lately there hadn't been enough normal. "Nick wants you to look like an Eden's Girl," he replied in a gruff tone after a lingering pause.

I stared at the storefront some more. "And what exactly is an Eden's Girl?" I asked, suddenly feeling anxious about my new role.

William looked at me with hunger in his eyes. I almost wished for his sunglasses again, hiding those heated orbs from my vision. His mask was more approachable. He reached out to stroke the top of my hand, and it made a warm tingling sensation kiss at my skin.

"An Eden's Girl is every man's deepest, darkest fantasy. She's soft and beautiful and unique. She's real, with real flaws, scars, and curves. An Eden's Girl creates her own definition of beautiful. She's not defined by her femininity, she defines it. Strong. Independent. Entertaining. Intelligent. Secretive. She embodies her namesake, a free, plentiful garden prone to sin."

I'd never heard William speak so poetically.

"And you think I'm capable of being an Eden's Girl? That sounds like a very high standard to live up to," I replied nervously.

William licked his lips. "I think you could be Eve herself,

Juliet."

I'd never been good at accepting the attention of others, and William was looking at me like I hung the moon. I averted my eyes. "So what is Bloom Apothecary?" I asked.

William turned off the car. "A lingerie shop."

I had a pretty good idea of what kind of establishment Eden's Place was, but knowing that I would be wearing as little as possible made me nervous. I was fairly confident with my body. I had a few stretch marks and curves, but I looked healthy and womanly. I'd never shied away from wearing a bikini to the local swimming pool, and I guess in some ways, it was the same thing as lingerie.

At least I was just the hostess. Malice made it very clear that I wasn't to be touched. It was a relief but also felt like one of his twisted games.

"I don't know how I'll explain this to Grams," I said, mostly to myself.

William softened. "You can keep the clothes at our house. If you need me to talk to the diner, I can have them keep you on the books for your Grams. Also, I really want to get you a car. I'm sure it's not easy relying on public transportation with her condition."

I was so stunned that I didn't know what to say. It made sense, William knew all my problems and had been paying attention. I just wasn't expecting him to be so thoughtful.

But also, I couldn't help but think…why now?

Not that I would have accepted his help sooner, but we could have been building a friendship all this time. What changed to make him go from my secret stranger to...well... he was still a secret stranger, just with more secrets and a soothing voice.

My stranger used to avert his gaze, but now he was staring affectionately at me. I wanted to understand the source of the shift.

"Thank you," I squeaked. "But I don't want one of the Civellas' unmarked cars. I've seen how Anthony scrubs DNA, and if I got pulled over, there's no telling what cops would find in that trunk."

William chuckled, and it was such a foreign look on him that I suddenly felt this strange urge to take a picture of the crooked smile on his handsome face.

"Come on," William said before getting out. I quickly followed after him, a blush rising to my cheeks. Unexpectedly, William held out his arm for me to take. The gesture wasn't really familiar, but since I was already stepping out of my comfort zone here, I figured when in Rome. I grabbed his arm, curling my fingers around the defined muscles in his bicep. A shopkeeper opened the door for us, letting us inside with a warm smile.

"William!" the shopkeeper exclaimed. Oh, so they were on a first-name basis? Her bright voice intruded on the intimacy of our moment. "It's so good to see you, dear," she said before leaning forward and kissing William on the cheek. She was a beautiful woman with bright red hair, brown eyes, and fair but freckled skin. She wore a tight black dress and Louis Vuitton heels.

"It's good to see you, Brittany," William replied. "I've got a new employee for you to dress. But she won't be like our other girls."

Brittany arched her brow at me. I felt her speculative gaze travel down my body, likely judging me. "I see," she began. "Is she special?" There was something nasally and intrusive about her question. However, William was not deterred.

"I guess you could say that. Nicholas wants her to be the face of Eden's Place. She needs to be classic and timeless. Suggestive. Addictive. She looks great in red. I'd prefer something a bit more conservative than what we usually select for our girls. Juliet is the kind of woman men dream about having. She's untouchable. Untouched. Think you can find something that will work?" William asked.

Against my better judgment, I preened at William's reverent words about me.

Brittany snorted, the sound like a car trying to start. "Well, of course I can find something for her," she exclaimed. Brittany was definitely getting on my nerves. "And her name is Juliet? What a romantic namesake! I think I have a collection that will perfectly fit your needs."

Didn't she know that Juliet died at the end of the play?

"If you'll just come with me," Brittany said. My arm was still hooked around William. I moved to detach myself from him, but he patted my hand instead.

"I'd like to see everything you pick out for her. It's of the utmost importance that we get this just right," William purred.

It was one thing to try on lingerie with Brittany, but something else entirely to do it in front of William. I guess I needed to get used to this, considering I was going to be a hostess at a sex club.

"Of course," Brittany gritted. Something told me she didn't like the amount of attention he was giving me.

Brittany guided me to the back of the store where collections with designer labels appeared to be. After taking my measurements, she quickly started piling garments up on her arm. William and I simply followed her with our eyes, only providing input when she held up a hanger for us to look at.

While she gathered items for the dressing room, I spoke to William. "So do you do this with all the girls?" I asked. It felt weird talking to him. For so long I pretended he had been a mere fly on the wall, but now I had a burning desire to find out more about what he was all about. My stranger was nothing like what I expected. Another question blurted out of me. "And what exactly do you do at Eden's Place?

Dress the talent?"

William cleared his throat. "Nick finances Eden's Place. He also brings in our elite clientele and abuses the privilege of the environment I've cultivated. But of the three of us, I am the one who crafts the aesthetic. My brother has no idea how to put together a club. I have expensive tastes and know how to appeal to the rich and powerful. And Brittany has supplied a lot of our costumes over the years. But no, I don't typically bring girls here. And I definitely don't watch them try on lingerie."

I swallowed. Luckily, Brittany had a dressing room ready for me, so I didn't have to respond. It was hard for me to decide what to say. William made his intentions quite clear, but I wasn't sure how I felt about it. Once again I found myself asking, why now?

This man had a dark and mysterious aura, but I was learning the elegance in his words and the swift patience he exhibited. William wasn't just the gruff man at Dick's Diner. He was luxurious. Thoughtful. Meticulous, almost. He cared for me, that much I knew. I guess, in a lot of ways, I cared for him too. William and Vicky were a package deal. One was never seen without the other. But now, I had to learn who the man behind the silence was.

"Now, some of these pieces can be kind of complicated. Let me know if you need any assistance." Brittany practically shoved me into a dressing room and slammed the curtain closed before running off to William's side. There was a velvet couch set up outside of the dressing room, and I imagined William sitting on it, his long frame leaned back and both legs parted in front of him. Relaxed. Confident. Goose bumps broke out over my arms at the thought of him seeing me like this.

I quickly undressed and gathered the first piece. It was a blush pink, silk night dress with a lace trim and a slit up the thigh. It was romantic but not too revealing. In fact, it was tamer than I was anticipating.

I opened the curtain and stepped outside, staring at the ground because I was too embarrassed to face William. "Look at me," William said in a gruff tone. Very slowly, I tipped my chin up, and with a steadying exhale looked him in the eye.

William nodded once, his eyes flaring with heat. "I want that in black," he said to Brittany without once tearing his eyes from my curves.

"Of course," Brittany said.

I ran the tips of my fingers down the lacy strap, and William's eyes followed the movement. He pulled out his cell phone and, without warning, took a photo of me. I wouldn't have even known he was doing that aside from the flash.

"What are you doing?" I asked.

"Asking Nicholas for his opinion," William replied. He

cleared his throat before nodding at me. "Try something else."

I went back into the changing room and put on the next piece. It was a bra and panties set. It made my already large breasts stand up so high they nearly touched my chin.

In contrast to the first outfit, this one was completely tasteless. It left nothing to be imagined. I definitely wouldn't be comfortable wearing it in front of a hypothetical boyfriend, much less a group of powerful strangers.

I called over the curtain, "I don't think this one is going to work."

Brittany laughed, likely finding amusement in my discomfort. What a cunt.

William's voice cut through her giggles. "Show me."

Pinching the meaty flesh of my thigh, I winced. "I really don't think this is the look you're going for," I argued. I averted my eyes from my reflection.

In a flash, the curtain was yanked open and William filled the small space. His bulky frame made the tiny dressing room feel even smaller. I wrapped my arms around myself, trying to hide the curves this lingerie showed off. I was normally a confident woman. I was all for body positivity, but that didn't mean I had to show off every curve I owned just to prove how much I loved myself. This was too much.

"You've never hidden yourself from me before, Juliet," William said in a soft, reverent tone. A cold sweat ran down my back. He slowly reached out and grabbed my arms and helped ease them away from my torso, almost as if he were opening a present. His eyes widened at the sight of me. He parted his lips in awe.

I felt beautiful but vulnerable. I felt seen. William knew every filthy part of me. For three years, I inadvertently opened up to him at the diner, and just two days ago, he saw what I was capable of in Anthony's death dungeon. And now, he saw my body for exactly what it was.

"You see?" I rasped. "I don't think it's what you're looking for."

Behind William, Brittany cleared her throat. "Leave us," William said forcefully. I couldn't see her look of frustration, but if the stomping step she took to the front of the store meant anything, then she was very upset. Was it wrong to savor that little victory?

"This is exactly what I'm looking for," William said while taking a step closer. He sounded so certain. I backed away, my back colliding with the full-length mirror in the room. "I'm going to buy this for you. But I'm the only person who gets to see you in it, okay?"

"That's a bit assuming, don't you think?" I said with an arched brow.

William groaned. "Oh, Miss Cross," he replied in a low dark tone. "I've seen you stripped bare since the day we met. You couldn't hide from me if you tried. I know every nuance. Every detail. In my mind, I've kissed you a thousand times. I've worshiped your body even more." He paused to lightly trace his fingers over my arm. A shiver traveled down my spine. "I tried to keep you out of this world. But now that you're here, I'm going to claim every last inch of you. I have spent the last three years eavesdropping on your soul. Next, I'll learn your body."

"Why now?" I boldly asked.

William licked his lips. "Vicky and I had a deal."

"What kind of deal?" I asked.

"It's not important anymore. The deal is off. I'm allowed to talk to you. Touch you." He paused to lean in and look me in the eye. "I paid my dues, and now you're mine, Miss Cross." I was shocked by the unfamiliar title, but the way it rolled off his talented tongue made the name feel overwhelmingly sensual and familiar. I wanted him to call me Miss Cross forever.

I'm not sure why I blurted out my response, but I did. "You saw me kiss Malice," I replied.

The lusty haze in William's expression faded a bit, but he didn't move to put space between us. "I learned a long time ago to let my brother have whatever he wants. The insufferable bastard likes to exercise his control any chance he gets. He kissed you because he wanted a reaction out of me. If given half a chance, he'll fuck you for the same reason. And then? He'll get bored of you. Kiss whoever you'd like. It won't matter in the long run. You've been mine for quite some time now. No one knows you like I do."

William backed away, leaving me in the fitting room all by myself. With shaky hands, I reached up and closed the curtain. The moment the velvet barrier was between us, I let out a shudder. What was wrong with me? Why was I so drawn to these dangerous men?

chapter ten

After William and I left Bloom Apothecary, he went to Eden's Place to get ready for the night, and I went back to the Civella Mansion to get ready. I had initially pushed to go to my own home, but explaining my new uniform to Grams would have been impossible. One of his men showed me a guest room tucked away on the first floor. Inside was all the makeup, hair tools, and beauty supplies a girl could ever need. Most of it still had the wrapping and price tags on it, and I couldn't help but wonder how often Malice had girls getting ready in his home that he needed to be stocked like this.

It only took about thirty minutes for me to get ready. I kept my makeup light and innocent, then curled my long hair. William was very clear about what made an Eden's Girl so unique. There was not a trace of pretense in her. She was confident and completely herself. As we made more lingerie selections, I realized that shopping for my uniform was more about what made me feel beautiful. Aside from the one outfit that William insisted I buy, everything else was selected based on my comfort level. Of course, it was all designer and chic. But it was uniquely me. It was an unusual experience to discover myself in a lingerie shop.

Something told me that William intended for it to be that way. He indulged in my secrets and collected them like gold tokens.

Keeping an eye on the clock, I spent my evening pacing the room while calling Grams and telling her that I was staying at Dick's for an extra shift. Her immediate reaction was to complain that I was working too much and needed a break, but her bingo buddy, Linda, stole the cell phone and told Grams to shut up and focus on the game. I giggled while listening to them bicker. The two of them played bingo at the community center once a week.

Although it might have escaped her notice tonight, I knew that she would soon be asking questions about where I was all the time. I wasn't sure how I would navigate that.

Around seven o'clock, someone brought me dinner.

Shockingly, it was my favorite dish: a medium rare steak and a loaded baked potato. I couldn't recall when the last time I had a meal like this was. I wondered if William was responsible for getting it delivered. Maybe it was a coincidence, or maybe he was once again showing me how well he knew me. I was questioning everything he did.

By nine, Hale collected me from my room and took me to a blacked out Escalade. The Civella Mansion was close to Eden's Place, so it was only about a five-minute drive. Although it felt like forty-five minutes, thanks to Hale's obvious stares.

There was something not right about that man. He had one hand on the steering wheel, and the other kept running over his greasy head and tugging at his pants. His beady eyes kept staring me down in the rearview mirror, and I wanted to claw them out of his skull.

Despite covering up with a cardigan and some jeans, the lacey outfit I wore still peeked through my clothes. I made a mental note to ask them if there was a locker room at Eden's Place for me to get ready there so I wouldn't have to travel in my work uniform—and I used the term uniform very loosely.

I wore a one-piece lace romper that clung to my body. It was a beautiful, bright red, the color of fresh blood, and it was so thin my nipples practically cut through it. It showed off the bottom half of my butt cheeks and accentuated my long legs. I paired it with some bright red pumps, but I knew I would regret my shoe choice within the first hour of my shift. Despite my aversion to wearing high heels, I couldn't help but feel sexy in them. I just prayed I'd figure out how to walk by the end of the night.

"Stop staring at me," I snapped at Hale when I caught his piercing gaze in the rearview mirror. He looked at the road but then right back to me. Dick. I knew that I needed to get used to being stared at. The entire purpose of this club was for men and women to gawk at the people working here. But there was something about Hale that made my skin crawl. It was like he didn't look at me appreciatively. He looked like a man imagining all the ways he could strangle me and hide the body.

I didn't like him. I didn't trust him.

Eden's Place was in an unpopulated part of town nestled in the business district. It was inconspicuous and didn't even have a parking lot, though I noticed a lot of luxury vehicles pulling around the back and disappearing through an alley.

Hale followed the drivers and pulled into a nearby parking garage that was hidden underground. I pressed both palms to the window as I stared out at the line of expensive cars and men in suits. The fluorescent lights flickered overhead. We parked, but Hale didn't unlock the door. "I don't want to be your babysitter," he growled.

"That makes two of us," I replied boldly.

"I think you need to learn your place around here. Just because you've got a nice pair of tits doesn't mean you have any power over me, you understand?" he said. "I'm the boss. You listen to me."

My tits had nothing to do with how I'd gotten here today. I'd killed a man. I'd navigated this new job with Malice and made decisions concerning my life without fucking Hale's input. I wouldn't let him diminish my abilities to having a nice rack.

"I listen to Malice, William, and Anthony," I quickly snapped back. "I listen to the people cutting my checks. And from the look of your shitty suit, I'm willing to bet you couldn't afford me."

Malice's words rang through my mind. Know your worth.

I didn't bother being polite to Hale. My gut was rarely wrong about people, and I trusted this man about as far as I could throw him. Hale growled and twisted in the front seat to glower at me. "When we get inside, don't do anything stupid. I'll introduce you to Kelsey, and she'll show you the ropes."

I breathed a sigh of relief. I didn't want Hale to be the one teaching me about this place. "Great," I replied in a snarky tone. Hale balled his hand into a fist, as if he were picturing crushing me in his palm.

"Boss wants to see you before we go," he said after a lingering moment before getting out of the Escalade. Boss? Which boss? I almost followed after him, but the passenger door across from me was yanked open, and Anthony slid inside, arriving with a grin on his angelic face.

"Well, look at you," he said with a smirk while scooting closer to me. Anthony had lost his beanie and was wearing dark jeans and a white undershirt. The outfit seemed out of place for an establishment like this, but something told me that Anthony didn't care about looking like he belonged. The shirt fit him tightly, showing off every defined muscle in his torso. He reached over to brush his knuckles along my cheek and pull at the cardigan I was wearing so he could see the outfit underneath. "I am so glad to see you. I wanted to take notes on the lye suggestion you made. What if your body doesn't fit in a fifty-gallon drum, should I like chop him up and liquify him in pieces?"

Anthony pulled out a notepad and pen and waited for me to answer him.

I blinked.

"Whatever is easiest."

He scribbled some more notes before speaking again. "And do you think it's environmentally irresponsible to pour the remains down the drain? There's not much research on it, but I think we should look into better waste management if this is the route we're going to take moving forward."

I gaped at him, speechless.

"You know what? I'll read up on it and get back to you. I'm so excited to test it out." Anthony pocketed his notepad and beamed at me.

"What are you doing here?" I asked. I'd also made a mental note that Hale called Anthony boss. If Anthony and Vicky were the closest, then that meant I trusted him the most in this place.

"Aside from chatting with you?" He grinned and then continued. "I'm putting on a show for all the rich assholes that like to get off," he replied. But I wasn't expecting that answer. His tone sounded almost bitter and definitely sarcastic. "It's fun. If you get tired of being a glorified door greeter, let me know."

"You're a performer?" I asked in disbelief.

"I guess you could call it that," Anthony replied with a bashful chuckle while scooting away from me. Was he embarrassed?

"Is it something I can watch?" I asked playfully, mostly curious how he would react.

"Hasn't anyone told you?" he answered my question with one of his own. "In our world, you can do whatever you want."

Once again, Anthony sounded bitter.

"I don't want to hurt anyone, and I get the feeling this

isn't just a game for you," I whispered.

"Intuitive, how refreshing," he murmured before licking his top teeth. I waited for him to tell me what he meant by that, but an explanation never came. He looked around the car, staring at the leather upholstery in a way that made me wonder if he was avoiding my gaze. "We don't have much time. I actually wanted to help you with something," he said, changing the subject.

I took his lead. If he didn't want to talk about it, then I wouldn't force him to, though it did bring up a lot of questions for me. "Oh? With what?" I asked.

He quickly pulled out his large cell phone from his pocket and opened a video chat. I watched it ring for a moment, and then my best friend's face filled the screen. "Vicky?!" I squealed the moment my eyes landed on her. It thrilled me to see her. Anthony's tense shoulders dropped some, and he playfully tossed his phone at me so I could hold it—covet it. I was so thankful to see her safe and sound.

Vicky's face filled most of the screen, but I could see beams of the early morning sun kissing her tan skin. She wore a soft pajama set and had her hair pulled back into a bun. She blinked away her sleepy expression a few times before seemingly becoming aware of who she was on the phone with. I didn't know exactly what time it was in Italy, but it was early.

"Are you fucking crazy?!" Vicky finally shrieked. "Anthony told me about Eden's. Juliet, what are you thinking?"

My excitement over seeing my best friend dried up quicker than a drop of water on a hot summer's day. My mouth twisted into a frown. Anthony winced. The excuse I'd been telling myself all day poured from my lips. "Vicky, your brother tied me up in his basement and held a gun to my head. If I didn't kill him—"

"I'm not talking about that," she quickly interrupted. "You did what you had to do." Vicky sounded so nonchalant and dismissive, it made me uncomfortable. She was just like her brothers, unbothered by the death that surrounded them. Would I ever get used to this?

My eyes were filled with hot tears as a forbidden grief barreled through me. Shameful wasn't enough of a word to describe the feeling I had.

Hearing Vicky talk about my crime made it feel more real somehow. Her brothers were virtual strangers to me, but this was a girl who had seen me through every high and low of my life for the last three years. She knew some of the darkest parts of my soul. I wasn't sure if it was her acceptance of me that was bringing tears to my eyes, or my inability to accept myself.

I did what I had to do.

I did what I had to do.

I did what I had to do.

I did what I had to do.

I refused to die. I refused to abandon Grams and Vicky. I refused to be a missing persons case that went unsolved. I refused to be like my mother. A cold case.

"I can't believe you're going to work at Eden's Place. Do you have any idea what you've done?"

Anthony leaned his forehead against the glass window, squeezing his eyes shut as if blocking out her voice.

"I know it's a sex club," I replied stiffly. Sometimes, Vicky treated me like I was naïve because our worlds were so different. My upbringing wasn't any easier than hers, though. Just different.

"But you don't know the type of men who go there!" she exclaimed. Anthony cleared his throat. Did she not know that her own brother was the performer?

"I suppose I don't know a lot of things about your life, Vicky," I snapped unexpectedly. "I didn't know you had three brothers. I didn't know that you were moving to Italy. I didn't realize —"

Vicky cut me off. "That never bothered you before. I told you when we first became friends that you had to be separate from this. I didn't tell you any of this, because I wanted to keep you out of the loop. I desperately wanted to tell you everything that was going on in my life, but I knew the only way I could keep you safe was if I kept you out of this. I never wanted you to have to deal with this. It's a burden I wouldn't wish on my worst enemy, let alone my best friend. This world will change you. Nicholas is..." Her voice trailed off, as if she couldn't find the words to describe her evil brother.

"I get that," I began. "I just felt blindsided by it all. A heads-up that you were moving would have been nice. You know how much I struggle with abandonment and being kept out of the loop. You were just going to disappear on me. And then everything happened, and I had no way to reach out to you for guidance, so I made the best of my situation."

Vicky bit her lip and looked off to the left before glaring back at me. "What did he offer you?"

I flinched at her question. I wasn't sure if it was the intrusiveness of her words or the assuming way she stared me down. Of course she knew that Malice had offered me something. They were blood. She probably knew better than anyone how he operated, it was why she was so determined to keep me away from it all.

"Who?" I asked.

"You know who. What did Nicholas—Malice—offer you, Juliet?"

I turned my head and looked at Anthony, stalling. Maybe it was because William was always sitting across the booth from us, but I wasn't embarrassed or uncomfortable to be having this conversation in front of a silent bystander. I guess every talk Vicky and I ever had was in front of a deadly audience.

Anthony stared back at me, waiting for my response. This felt like a test, but I didn't know the right answer.

Actually, I did know the right answer.

Honesty. Honesty was always the right answer. A lie was too close to a secret for me to be comfortable not admitting why I was here.

"Malice got Grams set up with one of the best doctors in the city. I couldn't afford her regular medicine, let alone an experimental drug. I was working sixty-five hours a week at that diner, barely surviving. I need the money. I need Grams to be okay. I don't want her to suffer, Vicky."

"I've tried to help you! I got you information about that assisted living place," she argued.

"I couldn't afford it, Vicky. I've been struggling so fucking much. I don't have time for a friend. I barely have time for school or my podcast. My hobbies include taking care of Grams, reading until I pass out, and visiting with you for forty-five minutes every Thursday night. I don't have a life. I don't have money. I walk both ways to work." I wasn't usually the type of person to complain about my situation. I didn't think that constantly getting down about things you couldn't change was helpful. But damn did it feel good to finally say what I'd been feeling ever since

Grams got her diagnosis.

I was tired. Miserable. I hadn't bought myself new shoes since sophomore year of high school. I spent all my time working. It was hard. Grueling. I valued Vicky because she was a very brief but also very bright part of my life, but that didn't mean she had the right to judge me for my decisions. Even if she understood this world better than I did, she didn't understand my situation. She didn't know what it was like to eat rejected food in the back alley behind Dick's Diner because I didn't have enough money for groceries until payday. She didn't know what it was like to save up for eighteen months for a shitty microphone so I could host my own podcast.

I wasn't secretive about my struggle, but she didn't attempt to truly see how hard it was for me to survive. And I guess I didn't take the time to see how much her own life was draining her. Maybe my best friend and I didn't know each other as well as we thought.

"I knew you were struggling, but…"

"But your world was so overwhelming that you didn't have the capacity to think about mine?" I asked. After being in the Civella circle for just a couple days, I knew how easy it was to get sucked into your own reality. I didn't fault Vicky for not understanding, but I would create a boundary right here. I didn't have the patience to be judged, and quite frankly, I was in this mess because of her. Malice now held murder over my head. I was lucky that he offered me anything at all. I would be helpless against him should he turn me in for murder. She was privileged enough to get away from this mess, but I didn't have the freedom of choice like she did.

"Can you at least admit that you're in way over your head?" Vicky asked solemnly.

I stared deeply into my best friend's eyes, taking in her bright blue gaze full of concern and hurt. I wondered if she was feeling the same way that I was. "I was already drowning, Vicky," I replied. "I'm in too deep."

Vicky sighed. I watched as she opened and closed her mouth, as if trying to force the thoughts swirling around her mind past her lips. "He makes it look so appetizing. He'll dangle your deepest desires over your head. My brother doesn't care about your Grams. He doesn't care about you. I don't think he's capable of caring about anything but his empire. I can't help you from here."

"Are we going to be okay?" I asked. I had already decided about working at the club. But it worried me that this decision would cause a wedge between Vicky and me. I already felt somewhat distant from her since the night at the diner. I was struggling to forgive her for abandoning me. She was going to walk out of my life without a second glance, knowing how traumatizing that was for me. But I didn't want to lose her.

"You're my best friend, Juliet. I'll always love you. I just want what's best for you. I can't support you getting close to my brother's business. I've spent my entire life wanting to get out, and I'm not sure I can forgive you for willingly putting yourself right in the middle of it all."

Vicky made it sound like this was some premeditated decision that I had made. It wasn't. Malice blackmailed me. He forced me to end that man's life. I had a feeling that it didn't matter what I said, though. Vicky had it in her mind that I was betraying her by being here. And I wanted to know why.

Before I could process the conversation between us, Anthony yanked the phone out of my hand and stared at his sister. "How's Italy?" he asked in a playful tone. "Did you know our family vacation home is two hours away from one of the oldest cemeteries in the world?"

"You know I only go to creepy cemeteries when you drag me to them, Anthony," Vicky replied dryly, though I sensed affection in her tone. "I suppose one good thing came from this. You got to finally meet Juliet. What do you think?"

Anthony gave me a sideways glance before responding to her. "You were right about us getting along. She has some great ideas for disposing of a body."

"I'd feel better if she were working with you instead of at the club. At least William will be there..."

Anthony's lips tightened into a brief line, but he forced a smile again. "I'll take good care of her. You just stay safe until we can figure out what's going on with this rat. We had another shipment of weapons stolen last night."

I leaned closer to listen to Vicky's response. "I think sending me to the other side of the world is overkill, but I am enjoying the sunshine. Be safe, okay?"

"Will do," Anthony replied before hanging up the phone.

Silence stretched between us for a long moment, and I wiggled anxiously in my seat while waiting for him to speak. "My sister really cares about you," he murmured. He placed his hand on the door handle and cleared his throat. "Guess that means I care about you too. Don't let this place change you, okay?"

I nodded, not sure what to say. There was something about Anthony that made my chest hurt, an instinct that there was more beneath the surface with him that I wasn't quite getting.

"I promise," I finally whispered, but he was already outside and walking through the back door.

chapter eleven

Kelsey was a blond bombshell with long legs and a corset tied so tight I wondered how she was breathing. Her stilettos were like stilts, and in the five minutes I'd been in her company, she'd run around this entire space without breaking a sweat or seemingly taking a breath. "Over here is the bar," she said in a bright tone while yanking me toward the middle of the club. I barely had the opportunity to take in my surroundings because she was moving around so quickly. The moment I was escorted through the door, Kelsey stood up and started running me places while talking a mile a minute.

There was no way to describe Eden's Place other than as a dark, gloomy place. Surprisingly, the common area lacked a certain sensuality that I'd expected. The black marble floors clicked under my feet with every step. Red lights illuminated the walls, and black velvet curtains sectioned off different areas of the open space. Lusty music boomed from speakers overhead. Diverse women in all stages of undress stalked around the club, carrying trays and flirting with the early patrons. They were the only sign that this was a sex club. Otherwise, it looked like a club for mobsters to hold meetings.

The bar was massive and served as a focal point for the main room. Lavishly finished tables surrounded the large bar, providing a cozy space for people to sit and visit. Hallways leading out of the main bar area were illuminated with deep red lighting on the floors. Kelsey hadn't taken me there yet.

"What's down the hall?" I asked, slightly out of breath from chasing her around the club.

"Those are the performance rooms. I'll take you there once more shows start. I want you to get the full experience," she said with a wink.

The full experience, huh? "Okay."

"Here is where most of our guests will start out for the night. Sometimes they play poker. Sometimes they sign billion-dollar business deals. Forget everything and anything you overhear. It's safer that way."

Her advice made sense, but I was supposed to be Malice's eyes and ears. "Good point," I choked out.

Kelsey gave me a pointed stare. "I'm serious. Keep your head down and act oblivious. You don't want to end up missing, okay?"

"Okay," I echoed.

"At midnight, we open the curtains, and a few of our performers get on stage behind a glass partition. Some of our guests are very particular about this, they like knowing who is performing when and where so they can reserve a seat close to the glass. Some men stick their faces up against it, and we have to clean the glass every hour. Disgusting."

Kelsey was talking so fast that I could barely keep up with her. "As the host, do I sit people here, or is it open seating?"

"Open seating," Kelsey replied while marching up to the bar top and grabbing a shot of clear liquid. I watched in awe as she tossed it back with a slight hiss. "The cocktail waitresses have this area handled. You will handle all of our clients' deepest, darkest fantasies." Kelsey slammed the shot glass on a dark wooden bar top and nodded toward the front of the club where people were walking in.

"That sounds a little intimidating," I said.

"Not really. You'll get used to it. But if you want to talk about intimidating"—she paused to nod toward our left—

"Nicholas Civella fits the bill." I followed her gaze, my heart beating erratically as Malice approached. Gleams of goose bumps started to appear on my skin. He was wearing an all-black suit. Black dress shoes. Black Gucci belt. Black button-up shirt. His hair was tamed with gel, and he had airpods in his ear. "Shit, he's walking this way. Don't say anything stupid," Kelsey stammered before patting her hair.

Malice stopped in front of us and looked me up and down. If he liked the outfit William picked out for me, then he didn't let it show. His lip twitched as I squirmed in place. His heavy stare felt like an anvil on my exposed skin.

"Is this the new hire?" he asked Kelsey, his voice slightly raised so people around us could hear. I was given strict instructions to pretend like I was just another employee and not to approach Malice in public.

"Yes, sir," Kelsey replied, her voice shaky.

We were supposed to be pretending to be strangers, but I couldn't help but still feel tension between us. It was palpable. Unforgettable. Overwhelmingly sensual, too. Certainly everyone else recognized it also. "She looks the part," he murmured before reaching out to run his finger along my side. My skin tingled everywhere he touched. Slowly, Malice leaned in to whisper in my ear. His hot breath feathered down my neck. "Come see me after your shift."

Malice pulled back and I nodded. "Yes, sir," I whispered. He paused about three inches from my face and breathed me in, a smile on his plush lips.

"You'll fit in here just fine," he replied before leaving us to go and sit in a corner booth.

The moment he was out of earshot, Kelsey let out a low whistle. "You are in trouble," she said. "You don't want to be on Mr. Civella's radar, honey."

I stared at him, seemingly transfixed. "Why not?" I asked. Little did she know, I was smack dab in the middle of whatever radar Malice had.

Kelsey teasingly grabbed a napkin and pretended to wipe drool from my chin. "Because that man is deadly," she replied, all humor from her voice gone.

I knew with complete certainty that she was absolutely correct. "I'll stay away from him," I promised, even though I didn't know how that was going to be possible anymore.

"Come on. Let's go." Kelsey smiled encouragingly before leading me back to the hostess stand. It was an enormous desk with two oversized computer screens. "Every guest has a card. The moment they walk through the door, they are expected to scan their card. A customized profile will show up on the computer." At the desk, Hale was leaning against the wall with his arms crossed over his chest and a frown on his face. I hoped he wasn't planning on staying there all night. Kelsey walked up to him and held out her palm. "Can I borrow your membership card? It's for training purposes." Hale huffed in annoyance before digging through his breast pocket and pulling out a black rectangular piece of plastic. "Thank you!" Kelsey sang before walking back over to the desk.

She scanned the card, and immediately a profile of Hale popped up. It had an unflattering photo of him, a list of every time he checked into the club, what rooms he went to, and what his preferences were. There was also a list of his favorite performers. His favorite...kinks. "The program is pretty intuitive," Kelsey explained. "It will provide suggestions based on his history, likes and dislikes. We also have a scheduling system for our clients. Guests can reserve rooms online, and it will show up here. Your job is to inform them of what is on the schedule. For example," Kelsey said, scanning Hale's profile, "it says here that Hale has a crush fetish."

"What's that?" I asked.

She waved her hand nonchalantly. "He likes watching women step on shit. Crushing it with their heels, ya know?" She leaned closer to read the notes on his profile. "It says he enjoys watching kittens, bugs, and puppies get crushed." She paused to wince. "But we don't abuse animals in this establishment. No kink shaming here, but Eden's Place has to have at least some standards, eh? We have a performer that steps on glass and food."

"Well, thank God for that," I whispered. I couldn't imagine what kind of monster liked watching innocent animals get crushed. It was fucking barbaric and told me everything I needed to know about Hale. I didn't trust him one bit.

I looked over her shoulder at the calendar. A performer labeled Crush Fetish was highlighted in red. Kelsey continued, calling over her shoulder at Hale. "Your girl is in the Calla Lily room tonight."

Hale marched over to us and grabbed his card back from Kelsey. "I'm good tonight," he began before looking down his nose at me. "I had my own private performance a couple days ago. It was hot, something I'd normally have to pay a premium to see."

Oh...oh my God.

No. Certainly he wasn't talking about—

But of course he was.

My stomach sank as I realized what his words meant. I'd fulfilled his disgusting fantasy. Watching me...crush... that man was his kink. I sold my soul, and he got off.

"Let's move on to the profile management of the job..." Kelsey said, oblivious to the existential crisis I was having. I had to press my hand to my mouth to stop myself from vomiting.

"She's going to puke," Hale said while cracking his knuckles. Pop. Pop. Pop.

Kelsey snapped her attention to me, confused. "Juliet? Are you okay?"

"I'm fine," I rushed out. "I just need to use the bathroom." I didn't even give Kelsey a chance to speak, I walked as fast as my death trap stilettos could carry me and as far away from Hale as possible. I didn't care where I went, I just needed to put some distance between us. It felt so wrong, knowing that one of the most traumatic moments of my life got him off. It was an invasive, nasty turn of events that made me feel sick to my stomach.

I went down one of the side halls, not really sure where I was going. The red, flashing lights made the space difficult to navigate. My vision was blurring, and my heart raced. I knew in my gut that I hadn't taken the time to process everything. I just kept pushing forward, but something about Hale sent me over the edge.

But stark white light caught my eye, jarring me out of my thoughts. The hallway was like a gigantic aquarium with waterless tanks. On both my left and right were glass walls separating me from the performers. Black curtains covered some sections. Some were already open for guests to see.

The first exhibit featured a man lightly kissing a blow-up doll. Tenderly. Slowly. He was a titan of a man, bulging muscles and glistening brown skin. His tongue slid across the blow-up's mouth with such passionate lust that I blushed. He didn't have an audience, but he was performing regardless.

I kept walking down the hall. The next room was bathed in a teal blue light. A woman was lying on a bed in the middle of the room, the pink sheets were ruffled and twisted around her. She was holding an oddly shaped dildo that looked...out of this world. Almost like the leg of an octopus. She was still wearing black panties and rubbing the plastic tentacle over her clit while arching her back off the mattress.

I watched in awe. Even though I knew that this was her job and the entire purpose of this club was to dive into the deepest fantasies of the rich and powerful, I couldn't help but feel like I was intruding on something by staring.

A woman wearing a deep ruby dress, with dark blue curly hair pinned on top of her head, took a seat in front of the mirror and watched with hungry eyes. The spectator looked rigid and fascinated.

I kept moving down the row of exhibits. Some performers had no one watching. Some had five or six men pressed up as close to the glass as they could get. The hallway was wide, and each glass wall had seats positioned in front of them.

On either side of me was every kink imaginable. Every race, gender, sexual orientation, and age was all represented at Eden's Place. A beautiful woman who looked to be over the age of sixty-five was dressed in all leather and was cracking a whip at a much younger man.

I did my best to remove any prejudiced bias from my mind. It was insane to me how big this warehouse of dreams was. There were some kinks I didn't understand. Men dressed like animals were chasing around naked women in one room. In another room was just a woman getting a tattoo on her vagina.

It wasn't until I got to the very end of the exhibit hall that I was truly shocked by what I saw. There, in his glass cage of pleasure, was Anthony Civella.

chapter twelve

Separated only by the glass wall, I shamelessly stared at Anthony Civella. His impressive body was fit and healthy. His brown, shaggy hair was tangled and damp like he just showered and haphazardly ran his hand through it. Every ridge and contour of his muscles was clearly defined. He had thick, long legs like tree trunks and a carved torso that looked like cut rock. The piercing look of his eyes flashed with danger when he saw me staring. He didn't look ashamed, but instead, resigned. It was a look of acceptance, as if he'd expected me to come tumbling into this playroom. He challenged me with his gaze. He wanted me to see him—really see him.

Grams once got us a season pass to the local zoo, and I fell in love with this bold tiger in the predatory animals section. As a little girl, I joked that he was my pet, and I'd make Grams sit with me in front of his exhibit for hours on end. We'd pack lunch and set up on the bench in front of his extravagant cage. Over time, I found myself feeling sorry for the powerful animal. He wasn't meant for the zoo; he wasn't meant for me, either.

Anthony was a lot like that tiger.

Naked. Primitive. Unique. Free yet somehow shackled, too. I wanted to know more.

He was completely bare, and my eyes slowly swept over his entire body. Anthony's cock was already hard. It was thick, long, and impressive.

Unlike the other rooms, this glass box was split in two by a thin black wall. His body was slick with oil, and he ran his trembling hands down his stomach while glaring at the wall separating him from the other side of the performance exhibit. There was a door leading into each side of the wall.

There were already a couple of men and women sitting down and preparing for the show. I found a seat in the front row. Maybe it wasn't ethical or professional of me to sit down and watch, but I was driven by dark curiosity. Anthony bit his lip, then turned around to face the door for a moment. I gasped at the site of his back.

Thick, raised scars lined every inch of his skin from the neck down. It was as if someone had taken a whip to his body and marked up every available part of him they could.

I was so shocked over the destruction on his flesh that I didn't notice a door opening on the other side of the wall. I tore my eyes from his damage to observe the woman who walked into their divided glass cage. She had beautiful creamy skin and dark brown hair. Her eyes were black and lined with thick eyeliner. She was fully naked with small breasts and an unshaved pussy.

Anthony rolled his neck and walked up to the wall. He placed both palms against the thick divider, and then, he did something unexpected.

There was honestly no way to describe it without sounding crude. He slid aside a partition, revealing a perfectly circular hole in the wall. I wondered what he was doing with that, but my question was quickly answered when he slid his hardened dick through the circular opening. I'd heard about glory holes before, but I'd never seen one in action. At the sight of Anthony's cock, the woman dropped to her knees in front of him and wrapped her lips around his pulsing penis. I blushed and placed my fingers over my mouth. I couldn't believe what I was seeing and didn't understand my reaction to it.

I was anxious for Anthony. The act was oddly

vulnerable. He didn't know who or what was on the other side of the wall. I was also slightly jealous. I wondered if he picked this exhibit or if this was something...else.

"If you're going to laugh, then get the fuck out of here," William's voice hissed. I jumped in my seat, surprised to hear him. A heavy hand rested on my shoulder as he crouched beside me. Next came so venomous a question that it practically burned. "What are you doing here?"

Shit. I was supposed to be working. I was both disgusted and embarrassed about what had happened with Hale. I ran away to put some space between us, but then I ended up going down the rabbit hole of Eden's Place. This club was intense and detailed. The way they set it up gave every desire a voice. What started as wanting to escape Hale turned into an exploration.

Instead of answering him, I asked a question of my own. I didn't care that Anthony had his own kinks. I wanted to know who hurt him. "What happened to Anthony?" Those scars on his back were abusive and cruel in nature.

"Come on," William said while nodding down the hall and away from Anthony's cage. I stood up just as another woman entered the showroom. And another woman. All of them lined up. Naked, glistening with sweat, and lust heavy in their eyes. All of them were prepared to drop to their knees and pleasure Anthony. Would he know the difference between each woman? Did it matter to him?

Were they just faceless pleasure for him to get off to? "Miss Cross?" William called once more. I couldn't tear my eyes away from the scene. It was sexual but also...sad. Anthony was all alone, standing there, his head tossed back and eyes squeezed shut. Like getting off was somehow painful to him.

Seeing the growing crowd on the other side of the partition made it look like an art exhibit more than anything. Anthony was reduced to only his cock. They didn't know the man behind the wall. They didn't know the scars on his skin.

And likewise, he didn't know them.

Tears filled my eyes as I watched him. His palms slammed against the wall. His muscles flexed. He groaned and bit his lip. Another woman dropped to her knees and started sucking him off.

William grabbed my wrist and gently pulled me up and away. "Come on," he whispered tenderly. I wasn't expecting to be so emotional, but there was something about this that made me sick to my stomach.

Once out of view of the showroom, William pushed me against the wall and cupped my cheeks with his hands. I felt his thumb brush along my skin, swatting at tears as he peered at me. "Someone hurt him," I whispered. It was so evident. How could all those people watch him when it was plain to see that something wasn't right? I didn't know

Anthony that well, but I recognized the pain within him.

William leaned closer for a moment, as if he wanted to kiss my forehead. I waited patiently, for some reason craving the comfort he offered.

"Anthony was taken by one of Cora's business partners a year ago. She ordered it," William admitted.

I still didn't know who this Cora bitch was, but a sudden wave of fury washed over me. I wanted to kill her. End her. Ruin her. William continued. "He's struggled to be physically intimate with people ever since. Even hugs bother him. Hell, he does better with the dead than the living."

I shook my head. This was terrible. "Why?" I asked. "Why did they take him?"

William pulled away, a flicker of pain flashing across his expression. "Our father raised Nicholas to be ambitious. But he grew too fast. The first year after our parents' death, he took over territories like it was nothing. It pissed a lot of people off, and I guess you could say we all were cocky. In a matter of eighteen months, we'd grown an empire our father could only dream of. We were motivated by grief. When our parents died, we wanted to build something in their memory."

I swallowed. "But everything comes at a cost," I whispered.

William nodded solemnly. "They had him for eight

days. Eight days was all it took to completely change him. He came back with his skin ripped to shreds. He'd wake up in the middle of the night screaming. The only person who could help him was Vicky. Hell, he still relies on her for most everything. Can't go a day without talking to her. She understands him."

"And Vicky's now halfway across the world," I said with a shudder. "Why would Malice send her away if she's the only person Anthony connects with? Did you not see what was happening in there? He didn't look happy, William."

"We didn't have a choice. Cora is vindictive and is ten steps ahead of us. Nicholas killed the partner who abused Anthony, and now she wants revenge. Nick refuses to let something happen to Vicky too. He might be a cocky, insane motherfucker, but he cares about his family, and he feels a lot of guilt about what happened to Anthony."

Even though I didn't really know Anthony that well, I felt a renewed sense of purpose about my role here at Eden's Place. I wasn't just finding a rat, I was finding a way for Vicky to come home. I was bringing some healing back into Anthony's life.

"We need to find the rat," I said, my voice stern. I thought back on what Malice had whispered to me when we bumped into one another earlier.

"And we will. I'm not sure how much we're realistically going to find out at the club," he replied. "Nicholas is convinced that we could find some sort of lead here."

I absorbed his words. "Why does Malice think that the rat is associated with Eden's Place?"

William looked around the dim hallway before answering me. "We made arrangements for a shipment of guns to arrive at a specific date and time. We met with the supplier at Eden's Place to discuss. Cora's army was at the exchange spot and stole our shipment. Killed three of our men, too."

"I really hate this bitch," I growled, suddenly feeling murderous.

William's lip twitched. "I think the problem is deeper, maybe even someone in our infrastructure. Nicholas doesn't want to believe someone close to us betrayed us. It's complicated, so be sure to stay diligent."

It was on the tip of my tongue to tell William that I didn't trust Hale. Something about him just felt wrong, but he was in their inner circle. Aside from knowing he had a ruthless kink, I didn't really know much else about him. And it wasn't like the Civellas didn't know already. They had an entire database dedicated to everyone's deepest, darkest desires.

William walked ahead of me back toward the hostess stand. I watched him walk, while trying to come up with how I was going to handle being around Hale without vomiting. I needed to talk to Malice about finding someone else to watch over me. It probably didn't help me keep a low profile to have one of his men watching over me, either.

Once I saw the hostess stand, Kelsey frantically waved me over. I slumped my shoulders. "Where did you disappear off to?" she hissed while following William with her eyes. He didn't look my direction and sat at the bar. "You can't just go wandering around. They'll fire you on the spot if they catch you slacking off, and you don't want to lose your job here on the first day. You haven't established your loyalty yet, and these people will do anything to keep their secrets from getting out, you feel me?"

"I'm sorry. I got lost," I lied before looking around. Hale was missing. "Where is Hale?"

"Nicholas came by with a job for him," she replied nonchalantly. "Look, I'm serious. You can't just walk off like that, okay? I'm saying this for your protection."

I gave her an apologetic smile. "I'm sorry. I just... Does Hale seem off to you?"

Awareness settled in Kelsey's features, and she nodded. "Ah, I see. Yeah, Hale is a fucking psychopath. I guess I'm just used to him. I promise, he has one of the darker fantasies here. Most people have fairly normal kinks. Malice doesn't let child predators walk through our doors, and everything we do here is consensual. Eden's Place actually has a full-time sex therapist to make sure that everything is handled in a safe way. I'm sure that was a little overwhelming to hear his kink right off the bat. Crusher fuckers are usually harmless, we just keep it on file so we are aware if he progresses, you know?"

I nodded. "What do you mean...progresses?"

Kelsey's lip pinched into a thin line, and she looked around. "I'm not qualified to explain this, but I'll do my best. We have protocols in place. Sometimes, Eden can be an outlet for clients, you know? Sometimes, it becomes an addiction. Sometimes, it becomes this rolling snowball that grows bigger and bigger. It gets dangerous. We like to give people a taste of their fantasies, but we don't want it to get out of hand. For all his terrifying business dealings, Mr. Civella is actually very particular about this."

"And what is Hale?" I asked, not sure I wanted the answer. "Is he here for the outlet, the addiction, or is he a snowball?"

"Hale is a fireball just waiting to happen," Kelsey whispered. "You can't give him even an inch with his kink."

Fuck. I'd just given him a mile.

chapter thirteen

By the end of my shift, my feet had surpassed the point of pain and were completely numb. Kelsey ran me through every detail of our job, and I saw more sex than I'd ever seen in porn. I learned about different kinks too. Some of it was strange and unsettling. A lot of it was hot and theatrical. A few things made me want to vomit.

It was an exhausting night—way harder than anything I'd experienced at Dick's Diner. I barely had time to stop and pee. In addition to running the welcome desk, Kelsey and I also provided support to the performers. The majority of my evening was spent running various supplies to them.

With her apparent inexhaustible energy, Kelsey continued to spit out orders through her headset.

"Denea needs a tampon on stage seven."

"Someone go remind Paige to take a break! Has she eaten yet? Fuck, someone bring her dinner."

"Sherrie! Do you mind taking a shift in the foot fetish room?"

"Someone go tell Cassandra to stop making out with Julius in the storage closet and get ready for her underwater masturbation display on stage eight."

"Nikki is our star performer. If I don't have at least thirty chairs ready to go at her stage, I will personally shove my stiletto up your ass."

"You need a foot rub, Brandy? I'll have a massage therapist here in twenty minutes. You just say the word."

"We have a pervert fucking with the talent on stage four. The guard needs backup."

"Nikita cannot perform under these conditions. She needs Vaseline, a can of whipped cream, some leather, and a decent pair of heels. We are serving fantasies here, not disasters, okay?"

I was in awe. Shocked. Honestly, I couldn't even keep up. I could see why they needed a second hostess. It was nearly impossible to coordinate with performers while checking people in.

Once we were done, I was bone-tired and starving.

I sat down once the last club member left, and let out a loud sigh. "Fuck, Kelsey. How did you do all of this on your own?" I asked.

She nonchalantly was typing up a report for a new member and smacking her gum. "You'll get used to it."

"My feet are killing me," I cried. "I mean, seriously, you just run around like it's nothing."

She eyed me. "Gel insoles for your shoes. Total game changer."

It was nearly three in the morning, and I was ready to go home. I pulled out my cell and checked where the nearest bus stop was and sighed when I realized it was about a half mile away. This wasn't a part of town I wanted to walk home in. Especially in these heels. It was the sort of place where you needed a solid pair of running sneakers and mace.

Hale was nowhere to be seen, though. Malice wanted to meet with me after my shift but had already gone home. Did he expect me to go back to his mansion? I didn't know where Anthony was, and William apparently stayed here until six a.m. to get ready for the next night.

"Well, that's a wrap," Kelsey said before grabbing a pair of sweats from a secret cabinet under her desk and slipping them on over her clothes. "You did good," she said with a smile. "Go home and get some rest."

"Thanks for all your help," I replied. "I really appreciate

it."

"Want to walk out with me?" she asked. Pride had me keeping my mouth shut about not having a car. I didn't want to have to explain that I had to walk to the nearest bus stop. I hated public transportation at night. I'd probably have to wait for about thirty minutes at the stop since fewer buses run after midnight. Maybe I could see how much an Uber cost. It would probably be more than I could afford at the moment, but pretty soon I wouldn't have to worry about it. My new salary made this entire crazy job worth it. I'd buy groceries that didn't have to cook in a microwave. I could go out to eat with Grams. Buy her those orthopedic shoes she'd been eyeing. I was so excited.

"I have to go to the bathroom," I lied. "Go ahead, I'll be out there soon."

She patted me on the shoulder. "See you tomorrow," she replied brightly before leaving. A bodyguard escorted her out of the building.

I dialed Malice's number on my cell phone. It rang and rang and rang. When it went to voicemail, I hung up instead of leaving a brief message. If he wanted to talk, he would have given me more instructions. It wasn't like I had anything to tell him, aside from my evidence-less assumptions about Hale.

I decided it was probably safer to ask William for a ride, but when I walked by his office, it was empty. Shit. It wasn't like I had his number either. I clicked on my Uber app and was horrified to discover that a ride home would cost sixty dollars. Considering I only had twelve dollars to my name, that wasn't an option. After much agonizing, I decided that the only way I was getting home was by walking and taking the bus.

Fuck.

The night air was humid but not miserably hot. It wasn't a well-lit part of town, but I used my cell phone to illuminate the streets. It might have drawn more attention to me, but at least I wasn't screaming at every shadow and every alley. I'd grown up in this town, and since meeting Malice, I knew that my fears weren't unfounded. I was very much in danger and would have to find an alternative ride moving forward. William had mentioned getting me a car before, and I just hoped that he meant it.

Thankfully, I still had my cardigan and jeans to hide my scandalous outfit. A few homeless men on the street watched me with their bloodshot eyes as I walked by. A couple catcalled me. One followed me for half a block before giving up.

My aching feet tingled with every quick step, and I prayed the bus would arrive quickly. Despite the exhaustion, I was full of adrenaline from my terrifying walk. Once at the stop, I breathed a sigh of relief. I knew it was just an illusion. I still wasn't feeling that safe, but at least I was under a structure and had finished the most difficult part of my trip.

I sat down at a bench and steadied my breathing while waiting for my ride.

"It's such a late night. Mind if I sit with you? Us girls have to stick together, yeah?" said a raspy voice with a slight Southern twang.

I jumped a little at the sound and turned to face my intruder. She was a beautiful woman with shoulder-length brown hair, brown eyes, and long lashes. Her lips were slightly chapped, and a light dusting of freckles was sprinkled across her nose. The harsh bus stop lights overhead cast shadows under her eyes, and she pulled at her soft silk shirt while assessing me.

"Have a seat," I said while scooting over on the bench. She seemed out of place for this part of town. But I supposed I did too.

"Just get off work?" she asked.

"Yeah," I replied. "Just ready to get home. What about you?"

The woman crossed her legs and stared out at the road. "I suppose I'm always working. Never really off, you know? Even when I am, I'm still taking care of my brother."

I knew that feeling well. The responsibilities never ended, and neither did the burdens. I loved my Grams and wanted the best life for her, but I also spent many nights crying myself to sleep because I wasn't sure how I was going to make it all work.

"My brother had so much potential...," she continued, as if baiting me. Maybe she just needed someone to talk to.

Deciding that I didn't have much else to do while waiting for my bus, I gave in. "What happened to him?"

Her answer was instant. "He was shot five times. Miraculously survived. Unfortunately, his life came at a cost. He's nothing but a shell of the human he used to be. It's tragic, really."

I felt for this strange woman, I really did. "Wow. I'm so sorry." I didn't really know what else to say.

"I'm determined to take down his shooter. I feel like it's consumed my life. And can you blame me? We'd do anything for the people we love, wouldn't we...Juliet?" The sound of my name turned my veins to ice. How did she know me? I shot up from my seat, but she merely smiled. "I hope you don't mind, but I just had to meet the girl that Nicholas Civella is all worked up about. You're just a child, hmm?"

"You're Cora," I stated, not bothering to ask if it was true, because I felt her identity in my gut.

"And you're Juliet Cross," she replied, a sly smile on her lips. "Nick thought you were my rat. I'm almost disappointed that I didn't learn of you sooner. You would have made a great rat. You still could, you know."

"What do you want?" I asked, because I knew this wasn't just a pleasant visit. She wanted something from me.

"I like your style. Straight to the point," she replied back. "I think it's obvious that you're in way over your head, Juliet. And I know you think you're doing right by your Grams, but Nicholas Civella doesn't care about you. He is incapable of understanding your struggle like I can. I know he has you in his fist, but I can protect you. I can save you."

Oddly, I found myself feeling drawn in by her offer. Cora didn't seem malicious to me. I didn't get that same bad feeling in my gut like I did with Hale. She spoke with such conviction that I genuinely believed that she could help me.

But Anthony's story kept me from believing her. "You hurt Anthony," I replied.

"My business associate hurt Anthony. And he paid the price for that with his life. Nicholas shot my brother five times. No one is innocent in this game."

Game. She called it a game.

In the distance, a bus was pulling up. I breathed a sigh of relief. "I think we could work together, Juliet," Cora persisted. "I have such a glorious vision for this city—for our futures. Don't allow yourself to die in the Civella web. Your Grams doesn't deserve to lose both her daughter and her granddaughter."

Tears started to fill my eyes. What she said sounded so right, but also felt so wrong in my heart. "B-but," I stuttered, not sure what to say.

"Just think about it, okay?" she said with a wink just as the bus pulled up. We briefly stared each other down. Her eyes were soft and compassionate. She didn't look like the crazy murderer villain that Nicholas made her out to be. "Okay," I whispered before turning around and sprinting onto the bus.

I sat in the far back row and looked out the window, but Cora was gone.

chapter fourteen

The Civella Mansion looked less impressive to me today. Perhaps it was the lack of sleep clouding my brain, or maybe it was the knowledge of all the secrets hiding within its fortress, but I wasn't as terrified now.

The early morning sunshine kissed my cheeks. It smelled like freshly cut grass outside. Walking up to the gate with a sense of confidence that felt forced, I rang the bell and waited patiently for a guard to let me in.

I ended my night with fear, but started my day with a decision. I was going to tell Malice everything that happened last night. It wasn't because I trusted Malice more. He was a twisted fuck. No, it was because I feared Cora less. If word got out that I was working with Cora, Malice would burn my life to the ground.

"What are you doing here?" Hale asked from the other side of the gate. I hadn't even noticed him approaching. He looked barely put together, as if he had spent all night pacing the floors. He had a stain on his shirt, and his pants were wrinkled. I looked down at his scuffed shoes. In the light of day, this man looked painfully human. Normal. Unimpressive and forgettable.

"I need to speak with Malice," I replied.

He looked me up and down, scrutinizing my oversized shirt, my faded jeans, and bare face. My hair was still wet from my shower, and my stomach was rumbling from lack of food. I was tired. Spent. Overwhelmed. But most of all, I was resigned to my fate.

"Boss is in a meeting."

"I can wait."

"He doesn't really take appointments. If he wants to see you, he will." Hale started walking away, so I pulled my cell phone out of my pocket and called the devil himself.

Ring.

Ring.

Ring.

"Hello?"

"Cora paid me a visit," I said in a bored tone. "I'm standing outside your house, and Hale won't let me in."

I waited a couple of beats. Then, Malice's raspy voice cursed. "Fuck."

The gates opened almost immediately. "See you soon," I sang before hanging up my phone and strutting past Hale like a proud flamingo. Of course, the bastard couldn't let me have my moment, because he was determined to follow me inside. I felt his eyes on my back as I ascended the winding path leading up to the house.

Malice was already standing in the foyer when I opened the front door. He looked like he'd just rolled out of bed and put on the first pair of pants and wrinkled button-down he could find. His blond hair was a ruffled mess, and it shouldn't have looked as sexy as it did. I suppose it was early. But I couldn't waste another minute.

"Tell me everything," he demanded.

And so I did.

—

"She knew where you were. She knew what bus station you'd be at and when."

I had my own personal theory on the matter, but the main culprit was hovering over me at the moment. Hale had to know I wouldn't have a ride back to my house after my shift.

"You need a car," William grumbled while stroking his

chin. "I'll get it sorted today."

"It should have been sorted yesterday," Malice snapped.

William's face was twisted with anger. "You're just as capable of coordinating these things. It was your idea to set her up at the club. What is it you always say? Protect your investments. Or what was it you called her, a toy? What difference does it make to you?"

Anthony piped in. The entire Civella family and Hale were sitting around a conference table. "He only cares about things after Cora gets her hands on them. Congratulations, Juliet. Your net worth just doubled."

Malice pulled a knife from his pocket and started scratching at the table top. I watched the entire exchange with my brows raised. "I'm not disillusioned about my worth, okay?" I said. "I know it doesn't really matter to anyone here if something happens to me. I'm sharing that Cora was in my space, because I'm being paid to provide information."

Malice locked eyes with me, an unfamiliar emotion flickering in his gaze. "Get her a fucking car. I want escorts for all my employees to their cars after their shifts."

Hale answered Malice. "I'll coordinate it."

"I can do it," William snapped. "I can fucking do something, you know."

William was still wearing his suit from the night before and had some scruff on his jaw. He looked like he needed a nap. Or a beer. Anthony was doodling on a notepad next to me. I got the impression that he didn't usually sit in on family meetings, but no one stopped him when he waltzed in and plopped down beside me.

"Fine," Malice replied. "You want to feel like you're actually useful for once, have at it. We need security increased tenfold at the club. Speaking of, where were you during all of this, Hale?"

We all turned to look at the beefy, greasy, nasty fucker. My appointed bodyguard had his response practiced. "We had an unruly guest I was taking care of. It's on the end-of-day report Kelsey sent."

Of course he did. Hale was the rat, and I was going to fucking prove it. "This just further proves that it's someone at the club," Malice said while circling the table.

"Or it could mean someone in your inner circle," William countered.

"Does this at least prove that I'm loyal to the cause?" I asked. More than anything, I wanted to be trusted. Ultimately, I decided to come forward with the truth today because the consequences of not telling Malice what happened last night were greater than the potential rewards of working with Cora. Malice hated rats, and I refused to become anything that this psychotic man hated.

"It means I distrust you marginally less. But don't get too excited about it," Malice replied.

Anthony chuckled.

"Great. Then I'll be leaving."

William perked up in his seat. Anthony stopped doodling to look at me. Malice bent over his table and tapped the top of it with his fingers. "Where do you think you're going?"

"Home?" I replied. "I haven't actually eaten since lunch yesterday, and I'm exhausted. I'm just the informant, not the mastermind behind whatever the fuck it is you plan to do about Cora. I did my job. I gave you information. Now, I'm off the clock."

Anthony reached out to brush his fingers over mine. "I can get you food, what do you want?" he asked softly. When Anthony wasn't chopping up bodies, he was actually incredibly sweet.

"It's okay. I have a long bus ride home—"

"No more goddamn buses!" Malice shouted before stabbing the tabletop with his knife.

I rolled my eyes. Anthony was right, the only reason Malice had his panties in a twist was because Cora got close to his property. He didn't actually give two fucks about my safety. "I'll get you one of our cars," William interrupted.

"Fine. But remember what I said about no murder cars. Anthony needs to work on his technique for scrubbing evidence," I said while teasingly nudging Anthony.

"I am very good about cleaning up DNA," he protested.

"You kept a dead girl's clothes in your death dungeon," I replied dryly. "Seriously, have you listened to any of my podcasts?"

"Hey now. You looked hot in her clothes. And it's a good thing I had them. You would've had to dispose of a dead body while naked," he popped back before staring at me with a...confusing expression. "Oh shit, I just got a boner."

I scooted away from Anthony. He cackled and continued to doodle.

"Fine. I'll buy you a new car. We can make a day of it if you'd like, Miss Cross. I'll even stop at your favorite restaurant on the way," William purred. His tone felt sensual and taunting, like he was somehow staking a claim with subtle suggestions. I turned to look at him. Even though I was tired, the idea of spending the day with him sounded appealing...

"No. Juliet is going to stay here and eat," Malice decided before turning to face me. "You need rest before your shift tonight so that you can be alert. You can take a nap in the guest room, and when you wake up, I want to discuss your shift for tonight and some potential suspects, okay?"

I didn't necessarily have to go home. Grams had plans with Linda today. She finally got her ticket to Palm Springs and was planning on buying some cute summer dresses for the trip, but I still didn't like spending yet another day away from her.

"I really need to go home."

"And that really isn't a decision you get to make. Get her some food, Anthony, and for fuck's sake, I don't ever want her walking after her shift ever again," Malice growled.

"Aw. Nicky cares," Anthony sang in a whiny voice. "I swear, Cora's got the magic touch." Malice glared at his brother, an unspoken warning in his gaze. Anthony lifted his hands in mock surrender. "It's okay, Nicky. You can't save everyoneeeee."

Malice turned to Hale. "And as for you? We have some things to discuss about your role here. Everyone but Hale is dismissed."

Nicholas Civella was like a fucking military sergeant. William and Anthony got up immediately, listening to their brother like this was normal. It was in my nature to question him.

I crossed my arms over my chest and stared him down. "I'd like to hear what you have to say to Hale."

Malice glared at me. Anthony, who apparently liked a good drama fest, stopped his exodus to watch the power struggle tennis match between his older brother and me. "Why?" he asked.

"He's supposedly my bodyguard. I just want to be made aware of how he plans to protect me from Cora should she show up again. He was gone the majority of my shift last night and coincidentally disappeared when I had to walk home. I just want to know how you plan to keep your employees safe."

Hale turned bright red, the anger so clearly prevalent in his expression that I had to bite back a smile. "Sir, I did my job. I've worked with you for four years. I'm not just a babysitter. I didn't realize I was responsible for her after her shift. What do you expect? Am I supposed to move in with the bitch?"

Absofuckinglutely not. Hale wasn't going to get within fifty feet of my Grams if I had anything to say about it. I was furious. "We will discuss the boundaries of your role later. Right now, I want to chat with Juliet," Malice said in a dark tone.

"Oooh, someone's in trouble," Anthony sang before exiting the conference room. William shook his head and sighed. Somehow, I felt like I'd made a mistake.

"Out. Everyone," Malice insisted.

William stared at me, as if silently begging me to ask him to stay. To be my hero. To be my person. But instead, I nodded.

The door to the conference room clicked shut, and Malice and I were left alone. "Do you think I'm incapable of keeping you safe, Little Fighter?" he whispered his question menacingly. The nickname was new to me. I watched as he circled the large rectangular table and approached me.

"I think Cora is closer than you think," I whispered back, antagonizing him for reasons I couldn't explain. "I think you're juggling too many plates and already have a list of people you feel responsible for. There's no room for strangers, right?"

Malice picked me up and sat me on the conference table. Slowly. Gently. "Is that so," he replied softly. "Are you a stranger still, Juliet?"

"Don't act like you know me. Don't act like you care. I see right through your games, Malice," I rasped. He was so fucking close. I breathed him in.

"Tell me. What game am I playing?"

I leaned back on the table, bracing my palms on the hard wood as I put some distance between us. "You sent Vicky away, knowing damn well that she's the only person who can get through to Anthony. Now, I'm suddenly put in all sorts of positions to spend time with him. You wouldn't happen to be filling that void, would you? Guilt can be a strong motivator, Malice."

His lip twitched. "Go on."

So he wasn't going to deny it? Interesting. I continued. "I don't know why, but you like punishing William. You kissed me to get back at him. But why? What did your brother do to make you want to hurt him?"

Malice grabbed the collar of my shirt and yanked me back toward him. "And what if I were to kiss you right now? What purpose would I have for that, Little Fighter? There's no one here to see. My brothers aren't watching."

I stared at his plush lips for a lingering moment. The tension between us was so thick I nearly choked on it. "I don't know. Maybe to feel something. Maybe because you're selfish. I don't trust you to take care of my body, Malice. I don't feel safe with you. I don't feel protected. I'll work for you. I'll tell you all the secrets. But I won't trust you. I've seen firsthand what happens to the people you supposedly love, and I want nothing to do with it. Vicky is in another country against her will. Anthony is covered in scars."

"I can keep you safe. I can protect everyone." His declaration was accompanied with a snarl.

"Show me you can protect the people you actually give a shit about, and then we'll talk, Malice," I replied before bracing both hands against his chest and shoving him away.

He stood speechless, and with as much confidence as I could muster, I got off the table and walked out of the conference room, feeling a bit more powerful than when I'd arrived.

CORALEE JUNE

chapter fifteen

"I don't think this swimsuit even fits me anymore," Grams said while staring at the black one piece in her hand. Grams wanted to dip her toes in her sister's hot tub in Palm Springs.

I grabbed it from her pale hands and folded it up. "It's your size!" I replied before putting my arm around her. After giving her a brief hug, I placed it in her large cheetah-print suitcase before continuing to work through an emergency folder with a list of all her medications and emergency contacts.

Was I nervous about Grams being all the way in

California without me? Absolutely. Was I still excited for her? Yes. Reluctantly, yes. It had been a full week since I had seen Cora at that bus stop, and Malice was trying to prove me wrong about his ability to keep me safe. I had a car—a BMW—and an escort every day before my shift and after it. Sometimes, I'd seen someone parked outside our house, but luckily it was never Hale.

Malice was sending a clear message to Cora if she was watching: I was his.

Malice also spoke with Dr. Hoffstead about Grams's trip, and they coordinated with another doctor in Los Angeles who agreed to be on call should she need anything while visiting her sister. Grams had another checkup yesterday and was cleared for her trip. Dr. Hoffstead seemed ecstatic to see us and thanked me profusely for whatever good word I'd put in with Malice.

Grams was happy. Really fucking happy. I'd catch her grinning to herself and humming.

"Agnes said that we could go to the casino and see a Bon Jovi cover band one night, so I will need a pretty dress for that," she said with a giddy grin. I hopped from her bed and started searching through her closet.

Grams had always been very close to her sister, Agnes. She probably would've visited her more often, but I kept her here. After Mom's disappearance, Grams didn't really feel comfortable leaving me. But this felt like a fresh start.

An exciting adventure. Even though I was really worried about her, I knew that she was going to be in good hands. And as painful as it was to admit, who knew how much longer she'd be able to do this? This was going to be good for Grams, and if I were being honest, I was happy to have her away from here while I did all this work with Malice. Lying to Grams was difficult. Trying to play detective while taking care of her was stretching both of us thin.

"I'm so excited," Grams said before looking at me. The smile on her face dipped some, and she cocked her head to the side. "You know I don't have to go. If you'd rather me stay here —"

I quickly cut her off. "I'm excited for you to go. I just worry about you. But I know Aunt Agnes will take good care of you. It will be weird being separated from you, though."

Grams shuffled over to me and wrapped her arms around my waist for a tender hug. I breathed in her lavender scent and sighed. "Maybe this will be a good thing. You work so hard, Juliet. Then, you come home and cook my food, fold my laundry, hover over me about my medicine. You need to relax every now and then and not worry about your grandmother. I feel like you've been scared ever since your mother disappeared. Like you're afraid to have me out of your sight. I don't want that for you."

I wanted to argue with my grandmother and tell her

that it wasn't true, that I wasn't the same little girl who was scared that all the people she loved would one day disappear. Parkinson's wasn't an abductor, it wasn't a police officer telling me that my mother was never coming back. But it was a slow disease that was eating at my grandmother, and I just felt like we didn't have enough time.

I loved her, and I wanted her to experience life. I wasn't going to let my fears stop her from seeing her sister.

"I'm excited for you to go, Grams," I emphasized, more for my own sake than hers. "It'll be good for you. I'm okay, I promise."

Grams looked like she wanted to talk some more, but the doorbell ringing made both of us pause. "Are you expecting anyone?" she asked.

I shook my head. "I'll go see who's at the door."

I wasn't expecting to see Malice standing on my grandmother's front porch. As soon as I saw his piercing eyes looking back at me, I wanted to slam my door in his face. He predicted my instinct immediately and reached out to push his palm against the door, preventing me from blocking him from my home. Asshole.

The slim black tie around his neck matched his black slacks and white button-up shirt. His blond hair was slicked to the side like he'd just gotten back from the barber shop. On the street, I could see one of his town cars and a couple of guards standing outside the driver's door.

"What are you doing here?" I hissed.

"I need you to work tonight," he said, pushing his way through the door with a smirk. I didn't want him anywhere near Grams.

"And you couldn't tell me that in a text message?" I asked.

He seemed to be lost in the midst of our small home. "I wanted to make sure she doesn't need anything for her trip. Dr. Hoffstead sent over a report. I am glad she will be taken care of there. What airline is she flying on?"

"Why do you want to know?" I asked. I rolled my shoulders back and looked down the hall where Grams was still in her bedroom. Pretty soon she would walk out here and want to talk with Malice. It was getting harder and harder to hide my double life.

Malice took a step closer to me. And another step. His eyes swept up and down my body. I was in shorts and a tank top, nothing overly revealing, especially when compared to the uniform at Eden's Place. But the way he stared at me made me feel stripped bare. "I figured I could anonymously upgrade her flight so that she's more comfortable."

His reasoning caught me off guard. Wow. Well. That would be nice, actually. "I can email you her flight information. But, Malice, I don't want to be in any more debt with you than I already am. I appreciate your kindness, but we are fine. We don't need—"

"Did you know that you didn't have a deadbolt on your door until yesterday, Juliet?" he asked, interrupting me. "That's not very safe…"

"Is this about what I said before? About you not protecting me? You've proven your point." I didn't need him to overcompensate. Didn't he have his own family to obsess over?

"I got a good look at your refrigerator. It's all cheap, quick meals. Not quite the sustenance I'd like for you."

"We are fine, Malice," I said through gritted teeth. "You can leave now. I appreciate it but—"

Malice got up in my space. He was always getting in my space. His dark presence made my breath hitch and a quick thrill jolt up my spine. "I come when I want to come. I'll leave when I want to leave. You can expect more checkups from me in the future. I like having my finger on the pulse of every employee in my empire. I'm just keeping you safe, Little Fighter." I didn't feel very safe with his hungry eyes staring me down.

Malice leaned even closer. Brushing his cheek along mine, he whispered in my ear. "Tell me to leave again and I'll take you with me," he threatened. Even though his voice was soft and tender, I felt a spike of fear turn my veins frosty.

I swallowed. Grams slowly exited her bedroom and started walking toward us, a smile on her face. I quickly whispered to Malice, "Please don't let her know that I'm working for you."

Malice didn't seem like the type of man who would listen to my pleas, but I just had to hope. "It's you again," Grams stuttered. She looked him up and down while stroking her chin. "Nicholas, right? You stopped by last week to drop off something for Juliet."

It was such an odd experience. I watched Malice's expression twist into this friendly, inviting look that made my heart stall. His smile was genuine. His eyes looked kind. He was a beautiful actor. If you didn't know any better, you would have never seen the death, destruction, and danger underneath. "I was in the area and decided to stop by and see you before your trip. Do you have everything you need, Ruthie?"

Ruthie? I rolled my eyes. Great.

She beamed at him. "Oh yes. I'm all packed and ready to go. I'm so excited! My flight leaves early in the morning."

"Should we go to the kitchen?" Grams asked. She paused for a moment, her hand shaking at her side. "Juliet made…made…cook. Cookies."

Grams was having a fairly good day, so hearing her stutter made me internally panic. Maybe she didn't need to leave? Grams kept eyeing me, and I couldn't tell if she was nervous about all the activity or if it was something else. Malice had this instinctive quality about him that made your skin light up with fear. I couldn't blame her if she was afraid of him.

But then my suspicions took a completely different turn when Grams winked. Winked! It was a mischievous move, and I started to wonder if she had different plans for Malice and me.

"That sounds lovely. I didn't know you could bake, Juliet?" he said while looking at me.

"There's a lot of things you don't know about me," I snapped back. And I wanted to keep it that way. If I wanted to survive, then I needed to keep this dangerous man at arm's length.

Malice led the way into the kitchen. He led the way everywhere.

Grams hooked her arm around me and whispered in my ear. "Oh, he likes you. So handsome. I'll b-be on my best behavior."

He sat down in our secondhand kitchen chair with scuffed white paint and a shaky wooden leg. Grams insisted on getting the platter of cookies. I watched with bated breath as she turned to grab it with both hands. She focused on the plate, and I focused on not grabbing Malice by his ear and tearing him out of our home. His kindness came at a cost. I needed to figure out what his ulterior motive was.

While she was distracted, Malice wrapped his fingers

around my wrist and pulled me close so that he could whisper in my ear. "Stop being so difficult, or I'll tell your sweet grandmother what I do know about you. I've seen you at your truest self. Don't forget who has the power here."

A shiver traveled down my spine. "What are you doing here?" I asked.

He stared at me and bit his bottom lip before releasing his hold on my wrist and letting me go. I waited for him to tell me what he meant by that, but an explanation never came.

Grams set the plate down with a loud clang and chuckled. "Chocolate chip. My favorite. I'd offer some milk, but we're out."

Malice's earlier words haunted me.

"I got a good look at your refrigerator. It's all cheap, quick meals. Not quite the sustenance I'd like for you."

He looked out of place in our dated home with his designer suit. "This looks lovely," he began. "Thank you."

I sat down beside him, but I didn't have any appetite. Grams was giddy. It was rare that I brought anyone home to meet her. I'd had friends and boyfriends over the years, but no one, aside from Vicky, seemed important enough to bring home. If Vicky hadn't been living such a dangerous double life, I probably would've brought her here to meet Grams, but otherwise, this was my sacred place. I was cautious about whom I let into my life. I was cautious about whom I cared for, too. Maybe it was my abandonment issues rearing their ugly head, but Grams was my person. I didn't just introduce her to anyone.

"Remind me again, how do you know my granddaughter?" Grams asked. Her voice had steadied some now that we were sitting. The kitchen was her domain. Even though she had stopped cooking as often since her Parkinson's diagnosis, she still thrived in this room. Heck, I got the sex talk while she was making my favorite chocolate cake.

I worried about what Malice would say. "I met her at the diner. I'm a bit of a regular, and we built up somewhat of a friendship."

It took every ounce of self-restraint that I possessed not to roll my eyes at him. "Well, you have quite a unique friendship. To give my granddaughter a new cell phone suggests that you're closer than acquaintances. Forgive me if I'm poking, but it's rare that my granddaughter introduces me to any of her…friends."

At this information, Malice preened. It was like he was having unfiltered access to the nuances of my life. It was intrusive, and yet I wasn't uncomfortable. Maybe if Malice knew how alone I was, he would trust me more.

"Well, I feel honored to be in Juliet's life," he said smoothly. I tried to sense if he was being sarcastic or teasing, but I found no hint of a lie. "I guess you could say I've taken on a particular interest in her well-being. I have a large family, it's second nature to me to care for the people in my life."

At his words, Grams smiled even bigger. She had no idea that she was being swindled by the devil. "That is just lovely. In fact, I'm glad that Juliet has someone. I've been anxious about going out of town for the next month, and it is quite a relief to know that someone will be here to look after her."

Malice looked at me and placed a heavy hand on top of mine. Grams stared at where our skin touched. "I promise to take very good care of Juliet while you're gone," he said earnestly. I didn't believe him for a second.

I stayed silent as Grams and Malice went into a long conversation about Palm Springs and Aunt Agnes. He was so smooth and gentle with my grandmother. Whenever she trembled or stumbled over her words, he patiently waited for her to find her sentence again. He was polite. Kind. It was almost like sitting next to a completely different person. I didn't recognize him, nor did I want to. I didn't want to believe that there was a side to this monster that could be nice.

"Palm Springs is in Southern California, right? I used to go to Los Angeles with my mother when we were kids. We'd go to a theme park and ride rides until we puked. My mother loved it. Some of my favorite memories happened there," Malice said with a smile. I was leaning so close to him that we almost touched. Hearing his version of their parents was new for me. I knew the man and woman Vicky missed dearly, but who were they to Malice?

"Oh, she sounds wonderful. Does she live in the area?" Grams asked.

At her question, a flash of the tortured Malice broke through his carefully constructed mask. It was a quick, vulnerable moment, but I recognized it clearly. "She passed away three years ago. I hope one day to bring my future children to the theme park there to keep her memory alive."

Grams gave him a tight pitied smile. "I'm sorry for your loss."

Malice nodded stiffly. "Thank you, Ruthie."

By the end of our little cookie date, Grams was smitten and Malice knew more about me than I wanted him to. But all I could do was sit there and smile and play nice. I walked him to the front door as my grandmother continued to pack, and once we were on the porch safely out of earshot, I let out a sigh. "While she's gone, I want you to stay at my estate," Malice immediately said. The smile in his eyes had faded. The politeness in his tone had completely disappeared.

"Why?" I asked.

Unexpectedly, a grin crossed his expression, and he

invaded my personal space. Both his hands clasped against my cheeks, the warmth of his palms making me shudder. Swiftly, he pulled me in for a savory kiss, and I completely drowned in the shock of it. His lips were soft and insistent. Passionate. Our bodies collided against one another with a frantic wave of need. He kissed me like a man on a mission, his tongue invaded my mouth, and he lapped me up like I was dessert or cocaine. In a terrible twist of fate, the devil tasted like my favorite dessert: chocolate chunk cookies.

He pulled away on a groan, and I...didn't know how to feel about his touch, his attention, or the flutter in my belly. Wrong. It was so wrong. I couldn't get involved with a man who would ultimately leave me.

"Grams was watching. Pack a bag. You move in tonight," he said, his demand leaving no room for protest as he walked down the sidewalk toward his waiting town car and guards.

Shit.

I couldn't help but wonder if Malice would ever kiss me with no one watching—with no ulterior motive.

CORALEE JUNE

chapter sixteen

Since I had to work tonight, Malice arranged for Grams to have a ride to the airport in the morning. She was tickled by his thoughtfulness and practically shoved me out the door when I mentioned that he offered for me to stay with him while she was gone. Grams always considered me a loner and blamed herself for it. She thought that she should have pushed me harder to go out and be social after Mom's disappearance, but honestly, I had no desire to act like a normal teen and make normal friends when the world felt so big. High school was nothing more than a social experiment. I'd gotten a taste of the real world and wasn't amused by teenage antics.

Vick was my one rebellious act. My connection to the outside world.

I stood outside the Civella Mansion for a long moment. Guards watched me in annoyance, waiting for me to walk inside. I had a small bag with a couple days' worth of clothes strapped to my back and a scowl perched on my face.

Despite already planning my exit, I hadn't fought Malice on this crazy idea of his. Part of me wanted to get closer and see how they lived. I wanted to taste their family dynamic and witness it firsthand. I was curious about what happened behind the scenes, and more so, I wanted to understand Malice's motivations for inviting me here. Did this mean he was starting to trust me? Or did this mean he didn't trust me at all?

"Miss?" one of the guards called out. I gripped the strap of my bag until my knuckles turned white. "Mr. Civella is waiting for you."

I cleared my throat, a question forming in my mind. Which brother was waiting for me? Anthony, the tragic yet quirky ally? William, the man I'd seen every week for three years but barely knew? Or Malice—Nicholas—the devil in a suit?

When I didn't move to enter the home, the guard cleared his throat. "William is in the guest suite. Has been working there for the last couple of hours."

So it was William, hmm? Why was he working in the guest suite? Curiosity piqued, I finally gathered my wits and marched through the front door. It was a familiar move. Even though there wasn't an inch of this property not under surveillance, it still felt intrusive to just walk through the doors. I supposed the Civella family was used to it though. Every day of their lives was spent under the watchful eye of their armed guards.

It felt strange to wander the halls of their mansion. I knew where I was going, but I half expected someone to jump out from a shadowed hallway and tell me that I wasn't supposed to be here. I moved quickly until I was at the guest bedroom door. I raised my fist to knock on it, but the door was yanked open before I could.

"You're here," William said with a smile. His outfit was something I never imagined I'd see him in. He was wearing casual jeans and a white shirt. His hair was messy and tousled. I tried to peer around him to see what he was doing in there, but he pushed himself past me and promptly shut the door.

"What are you doing in there?" I asked.

He bit his lip and wiped a bead of sweat on his brow. "Nicholas said you were coming to stay with us for a few weeks while Ruthie is out of town visiting her sister."

I cocked my head to the side. "Why are you on a first-name basis with Grams?" I asked, but he ignored me.

"I tried to make your room as comfortable as possible. I had a new vanity delivered so you could get ready here. And if you don't like the bedding, we can—"

"You've been decorating my room?" I asked. I couldn't tell if I was shocked or flattered. William was constantly surprising me. He was so much more than the quiet, stoic statue of a man who watched me with strength these last three years.

"I just wanted you to be comfortable," he whispered gently before pushing past me to open the door.

The first thing I noticed was a deep green comforter on the plush bed. "Your favorite color is green, right? I am having one of the guys deliver some soundproof padding for this wall for when you record your podcasts. I've noticed you missed an episode last week…"

"You listen to my podcast?" I asked.

"I was your second subscriber," he replied proudly. "I was disappointed last week when you didn't upload a new one."

"I didn't have time. There's been a lot of changes lately," I replied distractedly. If I were being honest, I'd been pretending like my podcast didn't exist. I wasn't sure I could handle talking about murderers and criminals, knowing that I too was deep in the dark world of killing.

"Do you like it?" William asked. I circled the room. On

the vanity were all my favorite floral lotions. There was a black and white abstract painting of Jack the Ripper on the wall, and a hanging rack of clothes in the corner was full of new outfits for work, all handpicked by William.

Each detail felt catered to my personality. A blank journal sat on the nightstand. I once told Vicky that I slept with a pad of paper and a pen by my bed so I could write down my dreams.

There was also a fluffy pair of slippers by the door. I had a thing for soft textures and comfort. I hated wearing shoes in the house but didn't like cold feet, either. A woven basket on the floor was filled with folded blankets of varying fluffiness. Vicky always joked that I was a cuddle comfort whore. I loved to wrap up in a soft blanket and watch murder mysteries every night.

It was a simple design, but it was all the little details that made me see myself through William's eyes. "You've really been paying attention all these years," I whispered while running my hand over a desk with a brand new laptop sitting proudly on top of it. Certainly that wasn't mine...

"Of course I paid attention," William replied.

"Why be quiet? All those visits, all those years. I sat across from you every single week, and you never said a word to me. And yet you know my favorite color. You know my hobbies. My fears. My preferences." I looked at the nightlight plugged into the wall. I'd once told Vick that I was afraid of the dark. "We could have been friends, too, you know?" I said. Surprisingly, I was frustrated by all the time that we missed out on.

He looked down at his designer shoes before responding to me. "I told you. Vicky and I had a deal…"

"Why?" I asked.

He looked at the ground. "I made Vicky promise that she'd do everything in her power to keep you safe. She agreed to my conditions as long as I kept quiet. She wanted one thing for herself. I can't even really blame her."

I shook my head in disbelief. "So wait. All this time…the rules were your idea?"

William licked his lips. "I never wanted this life for you."

"Guess it's too late," I whispered.

"We make do with what we're given. It should be wrong, but I have no regrets."

I looked up at William and tried to think about what I'd be doing right now if I'd just let Vicky walk out of my life. I'd probably be trying to figure out what happened to her. I'd still be working at Dick's. I'd be scraping by, and Grams wouldn't be on the new experimental drugs. She was thriving now. I had a car. A financial cushion.

And I had William. I had this entire new side of him that I never would have gotten before had I just kept to myself that night. "Why don't you regret it?" I asked.

He smiled and took a step closer to me. Another step. Another. "Because you wouldn't have opened up if you thought I was paying attention."

It was a romantic thing to say. I couldn't think of any man who just wanted to hear about every nuance of my life, but William did. He observed and learned. "I just feel like I'm at a disadvantage," I admitted.

"How so?"

"You know everything about me, and I know nothing about you."

My words had a dark effect on him, because William's face twisted into an expression that I couldn't place. "It's probably better that way," he admitted before cupping my cheek.

"Why?"

"The more you know, the less you'll like me back," he said before leaning even closer. His words were probably meant to push me away, but instead, it made me feel sorry for him. How many people did he push away because he didn't believe himself worthy of acceptance?

"Try me," I whispered.

His eyes darkened. He slipped his hand lower until it was wrapped around my throat. "I'm a murderer," he growled.

I arched my back. "So am I."

"I care only about myself," he added.

"This beautiful, thoughtful room says otherwise." He pressed his thigh between my legs, and I moaned when he pressed against my core.

"I like hurting people," he said while squeezing my neck.

I croaked out my response, taunting him. "I like pain." My heart thudded with the honesty of it. It felt like a damning proclamation. The start to a higher awareness.

His lips crashed into mine. It was like a car wreck. We left nothing but damage in our wake. He moved his hand and then gripped my heavy breast. My body enjoyed every move, squeeze, nip, bite, and lick. He savored me. He consumed me.

I wrapped my arms around his neck and pressed as close to him as possible, my body like a harsh wave, arching and colliding to feel all of him, to work out some of the pleasure rising like the tide in my veins. He pressed his thigh harder against my core, and I rode him as we kissed, shamelessly soaking my panties.

A knock on the door startled me, but William quickly wrapped his arms around my back and held me in place as the bedroom door opened. "Is Juliet here? I went to the old video store on K Avenue and found the holy grail of true crime documentaries," Anthony's voice rang out. William sunk his teeth into my bottom lip once more before pulling away. "You're here!" Anthony added excitedly. "I hope you're ready for a movie marathon. I already told Nicholas that we aren't working tonight."

William stepped back, his eyes wide as he took in the sight of his brother. Anthony, who was wearing his signature beanie and a gray Henley with black sweats, walked over to me, his arms full with a cardboard box. He stepped closer to me and swiftly leaned forward to kiss me on the cheek. It was a featherlight touch and so very brief, but it sent a wave down my spine. It was affectionate but didn't feel friendly. Didn't he see me making out with his brother just now?

It appeared that William was shocked by his brother's behavior, too. I knew that Anthony struggled with physical intimacy. Was this just a peck on the cheek, or did this mean something more? If I had to guess, I'd choose the latter based on William's mouth hanging open.

I cleared my throat. "I'm not sure I can just call out of work—"

"Of course you can. Nicholas can't and won't tell me no."

Anthony's response was swift and felt genuine. Anthony held a lot over Malice. "Oh really?" I asked.

Anthony shrugged in answer.

I chewed on the inside of my cheek. Malice's guilt over Anthony ran deep. It was a dynamic I was still working out. Seeing Anthony on stage at Eden's Place had revealed a lot about the trauma Anthony had to overcome. "Right. Well, I'll leave the two of you to it then...," William said, but he made no move to leave.

Anthony set down the box and bent over it to sift through the DVDs piled up in it. "Some of these are ancient. We should make a drinking game out of it. Every time a man with a seventies mustache stabs someone, we take a shot." I giggled. Anthony's sense of humor definitely vibed with mine, and his carefree attitude helped me process the intense kiss William and I had just shared. "But we might die of alcohol poisoning, so maybe that's not a good idea," he then added while straightening his spine and twisting to look at me.

"Probably," I agreed. "But that's half the fun."

He grinned. "Dark humor. I dig it." Anthony then turned to his brother. "Why are you still here? You hate crime shows."

William once again cleared his throat. "That's because most of the murderers are sloppy and leave a trace. It's frustrating to watch. If they just hired a decent cleanup crew and got rid of their weapons, they'd be significantly more successful."

"I personally love how careless they are," Anthony replied, his arm lifted in exasperation. "Not everyone has an Anthony Civella on their payroll. I'm the best cleanup man money can buy."

"I wouldn't say that," I interjected. Anthony arched a thick brow at me.

"Oh?"

"I mean, I was willing to boil a man's body with lye. All you have to do is drive the hearse to a funeral home. Takes the mystery and fun out of it."

Anthony tipped back his head and laughed. "First of all, the fact that you're able to joke about your murder tells me that you're coping beautifully." I blushed at his words. I wasn't sure if I was actually coping or if I was so busy and detached from my own emotions that it felt natural to joke about the distance between my awareness and my trauma. "Secondly, I feel like I've been challenged and now I have to prove myself worthy. Go kill someone, William. I'll do the cleanup for you."

I felt dread bloom from my chest. "Oh, you don't have to do that—"

"Do you have any preferences?" William asked, bored. Was he humoring him, or was he serious? Anthony's words filled my mind.

Nicholas can't and won't tell me no…

Did that go for all the Civella siblings? Did their guilt over what happened to him run that deep?

"Someone difficult to hide. Lots of muscle mass. Tall. Some bulky motherfucker."

William literally took out his damn phone and started taking notes. I started to breathe heavily. "Please don't kill someone just to prove something to me. It was a joke."

William rolled his eyes. "He can be, like, a rapist or something. Pick a menace to society, Batman, so Juliet doesn't have it on her conscience."

"So a large, muscular, evil man. Should be pretty easy to find. Tomorrow good? I have some bookkeeping to do at Eden's Place tonight."

"Perfect." Anthony rubbed his hands together, and I shook my head.

"Okay, I'm leaving for real now. Behave, please," William said with a small smile. It was nice to see him smiling, even if he was plotting to kill someone tomorrow on a whim.

Anthony reached out and laced his fingers through mine. I looked down at our joined hands before glancing at William. He was gaping at us. Okay, so Anthony truly wasn't used to touching people. This was big.

William eventually picked his jaw off the floor and left the guest room, and Anthony dragged me over to the bed and pulled me onto the mattress beside him. "You didn't do a podcast last week," he said. "I was really looking forward to your commentary on the Zodiac Killer."

I let out a deep sigh and put my hands behind my head. "Honestly, I wasn't feeling it. The podcast takes on a whole new vibe when you're a killer too," I whispered.

Anthony lay down beside me. We both stared at the ceiling for a moment before he spoke. "And here I was thinking you'd moved on. Wanna talk about it?"

"Not really," I replied. Avoiding was more fun.

He turned onto his side and propped up his head with his arm to stare at me. "Why'd you start the podcast? What made you want to do it?"

I swallowed. "It's kind of personal," I replied, my voice gruff.

"Well, considering William told you all about my touching issues and my glory hole sexcapades, I think it's only fair you share a bit of your damage with me too."

I chewed on my lip. I'd been hoping that Anthony and I could ignore what I'd seen. I didn't know how to talk about it with him. But he had a point. He seemed like the type of person to not drown me with pity or ask a bunch of stupid questions. "My mother disappeared during her walk home six years ago," I replied. "She worked at a grocery store. Night shift. Stocker. It was just a couple of blocks away. She would get off at two a.m., then walk the two blocks home. But one night, she never got home."

Anthony listened patiently as I told my story. As usual, my throat closed up, and I felt myself growing emotional. It was never easy. "The police showed up. There was only one traffic cam working at the time. It showed her heading down Gardenia Street. But she never made it to the other road. She just...disappeared. Almost out of thin air."

"Did the police have any leads?" Anthony asked.

"None. No one cared about a poor mother from the bad side of town. They asked Grams if she was a flight risk. She got in trouble for pot in high school, and it was on her record, so they labeled her a druggie too."

"Fucking cops, man."

"No one looked for her," I continued. "But I did. I ran every license plate in the footage she sent. There was an unmarked Nissan with temporary plates. Mom was beautiful. Gorgeous. I know she was taken. I know she didn't just willingly abandon me. I mean, shit was hard. She was frustrated with her life, but she wouldn't have left me." Tears were streaming down my face now. I could kill a man cold-blooded, but talking about my mother was like picking at a scab that just wouldn't heal. I let it fester over my soul and fill with puss. It was bloodied, diseased, feverish pain that stayed with me always.

"Not knowing why or how must be hard," Anthony whispered.

"Everyone thought she left on purpose. But I know the truth. My mom loved me, you know? She wouldn't have just walked away." I wiped at my eyes with my sleeves. "Some of her coworkers said she had a large backpack with her at work."

"Was that normal for her?"

I sniffled. "No. But she didn't leave me. She was a victim of a crime. I'll figure out what happened. And until that day, I analyze crime scenes. I learn. I watch. It's alienated me some. I let the mystery consume my life. It's both a distraction and a reminder of what I've lost." I stopped speaking for a moment and thought of all the things I'd missed out on because I was too afraid to give up—too afraid to lose her memory. "It's why Vicky and I get along so well. She believed me. She talked it out with me and provided insight to the crime scene. She never judged me. She never made me feel stupid for clinging to the truth. The world wanted me to move on, but Vicky took me as I am."

Anthony reached out and wiped a stray tear on my cheek before speaking. "She's good at that," he agreed. I knew that Vick and Anthony were very close. In a way, Anthony and I were bonded by her. We were both saved by her kindness. She helped Anthony navigate being captured and tortured. She helped me process my mother's disappearance. She was also the person who suggested I start a podcast. I couldn't rest unless I was doing something. I needed to feel like I was working toward a solution, even though sometimes it felt like there would never be a solution.

Anthony reached out to grab my hand. Once more, the touch made me pause. Why was Anthony comfortable touching me? As if answering my unspoken question, he then spoke. "I like this. Don't question it for now, okay?"

I nodded.

And we spent the rest of the day watching crime documentaries and holding hands.

chapter seventeen

Eden's Place was packed with people Saturday night. The moment I started my shift, a line of members at the door were making demands of me. I decided to wear something a little more modest because I had made the unfortunate discovery that at the hostess stand was a vent that constantly blew ice cold air. Despite the summer heat outside, it was frigid as winter at my desk. I wore short shorts, knee high boots, and a corset top. William surprised me with a lace sweater that looked both sexy and comfortable. It wasn't exactly the approved uniform, but I wasn't a performer, and I refused to be miserable for my entire shift. I also threw away every pair of heels William got me. I was wearing flats or nothing, so help me God.

"Please swipe your card," I said politely to the woman waiting at the front desk. I'd been working for a full week at Eden's Place and was starting to get the hang of things. The guest was wearing a long, navy blue evening gown that sparkled under the dim lights. She was a high-paying regular with a foot fetish and scowled at my flats every time she saw me. Tough shit, Meredith. You try being on your feet all day. Meredith also liked to roam around and sample the talent. I couldn't blame her, some of the performers were too intoxicating to resist.

"I already know where I'm going," she said with a giddy smile. "Anthony should be performing tonight." She flipped her hair back and waggled her eyebrows.

"Actually, Anthony canceled his show for tonight. I think another performer should be filling his spot though?" I shouldn't have been excited to correct her, but I was. I wasn't exactly jealous about Anthony being on stage. It just hurt me to think that people got off to his coping mechanisms. It's like he was slicing off a piece of his trauma and giving it to others to feast on. If he was empowered by it, then I supported him, but in my short time here, I'd gotten to know and care about him.

"Oh." The woman scowled. "I suppose I'll go to my

usual then." I smiled as she marched off, and rolled my eyes when she was out of sight.

"She's so annoying. At least she didn't comment on your flats this time," Kelsey said. She was updating the database beside me, adding new members, editing the profiles of existing ones. One of the cool things about Eden's Place was that people were constantly given the opportunity to discover new aspects of their sexuality. It was our job to keep their profiles updated so that we could offer them every chance to explore. "Speaking of, you're not exactly in uniform today."

I gave her an apologetic look. "It's just so cold up here. They have that vent turned on full blast. I need a jacket and heated blanket. Why do you keep it so cold? I'm glad William gave me this jacket to keep warm." I shivered to emphasize my point.

"It actually wasn't always like this. Someone started messing with the thermostat around the same time you started working. Maybe someone of authority wants you to cover up some," she teased.

"Maybe," I mused.

"Hey, I've got to go talk to William. You good?"

"I'm good! Go."

I rubbed my arms, and another client walked up. He was short and muscular. His bald head shone under the soft light, and his wrinkled suit barely met the dress code for here. "Welcome," I said politely before swiping his card. An alert popped up the moment I did. "Mr. Graves? It says here that you're two months behind on your membership dues. I apologize, but we cannot let you in until you settle your account."

I was advised how to handle a situation like this on my first day, but it was the first time I actually had encountered the problem. Of course, Hale, my appointed bodyguard, was nowhere to be found. He usually showed up with me but disappeared once I got to work. I wasn't complaining, because I wanted to be as far away from him as possible, but now that I was alone with a member of the club who I would have to turn away, I felt nervous.

"That's bullshit. I told Nicholas I would pay it next month," he growled.

I continued to search his profile. There was a note attached to his account. "It says here that you're not allowed in under any circumstances. I'm going to have to ask you to leave."

My voice wavered as I spoke. His face turned an angry shade of red, and I quickly looked around to see if there was anyone nearby who could help me. "Fuck you. I want to speak to a fucking manager!" he yelled. "I don't owe the Civella family shit, they owe me!"

I straightened my spine. "Sir, I'm going to have to ask you to calm down and leave. If you have any questions about our decision, you can schedule an appointment with William."

"I want to talk to the fucking boss now," he argued before circling the desk and walking up to me. My breath caught in my throat.

"Sir, you need to back away—"

"You need to shut the fuck up, whore!" he yelled. I saw a few people scurrying in the distance. I couldn't believe it, but I was actually hoping Hale would show up.

The man reached out and shoved my chest. "Little cock tease. You get off kicking me out?" he sneered. "Maybe I don't need a show. Maybe I just need to fucking show you who is boss."

He licked his lips menacingly, and I was about to make a run for it when two bulky men grabbed him by the arms and dragged him away from me.

Malice stood stoically on the other side of the desk, his muscular arms at his side and his expression flat.

"I was just fucking around, Nick. Get these guys off of me," Mr. Graves said.

Malice popped his knuckles one by one. No one spoke, and I felt like he was the performer now. All eyes were on us, and they got off watching their fearless leader basking in his brutality. "You don't get to call me Nick anymore, Graves. My enemies call me Malice, or have you forgotten?"

I'd become so accustomed to calling Nicholas Civella

by his menacing nickname that I didn't ever analyze what that meant. Apparently, this was a huge deal, because Mr. Graves paled immediately. "We've been partners for ages," he stuttered.

"You stopped paying your dues. You hassled my employee. You got cocky, Graves," Malice replied. His lip curled on the word employee.

"I'll pay. I promise!"

"You keep saying that. I've heard that you like to brag about your membership here, Graves. You've been chatty. You know what happens to people who can't keep their fucking mouth shut." Malice pulled out a gun, and as if on cue, everyone who was watching disappeared. It was like they knew exactly what was coming and what they were expected to do. Even the bartender in the lobby disappeared.

"Close your eyes, Juliet. I have a well-known rule at my establishment," Malice said. I didn't blink. I was frozen with fear and...curiosity.

Mr. Graves started sobbing uncontrollably, and he shook in the guard's grip.

Malice aimed his gun at Graves but kept his eyes locked on me. "You're only as safe as what you can testify in court, Juliet. If you see nothing, you risk nothing." We stared at one another for a few more frantic beats of my heart. Inhale. Exhale. I felt like every second was an act of defiance.

Malice pulled the trigger. I flinched. Blood splattered on the marble floors. Graves wheezed and gasped before falling in a heap on the floor. I watched it all. I took it in.

"You should have closed your eyes, Juliet," Malice said before grabbing a handkerchief from his pocket and wrapping his weapon in it.

I cleared my throat and stared at the man who was threatening me just minutes ago. "I guess you're going to have to learn to trust me, Malice," I whispered, making sure to emphasize the name I now knew had so much more weight than just a game between us. It was a play on words, a label for his enemies. His family and close friends knew him as Nick. I knew him as Malice because I was the enemy.

Malice inhaled and stepped over Graves's body to get to me. His eyes slithered up and down my body. There was something about his perusal that made me want to look and be strong. "Get back to work," he growled in a low voice before eyeing my upper thigh. I didn't dare follow his gaze.

Malice then crouched low, making him eye level with my center. Heat flooded my body as I looked down at him. There was so much power beneath me. I liked how he looked there, his lips level with my pussy.

He reached out with his thumb and wiped at a bead of

blood that had splattered on my thigh. The crimson stain smeared against my creamy skin, and his fingerprint was stamped on my body with the bloody ink. "Trust is earned," he said while standing up.

"Agreed," I replied.

"Someone find Hale. I want him to explain to me why he wasn't at his station," Malice called over his shoulder. I hadn't even noticed the guards dragging Graves's body away and the cleanup crew already bleaching the floor.

I smirked. "Hale is probably off trying to meet with Cora," I replied.

Malice's frown deepened. "Are you sharing evidence or making an assumption based on your own prejudice?"

"I don't trust him, Malice. He's never here. Do you even know Hale? Do you know where he goes during his shift here or what he's doing when you're not around? This is not the first time he's been conveniently missing from his post. Not that I'm complaining. I want that man as far away from me as possible." I shook away my nerves and kept speaking. "Something isn't right about him. You keep waiting for me to tell you about a rat, but I think there's one right under your nose."

"Unless you have some proper evidence, then—"

"He knew I was going to the bus that day, Malice."

Malice looked around. "We can discuss this later. I know you're shaken up about what happened here, but let's not throw out blame without proof, okay? Hale is a loyal employee."

I rolled my eyes. Why did no one see what I saw? "Fine."

Malice pressed his lips into a thin line. "I think you owe me something," he said.

I crossed my arms over my chest. The line of people wanting access to the club was growing again, but Malice had me rooted to the spot. "I owe you something?"

"I protected you today. Made sure you were safe."

Of course he'd want a pat on the back for saving me. "I could have handled it," I snapped back. "Even without my shady bodyguard, I would have been fine."

"Right. So no thank-you?" he asked.

"I don't think your ego needs the stroke," I replied, my voice a sensual rasp. Malice blew out a puff of air and fixed his tie.

"Killing people in the lobby, Nick?" William asked. I hadn't even heard him approach. In a swift move, my silent stranger wrapped his arms around me and looked me in the eye. "You okay?" William tenderly stroked my cheek.

I wasn't really sure how I felt. My secret hidden box of shit I was avoiding was getting filled to the brim. "Yeah. I'm good. Guess you don't need to find Anthony a body after all."

William chuckled. "And I was so looking forward to performing some vigilante justice today."

"Don't you have some fucking work to do?" Malice shouted, his anger reverberating across the room. William kept his arms wrapped around me. It felt like defiance.

"Don't you?" William countered.

Malice smiled at an onlooker closing the distance between the three of us. "Me doing my job has never been the problem, brother. Last I checked, it was you who wanted out. Get to fucking work and stop testing my patience, or Anthony will have two bodies to melt tonight."

chapter eighteen

"Close your eyes," Malice whispered, his face shadowed in the dark. "If you see my evil, I'll have to kill you."

I laughed and laughed. "What a way to die," I replied.

So much blood. Gore. I stepped on a bridge made of skulls to get to him. One step. Two steps. Crunching bones played an anthem of death as I walked.

"Don't go!" William begged me. I couldn't see him. My silent stranger watched. He always watched.

"Close your eyes, Juliet."

"Close your eyes…"

I woke up with a gasp. Sweat dripped down my face as I tried to calm my breathing. It was dark in my bedroom. The entire setting felt like an eerie continuation of the nightmare I'd just had. The wind outside my window was howling. If I listened closely, I could hear guards talking to themselves down the hall.

I was supposed to feel safe here, but I didn't. I wanted to go home.

I ended up riding back with Malice after my shift at work. I wondered if he was trying to keep me from going to the police after what I'd seen or if he had other reasons for wanting me close.

Even though he terrified me, I still felt like watching him murder Graves evened the playing field some. We both had something on each other. Not that I'd ever be able to act on it.

Hale never did show up the rest of my shift. Instead, Malice walked by the hostess stand multiple times throughout the night. He kept watching me with his dark eyes. I thought I was supposed to fly under the radar at Eden's Place, but now I felt like the center of attention. Even Kelsey was treating me differently. She was normally chatty but had kept silent the rest of our shift. I didn't know if I should address what had happened or not.

I'd slept all day. I was used to working late nights at

the diner, but adjusting to Eden's Place and staying at the Civella Mansion was exhausting. It was hard for me to feel safe and sleep soundly while here. I kept expecting Hale to show up or for Malice to decide that he didn't need his little spy anymore. I tossed and turned most nights, but I guess the exhaustion finally caught up to me.

A knock on the door stopped my thoughts, and I pulled my blankets up to my chin, as if some soft cotton could protect me from the evil living in this home. "Juliet?" Anthony's muffled voice cut through the thick door.

"Come in," I called out.

He waltzed in wearing a suit that made him look handsome but didn't quite fit his personality. I much preferred him in jeans, a faded shirt, and beanie. The expression on his face was a mixture of uncertainty and excitement. He kept biting his lip while averting his gaze.

"You sleep well?" he asked.

I yawned. "I had a pretty intense nightmare," I admitted. "I kind of want to go home. I don't sleep well here."

He stopped staring at the ceiling to look at me and furrowed his brow. "Why haven't you been sleeping well?"

I smiled politely. "I don't really feel safe here, Anthony," I admitted. "At any moment, your brother could decide to kill me. Doesn't exactly make for restful sleep." I didn't actually believe that Malice wanted to hurt me anymore. If anything, he was going out of his way to prove that I was safe with him. But still Malice seemed to have one of those personalities that flipped on a dime, and I never wanted to end up on his bad side.

Anthony sat down on the mattress at my feet and looked solemnly at me. "He won't hurt you, Juliet," he said softly. "I promise."

I wasn't exactly sure if that was a promise he could keep, but I nodded regardless. Anthony might have held his guilt over his brother's head, but it would only go so far. I wasn't convinced that Malice cared enough about his family to let Anthony control him like that.

"I heard about what happened at Eden's Place. You want to talk about it?" he then asked.

"Not really. I'm actually pretending it didn't happen. But it looks like you got your body," I joked. Humor and avoidance tactics were how I was going to survive this crazy world of crime that I was dropped into.

"Nope. That body is all Nick. You kill it, you clean it up."

I gaped at him. "Even the boss has to clean up his own bodies?"

Anthony patted my leg under the covers. "Especially the boss. He might enjoy it more than me. Gory motherfucker. I don't want to give you a big head or anything, but Nick doesn't just kill people in his club all willy-nilly. He saw that fucker threatening you and lost his cool. Everyone is talking about it now. The gossip is delicious," he cooed.

I frowned. "I don't know about all that. I saw Graves's account balance. He owed a fucking lot of money. He had a bar tab open that was six figures."

"Nick doesn't care about the money," Anthony replied. "He doesn't run Eden's Place for profit. He hosts it because the only thing worth more than money is information and connections. Graves stopped being useful months ago, which is why he had to start paying. Why else do you think he makes you and Kelsey keep such detailed reports on everyone?" I thought about what Anthony was saying. It was brilliant, actually. Malice had so much blackmail on everyone that he was invincible. "Graves used to own some shipping companies. Helped for smuggling weapons. But he started to get sloppy. Had a few ships repossessed. Made it more difficult for us to do what we needed to do."

"So that's why Malice killed him," I interjected.

"I wouldn't be so sure," Anthony replied with a tentative smile. "But let's not talk about him." He stopped speaking to tug at his collar. "I was wondering if you wanted to go to dinner?"

Based on how nervous Anthony seemed, I couldn't help but think that this was definitely more than dinner. "Like... on a date?"

He exhaled and stiffened. I tried to look him in the eye, but he was staring at the ground. "Yes. A date."

I liked Anthony a lot. I felt a deep connection with him, but I needed to be honest. I blurted my response and instantly regretted it. "I've kissed both your brothers."

He laughed. "Oh?" I watched as he playfully put his fist under his chin. "Tell me. How was it? William seems like the passionate, tragic type. Nick probably held you down and forced his mouth on you."

Anthony wasn't quite wrong on either account. "That's pretty accurate actually. I just want to be clear with what's going on so you don't think I'm leading you on or anything..." Disappointment hit me like a ton of bricks. I didn't realize he felt this way, and I wanted to explore it more. I just didn't know what the fuck I was doing with William and Malice. It was a clusterfuck of epic proportions. I knew on some level, I was just being used and confused. Nothing would come from this, but I didn't want to just be a doll passed around, either.

"Tell me something," Anthony began while pressing his palms into the mattress and crawling over me. "Do you want to kiss me, Juliet?"

I swallowed, but my response was almost instant. There was something about these men that pulled the truth from my lips. "Yes."

Anthony smiled before hovering just inches from my face. My heart raced. "I want to kiss you too," he admitted in a whisper. "And I haven't wanted to do that since..."

Anthony then reached out and lightly brushed his knuckles along my jaw. "You don't make my skin burn, Juliet. I want to explore that more."

I tried not to feel disappointed, but suddenly I felt like some experiment. Did he want me, or was this some sort of test for his boundaries and healing? "Okay," I croaked out.

"I like you," Anthony whispered. "You showed up and started talking about grinding bones and liquifying bodies. I've been listening to your voice for the past year on your podcast. You're funny and strong and caring and impressive. I. Like. You. I like how you make me feel. So go ahead and kiss my brothers. I'm not going to give up feeling normal because they're selfish and sexually confused bastards."

"But you like me?" I repeated. Why I needed this confirmed by this ridiculously attractive man was borderline pathetic.

"I really like you. Get dressed. I'm going to take you to my favorite restaurant."

I bit my lip. "Okay."

Anthony got up from the bed with this renewed smile on his beautiful face. Once he was at the door, I spoke up. "Hey, Anthony?"

He paused. "Yeah?"

"I really like you too."

—

Dinner was probably the worst food I'd ever had in my life. Anthony took me to this run-down restaurant that probably needed a health inspection, but I could see why he liked it. It was mostly empty and spaced out. He admitted on the ride here that sometimes crowds made him anxious. I suggested that I cook him dinner for a second date, and it made him grin.

I'd worn a lavender summer dress that was flirty but comfortable. My wedge heels were loud against the concrete as we walked back to his car. All in all, it was a really cute date. Anthony was attentive, flirty, and quirky. He asked me about my favorite podcast episodes and jokingly planned for our next body dump expedition.

The night air was warm and thick, and our hands brushed against one another as we made our way back to the car. I'd had a good time, but I struggled to understand where the line was with him.

I found myself wanting to reach out and hold his hand but stopped when I realized it might make him uncomfortable. At one point, he was scratching his jaw, and I licked my lips in appreciation. The strong angles of his face were tempting, but then I felt guilty for lusting after him.

With some people, attraction was instantaneous. It was this heated passion that flowed freely. You couldn't avoid it. You couldn't ignore it. With others, attraction was slow, intentional, and secretive. It moved like molasses. With Anthony, I wasn't sure what I was allowed to do. I wanted to touch and explore him but didn't want to overwhelm him, either. I was letting him take the lead, and I wasn't sure where this train was going.

"I'm not exactly sure what was in the pasta I just ate," he joked.

"Probably brains," I deadpanned. "Did you know that Peter Bryan killed his best friend, then fried his brains with butter before eating them?" I asked.

"Episode Thirty-three," Anthony replied with a smile. "I remember your cannibalism series. Can't say I've ever been tempted to eat any of the bodies I've handled. Fuck? Maybe, but never eat."

"You'd fuck a corpse?" I asked, not sure if I wanted the answer. It was a hard line for me. And selfishly, I couldn't compete with a cold dead body. I was completely alive. If that was his preference, there was no hope for us. I wasn't sure I could realistically date a necrophiliac, no matter how much I enjoyed their company.

"I've thought about it but never done it. Before Eden's Place, I thought it would be a good way to get off. Dead people can't hurt you. They can't move. Can't beat you until you pass out. I don't fear the dead. It's the living you have to look out for," Anthony said.

It was the first time I'd heard him openly talk about

what had happened to him, and I didn't know how to respond. My initial response was pity, but something told me it would upset Anthony. "I would never hurt you, Anthony," I whispered as we got to his car.

"I know," he replied softly. I wished I knew how to navigate this situation. I wanted to comfort him and kiss him all in the same breath. "Can I try something?"

I nodded, not sure what he wanted to try but trusting him anyway. He gently pushed me against the car and moved to cup my cheeks. My breath caught in my throat. "I'm going to kiss you, Killer," he said softly.

My heart started to race. Attraction and excitement ignited within me. "Okay," I replied, not sure what else to say.

Anthony's lips were soft and timid at first. I patiently waited for him to find his groove, and kept my fists balled at my side to keep myself from grabbing him. He smiled triumphantly against my lips, and I felt with complete certainty that there was definitely a spark between us. He moved more intentionally after a lingering moment. His tongue lapped at the seam of my lips. He moaned and pressed his body against mine. It took everything I had not to thread my fingers through his hair and tug at the wavy strands.

His hands lowered, and he touched the sensitive skin on my neck. He outlined my breast with his palm, and I felt his hard erection pressing against my stomach. "Fuck," he cursed. He had me panting. Melting. I wanted more, and with Anthony, there was no question of if this was right or wrong. I didn't feel disgusted with myself for liking him. He was the safe choice. The brother who liked me back.

"Touch me," he whispered between kisses. I accepted his demand and ran my hands up and down his chest. Slowly, slowly, slowly. I made sure he could predict every move of my hands. I noticed that his lips had stopped moving. And when I reached for his neck, he flinched.

"Sorry," I whispered before pulling away. He snapped his hands up and wrapped them around my wrists.

"Please don't apologize. That was...amazing. Incredible."

Happy tears filled his eyes, and I felt overwhelmed by his joy. His expression was so incredibly soft that I wanted to touch his cheeks and revel in it. It was such a vivid picture of relief. Our kiss was brilliant and beautiful. I couldn't imagine how amazing it felt to finally trust someone enough to do that. "You're a really good kisser," I choked out. My panties were drenched. He was leaving me wanting, but I wasn't upset. If anything, it made me more anxious for the next kiss—the next step.

He wiped a stray tear, and I found myself feeling thankful that he'd let me be a part of this moment. He quickly patted his pockets, then cursed. "Fuck. I left my keys inside. I'll be right back."

I watched his back as he jogged back up to the restaurant, a happy lift to his steps. Pressing the tips of my fingers to my plush lips, I mulled over what had just happened until I heard my phone ring. Reaching into my pocket, I pulled it out and answered without looking at the caller ID.

"Juliet?" Vicky's voice boomed into the receiver. "William just called me and said you were with Anthony. What are you doing?"

I winced. I didn't know how to tell my best friend what just happened. Not only had I broken every rule in girl code, but I'd also betrayed her trust. For the entirety of our relationship, she made it clear that she wanted me to stay away from this life—from her family. But I'd dove headfirst. I kissed them. I kissed all of them. I worked at their club. I was living in their home.

"We went to dinner," I whispered, feeling shame.

"Whatever. Anthony doesn't go to dinner with people. He doesn't like crowds. Hell, he eats in his death dungeon most days. What are you really doing, Juliet? I mean seriously. I'm not there, and I'm hearing things. Things I don't like." There was an edge to her tone. It sounded like a threat.

I didn't know how to respond. "You're not here," I whispered. "I feel like I'm forced to navigate something I don't understand. I miss my best friend."

"And I miss you too, but why are you spending so much

time with my brothers?" She wasn't letting me dance around the subject. I wasn't prepared for this confrontation, but I knew we needed to talk.

I shrugged, even though she couldn't see the move. "Anthony has been really nice to me. Grams went to California to visit her sister, and I miss you, and this whole thing has been pretty fucked up. He's been kind to me, Vicky. He's sweet and funny."

"He's sick, Juliet," Vicky hissed. I stared at the concrete. "He'll never live a normal life. He goes on killing sprees when he feels out of control of a situation. You talk about killers on your little podcast, so you think you know what you can handle, but I once found Anthony bathed in blood at the barber shop because a man that looked like his abuser walked in. Protecting him is a full-time job. You can think he's cute and fun. He loves deeply, but he's not safe. I'm saying this as someone who loves you both—stay the fuck away. All of my brothers are literally insane. You've only just scratched the surface. Anthony will always be controlled by the trauma he experienced."

I hadn't even realized that I was holding my breath. My eyes were locked on the ground. I struggled to come to terms with everything she'd said, but what upset me most was how little she thought of him. Anthony loved Vicky deeply. She comforted him. She helped him and treated him like a human. If Anthony heard what she'd just said, he'd be crushed. I loved Vicky, and I understood why she was trying to protect me, but it was still shitty of her to say. "I think you're wrong, Vicky. I think Anthony is so much more than what happened to him."

My phone was ripped from my hands before I could hear her response. I hadn't even heard Anthony walk up, and suddenly felt ashamed to know that he'd heard at least my side of the conversation. His face was blank, and I hated myself for it, but I found myself searching his expression for the uncontrollable rage hiding under the surface. "Hey, sis," Anthony said with a genuine smile. "I know you're worried about us. Love you too." And then he hung up the phone. I held out my hand for him to give it back to me, but his expression contorted. Fury seeped through every pore, every harsh angle. He reared back and tossed my cell phone as hard as he could into the distance before letting out a harsh scream.

It was blisteringly loud, covering the sound of the phone crashing against the concrete. The veins bulged in his neck as he yelled. I watched him without shame, taking in the full force of this moment.

His voice cracked, and he stopped yelling to pant. I let him steady his breath for a long moment before speaking. "Anthony?" I tenderly said. I wanted to reach out and touch him, comfort him.

"Let's go, Killer," he whispered.

And we got in his car. And we drove back to the Civella Mansion. And I wondered what was going on inside Anthony's beautiful mind.

chapter nineteen

The Rolex on William's wrist glimmered in the sunlight. He had one hand on the steering wheel of his Porsche convertible and one hand on my upper thigh. He'd given me a Chanel head wrap to hold my brown hair back and some Prada sunglasses to block out the early morning sun. I felt like an old Hollywood starlet as we cruised down the highway toward downtown. The destination was a surprise, but I was enjoying the trip, especially since the company looked so handsome.

Early this morning, William strutted into the guest room with a wardrobe bag draped over his arm, and he told me to be downstairs in twenty minutes. I eagerly got ready, excited to spend the day with my silent stranger despite his demanding early morning greeting. I was giddy for the chance to see him in his element—to learn more about him. I also wanted out of the house. It felt like every day was a revolving schedule of work, sleep, and more work.

We pulled up to a red light, and he grabbed my hand, lightly squeezing it. "Are you going to tell me where we're going?" I asked, my voice surprisingly low and suggestive. Seeing William behind this powerful luxury car and holding my hand was making my heart flutter.

He lowered his shades to look me in the eye. "I'm going to spoil you," he whispered. I liked the idea of being spoiled by my secret stranger.

After stopping for croissants and coffee, we arrived at a luxury spa on Briarcliff. William stopped at the valet and tossed his keys to the attendant before guiding me inside. The moment we walked through the doors, we were hit with a flurry of activity all at once. Suddenly, I was handed a glass of champagne by a thin woman, and then a man started softly trying to fluff my hair while whispering orders to his assistant. One person took William's jacket, and another, a bubbly woman with curly pink hair and thick-rimmed glasses, made her way toward me.

"Welcome to Penn Avenue Luxury Spa. We'll be

starting off with a couples massage, a myofascial cupping session, a body renewal scrub, full haircut, color, and style. Manicures. Pedicures. Mr. Civella requested every service on the book," she said with a giddy grin before lowering her voice to a whisper. "Girlll, tell me your secrets! This man ordered the works. No expense spared! So lucky. Does he have a brother?"

He had two, not that I was sharing.

As I looked back at William, I saw his calm and relaxed face, as if he were enjoying every bit of this.

"A day at the spa?" I inquired.

He licked his lips before responding. It was a slow, leisurely move full of intent. "Only the best for you, Miss Cross."

—

There was not a tight spot in my body. Each of my muscles was completely relaxed. The two-hour massage with William was beyond anything I'd ever experienced. It was sensual, relaxing, peaceful. It seemed to me that every time I looked at William, he had his eyes on me, as if I were the most beautiful woman he'd ever seen. I'd never been treated to something so luxurious. My skin was buffed, my nails were polished, and I was currently getting golden, sun-kissed highlights in my hair. I had enough foil in my hair to pick up the local news station, a joke my stylist didn't find very funny. I suppose it wasn't the first time he'd heard it.

I was sitting under a massive hairdryer and watching William. It was like taking an indulgent drink of fine champagne. I stared without shame or reservation. I looked at the skull tattoo on his neck, the way his eyelashes curled slightly, the veins in his hands. The steady bob of his Adam's apple.

I ran my fingers over the soft robe wrapped around my body and hummed in appreciation. "I love this robe," I whispered.

William was sitting in a nearby leather chair, legs crossed, sleeves rolled up. He had his iPad in hand and was reading an e-book. He peered at me over the edge of his iPad. "You can have it."

I blushed. "Thank you for today," I whispered. "But…"

He looked up at me and powered off his iPad. I loved that I never felt like I was fighting for William's attention. He was completely attuned to me.

"But what?"

"Why? This feels like an excessive treat."

William grinned while leaning forward to rest his chin on his fist. "Excessive?"

"I'm not complaining. It just feels…" William waited patiently for me to answer. I couldn't even finish my thought. "Why? Why me?"

"I like excessive things," he murmured. "And it makes

me happy to give you all the things you deserve, Miss Cross." I shifted in my seat. "You're not used to this," he observed.

"I'm not," I replied with an uncomfortable chuckle.

"You know what I've noticed about you?" he asked.

I shook my head, the foils on my hair shaking with me. "What?"

"You do everything for everyone else. I watched you work your ass off and never once complain. So many times I wanted to help you, but…"

"The deal," I finished for him. I refused to resent my best friend for making that arrangement with William, but still, it stung. "Can you tell me something?"

"Anything."

"What happened between you and Malice?"

My question made William shift in his seat. I watched him inhale and then exhale, stalling. "I'm very good at business," William admitted. "A majority of our…legal… fortune is a result of my tedious efforts with the stock market and dabbling in hard investments across the country. I've always been good at it."

"That still doesn't explain why he…"

"Hates me? My brother was trained from birth to be competitive. He's the firstborn. There's a phrase in royal families that can be applied to my family. He's the heir, I'm the spare. I guess it created a lot of friction between us. He has to constantly prove himself with others in our organization, and as a result, he is forced to put me in my place. There are some who think I'm more suited for his job."

"Do you want his job?" I asked.

William took a sip of his drink. "It's not worth challenging him now. For the most part, I like being the spare. Sometimes I wonder if it would be easier. Nicholas hates me because he knows I'm very capable of taking over. I'm fine with biding my time, though. Right now, I'm sitting across from one of the most beautiful women I've ever seen, and my brother is off somewhere sniffing out a rat."

That got my attention. I leaned closer to hear him. "What are you talking about?"

William looked uncomfortable, like he wasn't supposed to say something. "Nick is looking into the Hale situation for you."

My brows raised. "He is?"

"We decided it might be best if you were away from the mansion until things are sorted. I was going to take you to dinner tonight too."

"So, is Hale guilty? What did you find? Where is Malice now?" I had a million questions. Malice actually was listening to me? And he'd sent me away? With William of all people.

"Hale is up to something," William replied. "Don't worry, Nick is taking care of it." I leaned back in my seat. Hot damn. I couldn't help but smile. "Why are you grinning like that?"

"Because I'm right!" I exclaimed. "I knew that fucker was a creep. Vindication is sweet." I basked in the glory of being right as the hairstylist finished up my trim and color. It took every ounce of restraint I possessed to not text Malice. I wanted to see Hale's greasy face the moment he was caught.

It wasn't until I was getting dressed that I realized my job was done.

Done. I'd found the rat. I did what Malice hired me to do. Did this mean I could go back home? It all felt anticlimactic.

I walked out into the lobby feeling less enthusiastic. I wasn't sure what this meant for my future at Eden's Place or my role in the Civella family. Would Malice stop funding my grandmother's medicine now that my job was done? I mulled over my concerns while William paid the bill.

I cleared my throat to gather his attention, and the moment his eyes landed on me, I felt my skin buzz from his heavy gaze. "You look stunning," he whispered.

I shifted my weight and stared at the ground. "Amazing what trained professionals can do with a hairbrush."

I felt William's hand under my chin. He eased my

attention up until I couldn't avoid him. "Don't do that," he whispered.

"Do what?"

"You've got these big brown eyes that haunt me, Miss Cross." My eyes filled with emotion at his words. "I like you just as much in a stained Dick's Diner tank top as I do now. I used to dream about those damn dark circles under your eyes. Skin covered in grease. Pen ink on your fingers from doing your homework in the kitchen during lulls." William picked up my hand and inspected my freshly painted nails. "You would bite your nails down to the stub when you were anxious." He tucked my highlighted hair behind my ear. "I remember the first time I saw you with your hair down." He brushed his cheek against mine and breathed me in. "I wanted to wrap it around my fist and pull you in for a kiss."

I closed my eyes, my lips parted, and I shivered at the smooth sound of his voice. William placed his hand at my lower back and guided me outside to where his car was waiting for us. My legs shook with every step. I wanted him.

Once both of us were in the car, a brave moment of insanity hit me like a punch. He moved to put the car in drive, but I leaned over the center console and slammed my lips to his. It took William a second to realize what was happening. I felt every emotion reflected in his kiss. Shock.

Awe. Lust.

I pressed my hand against his chest and dragged my teeth along his mouth. He moaned and threaded his fingers through my hair, tugging lightly. "Thank you for today," I whispered between kisses before moving to suck on his neck. I didn't care if everyone in that damn spa was watching us from the windows. I needed this. Right here. Right now.

William grabbed my breast and moaned. I sucked on his skin until it bloomed a blue hue, a bruise in the shape of my lips. We made out, hot and heavy like horny teens until his cock was so hard that I could clearly see it through the outline of his pants. I slowly eased my hand lower, but he grabbed my wrist, stopping me.

"Fuck," he cursed before pulling his phone out of his pocket and answering it. No, no. I wanted to keep going. I pouted as he spoke. "What do you want, Nick?"

It stung a little, that William stopped us to answer his phone. I ended up sitting back in my seat to sulk.

"What do you mean he's gone? How did you let him get away?"

I snapped my attention to William. Were they talking about Hale?

"Fuck. Fine. We're headed back....No. She's fine....Yeah. She enjoyed it a lot." I listened intently. "No shit, I'll keep her safe....Yes. Yes, I'll come straight back, Nick. Can you just let me—" William rolled his eyes and tossed his cell onto the center console. "He hung up on me."

"Hale ran away?" I asked in a bored tone as William closed the top to his convertible. Seemed fitting the slimy bastard would make a run for it; he'd probably had a contingency plan all along.

"Yep," William replied with a curse. "And Nicholas is now going on his usual overprotective tirade."

I shook my head. "Anthony pretty much lives in a dungeon, Vicky is halfway across the world. What's next? Is he going to lock you in your office?" I asked. Malice couldn't control everything and everyone.

"My brother doesn't care what happens to me," William replied in an ominous tone. "But he'll probably keep you at home for the foreseeable future."

"Me?" I asked, palm placed over my chest in surprise. "Why me?"

William gave me an exasperated look before pulling out of the parking lot. "Let's go home before he sends an army to collect us."

chapter twenty

I stared at my reflection as Grams spoke. Anthony had replaced my phone since he'd broken the last one. Malice wanted me to be accessible at all times, the overbearing asshole.

"Oh, Juliet. You'd love it here. I wish I could fly you out," Grams said. She sounded damn good—better than she'd sounded in months. It was like a weight was off her shoulders.

"I'm glad you're enjoying yourself," I replied, genuinely thrilled that she was having such a good time with her sister. She needed this vacation. They'd been out to watch jazz bands, the beach, up the mountains. Grams was moving every day, and based on the updates from Aunt Agnes, she was doing phenomenal. I wasn't sure if it was the change of scenery and being with her sister, or the medicine from Dr. Hoffstead. Either way, it made me feel incredibly relieved to know that Grams was doing so well. She was thriving. I wished I could see it in person.

"How is Nicholas doing? Is he keeping a good eye on my girl?" It was so strange to hear Grams use his name when I was still calling him by his evil alter ego.

Honestly, I hadn't really seen Malice since the shooting at Eden's Place. Three days had passed since my spa day with William, and even though I hadn't seen him, he had me on house arrest. There was a guard constantly poised outside my door. It was driving me absolutely crazy to stay here every day.

William and Malice left this morning to follow a lead on Hale, but I hadn't heard anything else. I wasn't sure I ever would. Something told me that Hale had weaseled his way deep into the organization, and it would be a while before Malice got his revenge.

"I haven't seen him, but I'm doing well. Working and keeping busy," I assured her. Malice had agreed to let me go to Eden's Place tonight, mostly because Kelsey was swamped and overwhelmed. Again, Malice never spoke directly to me. I only got random text messages with demands or verbal directives from his army of suits.

"Mr. Jonas called the other day and said he hadn't seen you at the diner recently. Did you change your shift?" Grams asked. I hated lying to her, but I wasn't about to tell her that I was working at a sex club with dangerous Mafia men and doubling as a spy.

"I'm working the overnight shift these days, Grams," I lied.

"Oh, you know I hate that," she said in an angry tone. "It's not safe for a pretty girl like you to be working overnight in that part of town. Ma-maybe we could find you a better job with more consistent hours. You're a smart gir-girl." I could tell she was getting worked up because she was struggling to get her words out. I felt bad for worrying her.

"I think that's a great idea. We can talk more about it when you get back. Polish up my resume and see who is hiring, okay?" I offered, mostly to placate her. I'd already gotten my first check from Malice, and the money was too good to pass up. I'd just have to come up with another lie. It was all really starting to pile up. First Grams. Vicky. Myself.

"Okay. Well, Aunt Agnes and I are going swimming again. It feels so good on these old bones to be in the water and just sit. Let me know if you need anything, okay? And don't be working too hard."

"I won't, Grams," I promised. "Love you bunches."

"Have a happy day, my sweet. Love you too."

I hung up the phone and turned on my curling iron. It was my first shift back at Eden's Place tonight since the shooting, and I was not looking forward to it. I kept seeing Malice's angry face as he pulled the trigger. Mr. Graves was a shady character, but when did I start becoming desensitized to death? The night after I saw him killed, I slept like a baby, not once considering the legal implications of what I'd witnessed or the moral obligation I had to feel something about the murder. In just over three weeks, I'd started to slowly trust Malice and his empire. I understood that he controlled this town. Hell, maybe even the entire country. His connections far surpassed my own, and murder wasn't the damning thing I once believed it to be. I was still having nightmares about the death of my soul, but I was learning to cope. I was enjoying the darkness.

I'd become one of the monsters I'd once obsessed over.

I thumbed through my makeup, trying to decide on the look I wanted to go for this evening. Someone gently knocked on my door. "Come in," I said absentmindedly while adjusting my robe.

"Fucking cunt," a familiar voice growled.

My eyes searched for the source.

My stomach dropped at the tone.

No. No. It couldn't be.

My entire body turned cold.

Immediately, my eyes found his reflection. He was standing in the doorway, his arms crossed over his chest. He had a manic smile on his face, one that reminded me of all the twisted things he was capable of. I quickly stood up to face him, a stern expression on my face.

"What do you want?" I asked. I scanned his face and noted a black eye, swollen and angry on his face.

He ignored my question and stalked closer. "Everything was great before you came along," he growled.

I inhaled deeply, forcing my shaking bones to settle. I couldn't get out of this if I was afraid. All I'd have to do was scream and one of the dozens of guards would storm in here. Hale had to have known this, right? He wouldn't hurt me. Or was he unhinged? "You would have been caught eventually," I replied, my chin tilted high and my shoulders rolled back.

Hale stepped closer. I suddenly wished I had a knife or something to defend myself against this fucking creep. "You asked too many questions. You made him doubt me."

"You did that all on your own. How long have you been working with Cora, Hale? How long have you been betraying Malice?"

He grinned. "Months. The pay is better. I'm only as loyal as the money in my wallet, and Cora's got loads of it."

"So why come back, huh? You got paid."

"I didn't get everything I wanted," he rasped while stalking closer to me.

I looked around for something—anything—to use to defend myself. "What are you talking about?"

Hale's nostrils flared, and he closed the remaining distance between us. "I couldn't stop thinking about you. The way you crushed his skull with your foot." He stopped speaking to rub his hand over his hard dick in his pants. Bile traveled up my throat. I wanted to puke all over him. "Blood just splattered everywhere. It was the hottest thing I'd ever seen," he said with reverence before grabbing my arm and pinning me against the wall. His breath was rancid. His beady eyes soaked me in. "It was beautiful," he whispered, awe in his tone. "I want you to do it for me again."

I wiggled and shoved against him. For some reason, I couldn't seem to move my feet. I had them planted on the ground from fear. It was this chronic awareness of the murder weapons attached to my legs. My own body was betraying me and fueling my enemy. "Fuck off," I cursed.

"Such a nasty mouth. So foul. You have no idea what you're getting yourself into."

I looked up at him, my eyes angry slits. "People keep saying that to me. But I know exactly what I'm getting into. Why are you here? We both know Malice will kick your ass for touching me."

Hale tipped his head back and laughed. "You think any of the Civellas give a shit about you? I've seen girls come and go. You entertained Nick for half a second, and now you think you mean something. This room gets used all the time. The girls at Eden's Place get recycled by the brothers too."

I shoved and twisted, trying to get away from the unhinged man. "So what? It doesn't change the fact that Malice hates rats."

Hale laughed. "Does he, though? I'm still here, aren't I? I was able to practically walk through the front door."

I stared at his black eye once more. "He gave you that black eye, didn't he? And he'll fucking end whoever let you in here."

Hale frowned. "There will be no one left for him to end."

That ominous threat terrified me. Had Hale killed everyone? I shoved again, but he was like a brick wall—impossible to move. "What's your plan then, huh? Come here and scare me?"

And then, in a sickening move, Hale reached down and unzipped his pants. "I'm here to show you how worthless you are. I'm here to remind you that you're nothing. No one. You can snitch all you want, but no one will believe you. No one cares about you. You're completely alone. I'm going to fuck you right here, I'm going to fill this entire mansion with your screams, and there won't be a single person that runs to your rescue."

I'd never felt this much fear in my life. It was overwhelming and damning. My legs shook. My eyes widened. I felt frozen with inaction. My flight or fight was broken. I was just standing there helplessly as his terrifying words simmered in my soul.

I'd never understood the women who didn't fight for their lives against evil men. I'd always thought about what I would do in this sort of situation, how I would kick, scratch, scream, and punch my way out of this no matter what. But the shock was too much. My body was completely frozen.

He ripped at my robe with his nasty, meaty hands, exposing my bare breasts. I released the breath I was holding and realized I had to do something. Fucking something.

I screamed loudly.

It tore through my throat. It ripped my vocal chords to shreds. My veins bulged. Hale laughed and laughed and laughed. He slammed his hand between my legs. I pushed my thighs together, but it was impossible to avoid his invasion. I hated the way his rough fingertips slammed against my most private parts. I hated the tears streaming down my face.

More screams. I slapped him. I finally moved. I finally fought. But I wasn't strong enough. How could I be so fucking weak?

"Help! Please help me."

Maybe Hale was right. I was a nobody. I wasn't special. I was completely alone. Just like my mother was the night she disappeared.

He pinned me. He roughly rubbed along my sex. I felt like vomiting, I wished I could. I wanted to piss all over him. Shit myself, even. I wanted to disgust him. Anything to get him away, but I had no control over myself.

And then, like a knight in a Gucci suit, Malice walked through the door.

Time slowed.

Relief hit me.

Oh God, I was going to live. I was going to survive.

My eyes widened as he marched up to Hale and yanked him off me with strength I didn't even know he had. Hale was surprised by the attack but quickly fought. Malice didn't even flinch when a fist came flying at his face. They both grappled on the floor, rolling and hitting and punching. I screamed for more help. Where were the fucking guards?

Malice managed to pull a thin wire from his pocket and wrap it around Hale's throat. His legs were around Hale's torso, and his arms were pulling the wire so tight that it cut through his skin and forced beads of blood to form along Hale's meaty neck.

I heaved as I watched in horror and satisfaction.

Nicholas had come for me. No, Malice had come for me.

"Fucking pass out," he cursed as Hale's movements slowed and his face turned blue.

I watched as Hale's body turned impossibly still. And eventually, he stopped moving altogether.

Malice removed the wire and checked his pulse. "That's right, motherfucker, you don't get to die that easily." Malice then looked up at me. "You okay?"

I didn't even know how to answer that question. Apparently, my hesitation was answer enough. Malice took the wire and quickly tied Hale's hands together. Then, he rolled him on his stomach all while cursing. "Fucking rat ass pervert." Hale groaned. Yep. He was definitely alive. What was Malice planning?

"He's the rat," I whispered. "He tried to…"

Malice stopped his work to look at me. Once again he asked a question I could not answer just yet. "Are you okay?"

"Sure," I replied. What else was there to say? Apparently, my answer wasn't good enough, because Malice let out a literal growl through his clenched teeth. He bent over and grabbed at the waistband of Hale's pants and pulled them down, revealing his pasty ass. "What are you doing?" I asked.

"Hand me that curling iron," he snapped.

I froze. "What?"

"Hand me the fucking curling iron," Malice growled.

His eyes were wild with intent. It was the first time I'd ever seen him out of control. He was usually so...calculating.

"I don't understand," I replied. What was he going to do, curl Hale's hair?

Malice huffed and shoved past me to pick up the curling iron off my vanity. It was a thick wand, perfect for bouncy waves. I still didn't understand—

Malice pulled one of Hale's hairy ass cheeks to the side and swiftly shoved the heated iron up Hale's ass. The smell of burnt skin filled my nose. Hale's back arched, and he woke with a start, screaming bloody murder as the curling iron literally burned him from the inside out.

I cupped my hand over my mouth in horror, but a thrill also traveled through me. Retribution. It was gruesome. Blood poured from his ass. Smoke filled the air. Burning, burning, burning. He struggled against the wire tied around his wrists. Malice laughed maniacally as he pressed his knee into Hale's back, pushing him down as he essentially burned alive.

"You thought you could fuck me over? Fuck my girl? You thought you could feed Cora secrets and I wouldn't know?"

Hale screamed and screamed. I wrapped my robe around my body and watched in awe. I sensed his consciousness fading, fading, fading. He spasmed on the floor but once again grew very weak. I felt a sudden urge to tell him something.

I wanted to tell him the very thing he said to me.

My voice was surprisingly strong, despite all the trauma I'd experienced. "You're nothing. No one. No one cares about you. You're completely alone. You filled this entire mansion with your screams, and not a single person ran to your rescue."

And Hale, the creep, died from a hot curling iron up the ass.

chapter twenty one

"You killed him," I said.

Malice smirked, as if this was funny. As if the brutal death in his guest room was nothing more than an outlet for his destruction. "I did."

I was trembling, my entire body shaking from the adrenaline and fear. "You...you tortured him," I whispered.

"I did."

"You saved me."

At my awed tone, Malice softened some. "I did," he echoed once more. Simple words packed with sentimental meaning. He cared. "And I'd do it again. Now come here and fuck me while his corpse watches."

I gasped at the sudden shift in the room. His attention was fully on me. I clutched my robe and fisted the silk fabric. "What?" I asked.

Malice straightened his spine, stepped over Hale's lifeless body, and stalked closer to me. "Take off your robe."

"No."

"Let me see what's mine," he insisted.

"I was just assaulted," I snapped back. I wasn't sure I wanted to be touched. "And I'm not yours," I quickly added. This was wrong, so, so wrong. My skin felt flushed. The power rolling off of him hit me in waves.

"You live in my house," he insisted.

"I'll leave." Closer. He grew closer.

"I sign your checks."

"I'll quit."

He wrapped his hand around my neck. "I ruined your soul," he whispered.

"Maybe it was ruined to begin with."

Malice slammed his lips against mine with white hot passion. I felt my body tense up at the hard presence of his body pressing against my torso. He threaded his hands through my hair and pulled at the roots until I moaned. He then ripped at my robe and exposed my skin. It didn't feel intrusive like when Hale touched me. It was pure, raw pleasure thumping through my system. He was like a hit of heroin.

I kissed him deeply, but I saw Hale's body twitch, like the dead nerve endings in his body were cracking and popping with little last moments of defiance. It made my lips still and my awareness grow heavy.

"Fuck," Malice cursed when he realized I was staring at Hale. He might be fine putting a show on for a corpse, but I wasn't. "Come for me and I'll get you out of here," he said, his tone a harsh demand. Malice then touched me where Hale had his nasty fingers just minutes ago. I was now soaking wet, my slick desire coating my thighs. I didn't bother asking myself what the fuck was wrong with me. Malice had already twisted my perception of right and wrong.

I curled my arm around his neck as he worked my pussy. I kept my eyes on Hale. His lifeless body felt like winning. He got off to me murdering someone, now I was about to get off to his humiliating death as well.

"I knew you needed this," Malice cooed. "That's right, Little Fighter. Show that fucking bastard how good it feels to come on your own terms."

Faster, faster, faster. Malice worked my greedy clit. I arched and moaned. I cried out. I sunk my teeth into Malice's neck as he rubbed my swollen nub. I was so fucking sensitive. Every jolt sent a shockwave through my body. I could barely stand, the pleasure was so strong, and when

I came, I didn't bother holding back my scream. I let my voice ring through the halls, the same way Hale threatened me. He said the entire mansion would hear my screams after all. Fuck him.

Wave after wave of pleasure rocked through me. The adrenaline from the kill intensified every sensation. My muscles contracted, then all relaxed at once. I panted and would have collapsed if it weren't for Malice's strong arms holding me upright. "So good, my Little Fighter. I'll get you out of here."

Malice lifted me up, and I wrapped my legs around his waist before nuzzling my face into the crook of his neck. Now that the high of my orgasm had worn off, I felt overwhelmed by what had happened. Hale was dead, and I metaphorically danced on his grave.

Zero regrets.

Malice walked me out of the bedroom and paused at an intercom outside of my room. He pressed the button. "Why was no one watching guard in the house?" his voice boomed.

It took a lingering moment for someone to respond, and every tick of the clock, I could feel Malice's body tensing against mine. "A group of men were spotted at the south entrance. We've been sweeping it for the last forty-five minutes and found a shady looking suitcase with wires. Waiting for our bomb expert to show up, boss. I set off the alarm for a full mansion evacuation an hour ago."

Malice cursed. I held him tighter, and the move made him reach up to pat my back as if to comfort me. It was unexpected, but I welcomed it. I would have plenty of time to obsess over all that had happened today. "I'm in the house right now, and there's no alarm going off. I want to know who was scheduled to be in charge of Juliet Cross today, and I want him buried with Hale."

A pause greeted Malice's demand. "Hale, sir?" he asked.

"Hale is now dead in Miss Cross's bedroom. I need a cleanup crew here now, and I want a full report on my desk in six hours about Hale's known alliances, contacts. I want every fucking password in this house changed. I want a sweep of his laptop, cell phone, and car. Every fucking security video footage you can find on the fucker delivered to me with the report, or I'm going to start lodging bullets in skulls."

I chewed on my lip as a round of Yes, bosses rang out on the intercom. "What level of threat is the bomb?"

"What do you mean, sir?"

"Do you think I'm safe to fuck my girl in my own home, or should we leave?"

I wanted to claw his eyes out. Malice grinned. "It's fairly small, sir. About thirty yards from the home. It looks to be more of a diversion than anything. However, I suggest you leave for your safety—"

Malice ended the communication, let out a huff, and started walking me down the hall toward a room at the end.

I chewed on my lip again as he set me down on a plush bed. Fuck. I probably shouldn't be telling the terrifying, angry mob boss I told you so. "I had a plan. I had it all fucking under control!" he screamed before pulling his phone out of his pocket and dialing. I found a spare blanket and wrapped it around my body, but Malice marched up to me and yanked it away from me. Fucking dick.

"Cancel the diversion. Hale is dead," Malice said whenever the other person on the line picked up. I looked around the room. Dark furniture. Black walls. Black bedding. Black and white abstract paintings filled the wall. Dark curtains covered the floor-to-ceiling windows too. It was a moody bedroom that fit Malice's personality perfectly. I had no idea he slept so close to where I was staying.

"As in fucking dead, William," Malice continued. "I shoved a hot curling iron up his ass. He's currently lying on Juliet's bedroom floor, cooking like a spit roast."

The image made me press my hand to my mouth. Vomit traveled up my throat, but I swallowed it. I refused to be distressed by what we'd done. It was either him or me, and once again I chose me.

"Must have figured out that we let him go on purpose.

Guards found a bomb on the south lawn, and the fucker disabled the alarm. He thought he'd get one last fuck before fleeing. And of course he picked a time when he thought I'd be gone for the day. I just so happened to come back to grab my wallet when I heard Juliet scream."

Thank fuck Malice had come back. He looked me up and down. "Yeah...," he said to William. "She's fine." William must have been yelling on the other line, because Malice pulled the phone away from his ear for a moment. Not once did he take his eyes off me. "William?" He paused. "William!" More pausing. I felt my chest begin to rise and fall. The tension was thick between us. We obviously had unfinished business. "Goddamn it, William. Goodbye. I've got something very important I need to do."

He hung up his cell and tossed it on the floor. "Open your legs, Little Fighter."

I didn't obey him. "Don't you have work to do? A possible bomb to deal with and a dead body in your guest room?" I taunted him. For some reason, I felt this inexplicable urge to deny this man of the control he so desperately craved. I wanted to be in charge.

"Spread your fucking thighs," he demanded.

I slammed them together even harder. "What are you trying to prove?" I asked.

He licked his lips, as if he was savoring the taste of my mouth on his. I might have had a moment of weakness back in the guest room, but I wasn't about to give in again. I'd gotten my orgasm, I didn't need Malice's twisted back and forth.

Malice walked over to me and dropped to his knees. He lightly kissed both my knees. Softly. Tenderly. Briefly. Then, with his tattooed hands, he ripped my thighs apart and bent over to breathe me in. I wanted to resist him and hide. It was so bold of him to expose me like this.

But Malice's eyes rolled back in his head. He moaned and rubbed his face along pussy. He delighted himself with my scent, my heat, my lust. "I have nothing to prove, Little Fighter. Right now I want you. Tomorrow, I might kill you. Yesterday, I hated you. Monsters operate on their base needs."

He licked a slow line up my slit, and I nearly jumped off the bed. "So this is just about getting off?" I asked, my voice shaky.

"It's about how good you taste." He paused before licking me again. I squirmed on the mattress. "It's about making you scream." He dug his fingers into my flesh, likely leaving behind little bruises in the shape of his fingertips.

I threaded my hands in his hair and forced him to look up at me. "You just want to feel like the hero for a bit longer," I whispered. I knew his past. I knew he was driven by building and protecting his empire, just as I was driven by protecting myself and finding answers.

Malice growled, and I knew I had hit him where it hurt. He wrapped his hand around my wrist and removed my hand from his head. Then, he got up and shoved me on my back on the bed so that he wouldn't have to look me in the eye. Something told me that Malice struggled with the reality in my gaze.

"Shut up and feel me, Little Fighter," he whispered before kissing my stomach, my chest, my jaw.

I moved to lift his chin up, once more challenging him to look me in the eye. "Thank you for saving me, Malice," I replied.

My words spurred him on. Malice frantically took off his belt, his shirt, his pants. He kept his emerald eyes on me as he worked his clothes from his body.

And oh, what a beautiful body he had. The intricate ink covered every inch of his skin. Beautiful, striking art designed by a genuine artist. The lines were impeccable. They healed perfectly and flowed seamlessly with every line of his body. On his chest was an angry owl with a snarling expression and beautiful wings stretched wide over his pecs. I wondered if the symbolism spoke to Malice's quiet wisdom.

On his neck was a black and white lotus with cursive script wrapped around it. I read it and bit my lip.

Civella.

He was literally branded with his family name.

When he slipped down his black briefs, I gasped at the shiny metal piercing his hard, long cock. I debated on asking if the barbells lining his shaft had hurt, but I got the impression nothing hurt him. Malice was invincible. Brutal. Hardened by the deadly organization he was raised to lead.

He crawled over me, his muscles tense and defined. I reached out and ran my hand over a bold year tattooed across his abs. 2018. "What's this mean?" I asked. I wanted to understand him. Malice let out a little gasp as I sensually traced the bold numbers.

"It's the year I watched both my parents get murdered," he admitted before gently pushing my hand away. I wasn't expecting that answer, and my heart broke for him. What kind of life did he live? "It reminds me to never be complacent. Trust no one. Let no one in."

I understood it. I myself had built a wall around myself so high that even my best friend was barely looking over the edge. This man had lived a life of bloodshed. He'd watched the people closest to him suffer and die.

"Fuck me, Malice," I whispered. This was reckless, wrong, and so fucked up. This man had forced me to kill a man. He wouldn't protect my heart. He wouldn't care for me. He was dangerous and unpredictable.

But I wanted to feel him just once. I wanted to be reckless. Malice was right, this was about base needs and nothing more. I wanted to understand the most raw, physical parts of him. If I was going to hell, then I'd ride the devil's lap on the way down.

Malice pinned my hands over my head and settled between my shaking thighs. I jerked up at the harsh invasion of his cock. He pressed against my entrance, teasing and taunting me. "I can't control myself when I'm with you," he rasped. I didn't want his control. I wanted his cock. I wanted his wild.

He thrust inside of me with one quick movement that had me moaning loudly and arching off the bed. So fucking thick. The piercings on his dick made me feel full, and each one hit a sensitive spot within me. He stretched along my body, continuing to hold me down with his hands, and I loved the look of his bulging muscles as he slid in and out of my slick cunt.

"You're so fucking tight," he said before grunting a curse. "Like your pussy was made for my cock." He bent down to wrap his mouth around my nipple, pausing his thrusts to scrape his sharp teeth along my sensitive flesh. I writhed and moaned while wrapping my legs around his waist.

He then moved to my cleavage and sunk his teeth into my skin, drawing blood. I cried out from the sharp pain just as he started fucking me harder. Drops of my blood spilled down his mouth, and I looked at the imprint his teeth made on my breast. Violent, angry cuts in the shape of his cruel smile stared back at me.

I pushed at his chest, angry that he'd bitten me so hard, but also slightly turned on by the brutality of it all. "Come on, Little Fighter. Fight the big, bad monster," he taunted before grabbing my waist and punishing me with his cock. Every hard pulse of his body was damning. I ran my nails down his back. I wanted to mark his skin like he'd marked mine. I wanted to ruin his beautiful tattoos and dig so deep I found some permanence in his soul.

I bucked and squeezed my legs tighter around him. I bit his shoulder, sucked on his neck, licked his bottom lip and tugged at the cool nipple ring in his inked skin.

Fuck, fuck, fuck. Harder. Faster. Deep, deep, deep, and deeper. It was rough passion shared between two people who were both strangers and intimately acquainted. We'd witnessed each other's deepest sins. We'd sworn allegiance with our bodies, our trust, and our dirtiest intentions.

We continued to fuck and fuck and fuck. We didn't change positions. As it turned out, Malice liked looking me in the eye. Maybe because he saw bits of himself in my gaze.

And when I came, it was the sweetest release. We didn't both cry out, it was one of those silent little deaths. A wave of completion that left us both spent and heaving. He collapsed on top of me and licked a bead of sweat off my neck.

"Wow," I whispered. I hadn't expected it to be so intense—so much.

Malice was silent. He was quiet when he pulled out of me. He didn't say a fucking word when he went to clean himself up. Not even a whisper escaped his lips when I asked if he was okay.

The finality of it all made me feel empty. I just lay there with his cum seeping out of me. No cuddles or sweet words. No tender kisses. No...nothing.

I was lying there when the door was pushed open and Anthony came jogging inside. He sighed in relief at the sight of me, then quickly realized I was naked. Thoughtfully, Anthony assessed the situation in moments. I wasn't sure how much he knew about what had happened or if this would trigger him. Malice was still in his connected bathroom doing God knew what.

"Are you okay? Did he hurt you?" Anthony asked gently while easing closer to me. My eyes filled with tears. I wasn't sure why I was crying. Shame for what I'd done with Malice. Fear over what happened with Hale. Terror over the brutal murder I'd witnessed.

Anthony gently took off his shoes and grabbed a blanket. He stared at me for a brief moment and let out a shudder before covering me with the soft fabric. "I'm here."

I didn't think twice when he crawled onto the bed

beside me—the bed that smelled like sex. The bed I'd just fucked his brother on.

He wrapped his arms around me, and I let out a sigh of relief. This was the comfort I needed. Even if it was wrong and selfish. He gently kissed the top of my head and held me close. He didn't let go when Malice walked out of the bathroom, stark naked and covered in scratches and my blood. He walked proudly toward the bed, wearing the brutality of our fuck like a medal of honor. If he was shocked that Anthony was touching me, he didn't show it. It wasn't until Anthony glared at him, then turned my head to place a wet, hot kiss on my mouth that Malice's mask faded into nothing. Shock covered his expression. I kissed Anthony with my eyes on Malice, worried about what this meant—confused by everything that had happened.

"I'll protect you," Anthony whispered. "I'll always keep you safe," he promised before glaring at his brother.

Malice grabbed his clothes and left us alone in his bedroom without a single word.

chapter twenty two

Anxiety was almost like having a rogue fly show up in your bedroom. Maybe a deadly wasp was more accurate. Or an elephant sitting on your chest. But tonight? Tonight, I had a fly buzzing around my head. Landing on my skin. Crawling across my cheeks. I tried desperately to lie on Malice's bed, eyes squeezed shut, but I could still hear that constant whirring in my ears. Round and round and round. If I opened my mouth, would it land on my tongue? If I opened my eyes, would it drink from my tears? If I swallowed a fly, would it build a home for itself in my stomach? No one would see the fly, but I would feel it. No butterflies for the fly lady.

Anthony and I lay in Malice's bed, and I couldn't help but think of flies in my stomach, eating on the death buried within me. They liked that shit, didn't they? They flocked to it. I'd probably have flies following me around for the rest of my goddamn life. They'd leave a trail of destruction in their wake.

The Civella home had flies in the walls.

On the furniture.

They kept the little bugs loaded in their guns.

Anthony moaned.

He had one hand resting on my body, but he snapped it back, like my touch burned him. People were vulnerable when they slept. He was talking to someone in his dreams. Telling them to fuck off. Anthony was fighting flies of his own.

I wanted to reach out and wipe the sweaty hair from his forehead, but I had a fly in my brain that I just couldn't get rid of.

I got up and cleaned myself up. Dried cum coated my skin. My hair was tangled. The air smelled like burning flesh. Bzzz.

That fucking fly had to die.

I found neatly folded clothes in the bathroom in my size. I found the fabric to be soft to the touch. It felt very luxurious. William was here. Did he know what I'd done?

MALICE

Was he as disgusted by me as I was by myself?

While he was sleeping, Anthony let out a cry. I needed to kill all my flies for him. I couldn't hold him and comfort him until I did.

The guard outside our room asked where I was going. I told him I needed to kill a fly.

He spoke into his radio and followed after me, curious.

Bzz.

Bzz.

Bzz.

Bzz.

He was nothing more than a faceless, nameless man. Mercifully, he didn't stop me. The king on his radio said to let me be. Freedom to kill the fly, how lucky was I? I laughed while grabbing my purse and keys.

They followed me down the street. A convoy of men. Witnesses to my hunt.

My fingers twitched as I drove after the fly. I knew where it was going, it followed death, didn't it?

Shock was almost like being given a reason to escape.

—

Ringing. Ringing. A man stood behind me, arms crossed over his chest. "Answer the phone, Vicky," I cursed. I had important things to do.

"Hello?"

"Oh good, you're here," I sighed in relief while pacing

the hard concrete. I was barefoot. Until I wasn't barefoot anymore. A man in a suit handed me flip-flops. "Mom left her job at 2:36 a.m.," I said into the phone. Vicky went deathly silent. She always did when I talked about this. "The cameras saw her leaving with a backpack. She never had a backpack. But that day she did."

"Oh, Juliet," Vicky said tenderly. "Are you on Gwendola Lane? Are you alone?"

I wasn't alone. I was never alone. I had the fly in my stomach and the wall of Malice's men at my back.

"She would have taken this route home. It's the direct way to Grams's house. But what if she was going to stop somewhere? What if she had laundry in that backpack, Vicky? There is a twenty-four-hour laundromat on Hannah Street. She could have walked there—"

"We already checked the security footage for Hannah Street, and no one at the laundromat saw her, Juliet," Vicky replied quietly. I knew this. I really did. No rock unturned. It was a theory, a lead, a dead end. A nothing. Flies everywhere.

"Okay. So what if she was abducted—"

Vicky cut me off. "Juliet. Can you sit down? Let's do our breathing exercises. The ones we practiced last time," she whispered.

Her tone angered me. Didn't she get it? "I don't want to breathe. I want to find my fucking mother."

She sighed into the receiver. "Okay. Give me just a second. I'm going to text someone."

I counted my steps between stores. I looked at the sun rising in the east. I found a piece of old gum on the concrete. Evidence. Get all the evidence.

"Okay, Juliet? Are you still there?"

"What if she took a cab home? What if she didn't feel—"

"She didn't take a cab, sweetie."

Right, right. "Do you hear that?"

"Hear what?"

"That fly. It won't stop buzzing." This would be so much easier if Vicky were here. "When are you coming home?"

Vicky's response was immediate. "Soon, sweetie. Did something happen today?"

Tears for the flies started rolling down my cheeks. Salty. Hot. "Hale is dead," I whispered. "He hurt me, Juliet."

Vicky gasped. The men watching me stood taller. Someone was coming.

"Oh my God, Juliet. Are you okay? That's it, I don't care what Nick says, I'm coming home."

More tears started to flow down my cheeks. I wanted my best friend. I wanted to find out what happened to my mother. I wanted to watch Hale die again and again and again. I wanted Malice to hold me after we fucked. I wanted to take away Anthony's nightmares. I wanted to get lost with my secret stranger.

I wanted to kill the fucking fly.

The streets were made of flapping wings. Eyes followed me everywhere I went. They covered every surface. They crawled over my skin. They were digging in my ears, my eyes, my nose, my mouth.

"I miss you, Vicky. I'm not okay."

She let out a slow breath over the receiver. Time passed. I sobbed into the phone. The wall of guards shifted on their feet. "Maybe your mom wasn't walking home. She said she had a crush on that single dad that frequented the store. Maybe she finally made her move," Vicky offered, distracting me. It was a theory we discussed often.

"Jeffrey Dahmer disguised as a single dad working the night shift," I said, disgusted.

"It's possible," Vicky offered, placating me. "Hey, Juliet? Is anyone there?"

I looked up just as Malice, Anthony, and William exited a car. "They're all here."

Vicky whispered in my ear. "Great. Why don't you go home and get some rest? I'll stay on the line if you want? We can talk about theories again. I got a notepad to take notes."

William held his hand out to me, and I stared at it like his body was a weapon. Anthony started pacing the concrete, staring at trash on the ground, smudges on the windows, and shops lining the street. Malice wore a shirt splattered with blood.

"Let's go home, Miss Cross," William said.

The reality of this moment felt very heavy all of a sudden. "But...but I have to kill the fly..." My words weren't real. There was no fly.

"Where is the fly, Killer?" Anthony asked while taking off his shoe. More tears streamed down my cheeks. It was this never-ending grief. No closure. No answers. This was a pain that would never let up.

I nodded at the shop that was too cheap to invest in video cameras. "There," I whispered. Anthony nodded, moved to the window, and swatted it with his shoe. The loud smack was satisfying.

"Where else, Killer?"

I swallowed. I both hated and loved that nickname. Pointing at the ground, I said, "There."

Anthony stomped. He looked ridiculous, swatting at my imaginary demons.

Malice finally spoke up, his words dark and cruel. "Where else, Little Fighter?" I looked at him for a moment, memories of what we'd done together still haunting me. Did he deserve to know about my flies? "Tell me," he insisted once more. I then pointed at the stoplight. Malice got out his gun, aimed it at the street light, and fired a bullet. Glass shattered, and the boom got rid of one more fly buzzing in my brain.

"Show me where all the flies are, Miss Cross," William begged.

My face twisted into agony, and I looked down at my chest. "Here," I whispered while pointing at my heart. "It's here."

I hung up on Vicky and walked to the car. The shock was wearing off, and all that was left was overwhelming sadness. The Civella brothers followed me. Anthony started talking about electric fly swatters. Malice insisted I sit in his lap. William drove.

Shaking.

Sobbing.

Laughing.

Dying a little, too.

The buzzing stopped.

My heroes had killed the fly.

And we never spoke of it again.

chapter twenty three

After a couple self-care days, I demanded normalcy. The shock I'd experienced was intense but not necessarily unfamiliar. Vicky called twice a day to make sure I wasn't pacing the streets again. Malice wouldn't talk to me. William practically lived at work. Anthony was building a sophisticated fly trap in his dungeon of doom.

I was embarrassed.

I knew what shock was. I knew that I had a temporary moment of insanity. I knew it was reasonable. I knew. I knew. I knew.

I needed out of the Civella home. I couldn't sleep in the guest room because, despite the team scrubbing every inch of evidence from the room, it still reminded me of Hale. I was tempted to knock on Malice's door and sleep in his bed, but every time I worked up the courage to do so, I convinced myself that it was for the best that I didn't. Malice didn't have to say a single word in order to let me know how he felt about what we'd done. He'd shown up to fight my demons on Gwendola Lane because I was a security risk, not because he cared. I wasn't the girl who tamed the beast. I was a body to pass the time with.

This morning, I left to stay at Grams's house. I craved something familiar, and I needed to check on things, anyway. I had a pile of mail waiting for me, and my cheap but warm mattress. After tossing and turning for hours, I got up to get ready for my shift at Eden's Place. Maybe keeping my distance was better. Staying at Grams's house made it easier for me to go back to my life.

"You okay, hon?" Kelsey asked as I updated some client profiles.

"Yeah, why?"

"You keep huffing and seem distracted today." She paused to lower her voice. "Is it the shooting that happened? You'll get used to it. Next time, close your eyes though, okay? See nothing, say nothing, babe."

Mr. Graves's death seemed so far away now. I'd almost

forgotten it. I nodded. It was probably easier to go along with her assumptions about why I was feeling the way I did. I wasn't sure I could trust her enough to say what was truly bothering me. Was it crazy to be offended by Malice's silence? I was about to say fuck it and spill the beans to her anyway, but a strong presence strolled through the front door, nearly knocking the air from my chest.

Malice walked past me like I was nothing more than a painting on the wall. He made me feel invisible. Perhaps he got what he wanted from me. I knew plenty of men who treated women like conquests or notches in their bedpost. Once he used up my body, I was useless to him.

And I hated how that made me feel. Of all the things to obsess over, this was the most ridiculous one on the list.

I'd had this strange notion that I could be the one to change him. Being desired by Malice was like a drug. Being protected by him was an indescribable high. It was like balancing on the sharp edge of a blade. Dangerous. Safe. He was all those things.

Part of me was sick with myself for feeling this way, part of me was thankful that he no longer invaded my personal space and demanded things from me I felt uncomfortable giving. It was wrong to want him. I knew that. There was nothing good that could come from a relationship with him—or with any of them for that matter. However, his dismissal hurt a lot more than I wanted to admit.

"Oh girl," Kelsey said with a low whistle. "You've got it bad."

I snapped my attention to her and tried to look inconspicuous. "I don't know what you mean," I replied, nose tipped in the air like I could fake my way through the truth with my pride intact.

"You got the hots for Boss man," she replied before nudging me. "Can't say I blame you. He's got this dangerous vibe and a body to match. Hot." She fanned herself for emphasis. "But, girl, that man is not to be fucked with."

I let out a huff. There was no use denying it. "I fucked him," I replied.

She squealed the kind of squeal women do when they get a juicy bit of gossip. She started jumping up and down and nudging me. "I just know his dick is big. Massive right?"

"Huge. And pierced."

She swooned. "Damn. Was he good? Did he spank you? He seems like he would be into that. Boss man doesn't have a club profile, but I've made a few observations. He likes to go to the blood kink room to unwind. Did he cut you up? Oh my God, that's so hot."

I held my hands up, wordlessly begging Kelsey to slow down. "He bit me," I admitted reluctantly. At the time, it didn't feel like a kink. It just felt like need overflowing. Like my pulse was too erratic for my body to contain it all. I wanted to explore it more, but… No—no future fucks for the devil and me. "He was rough and passionate and just kind of took control."

"I love a man that takes control, slams you into the mattress, and fucks you raw," Kelsey said in a dreamy voice.

"It was hot," I agreed. "Very hot. He knows what he's doing, but..."

"But he's now pretending you don't exist?" she asked. "Sounds very on-brand for the general population of penis-having assholes."

I tried to shrug and act like this was nothing. "I just need to get over it and move on. I've kissed both his brothers, so it's probably better if—"

"Wait. You kissed Anthony and William?" she shrieked. I pressed my index finger to my lip, encouraging her to slow down.

"What was it like? Oh my goodness. I can't believe—"

"Yes, Juliet. Tell me what it was like...," a deep voice interrupted. It had that raspy tone of someone who hadn't used his words in a while. I knew it was my silent stranger before turning around and meeting his cruel gaze.

"William," I greeted. Kelsey looked like she wanted to grab a bag of popcorn and watch our exchange.

"I need to speak with you. Now," he said before grabbing my arm and tugging me along the hallway to his office. Kelsey grinned like a schoolgirl as he dragged me away from the front desk.

"You don't have to manhandle me," I growled when we got in front of the door.

"Weren't you and Kelsey just talking about how you loved a man who takes control," he challenged while looking down at me. My heart raced.

"In the bedroom," I countered, my tone dripping with snark.

My silent stranger pressed his tongue against the inside of his cheek and shook his head. "Don't you know, Miss Cross? You can have plenty of fun outside of the bedroom." He then opened his office door and pressed on my lower back to guide me inside.

I crossed my arms over my chest. "What do you want, William?" I asked while looking around. His office was clean and luxurious. High-end details could be found in the brown furnishings and plush chair. His laptop was open on the desk, and he had a neat stack of papers in the corner. It was spacious and moody, with a black accent wall and photographs of the performers acting as a focal point in the background.

"I wanted to check on you. I noticed that you slept at your house last night."

"Oh, so now you care? I haven't seen you in three days. Not since..."

William licked his lips. "I needed time to think. I didn't

want to make things worse for you." He ran his hand through his hair nervously.

"Worse as in?" I asked.

"As in swatting imaginary flies on the street where your mother was abducted. We've helped you before, but it's never been that bad."

I felt embarrassed. I would probably never live down my moment of weakness.

I let out an annoyed breath. "Well, I've also never killed someone, been assaulted, and then watched that man die."

"Fair enough. You left last night. Why?"

"I wasn't really fond of sleeping in the same room as Hale's ghost. It still smells like burnt asshole in there," I complained, trying to make light of a truly disturbing memory. I couldn't wipe it from my mind.

"Joking to cope, how Anthony of you." My stranger looked me up and down. I didn't put much effort into my appearance today. He'd probably give me a write-up for being out of dress code. My shorts were denim, and my corset top and lace sleeves covered most of my skin. For some reason, all my other outfits made me feel vulnerable. Hale had seen me in them. I wanted to burn my entire wardrobe.

"You didn't have to come here today," he said softly. Those inquisitive eyes of his took every inch of me in. He didn't have to voice his thoughts for me to know what he was thinking. My silent stranger knew me at a cellular level. He knew I was hanging to my sanity by my pinky finger.

"Malice said I could go back," I replied. Unexpectedly, William slammed his fist onto his desk.

"And whatever Nicholas says goes, right?" he growled. "I run this fucking place, but he's the boss, right?" William had a naturally grumpy disposition, but seeing him like this was a different level of anger. "Did you like it?"

"Did I like what?"

William picked me up and put me on his desk. I stared up at him.

"Fucking the boss."

I scowled. "That's none of your goddamn business."

He tugged at my corset top, exposing the tops of my breasts. "Do you like being marked, Juliet? Come on, tell me. Pretend we're back at the diner and you're spilling your pathetic guts all over the table. Want to talk about how he fucked you? The dirty things he said? Or we can talk about your mother's disappearance. Want to cry to me again, Miss Cross?"

"That's enough," I snapped.

"Is it though? Now that I'm not a stranger, you suddenly don't want to tell me your secrets. Does it scare you that I'm human? That I can hear all the filthy shit you've got in your soul?"

"Fuck off," I growled at him. This wasn't the William that treated me to spa days and spilled poetry at my feet. This was an angry version of my silent stranger. A hurt man who was jealous. The man who had to compete for space in this family every day of his life. William was a man with something to prove, and right now I was his victim.

Feeling alive for the first time in days, I challenged him. "What pisses you off more, knowing that I fucked your brother or knowing that I enjoyed it?"

William grinned. "You can fuck whoever you want, Miss Cross. But with you, I don't share. I'll let them have the dirty, damaged pieces of your soul, but I get your heart."

I heaved, my breasts rising and falling with every breath. "You think I gave Malice my heart?" I scoffed.

"I think he stole it," William snapped back before leaning in to scrape his teeth along my neck. "Just like every other damn thing in my life."

William quickly pulled away and circled his desk. I watched with hooded eyes as he bent down under his chair and pulled out a large black velvet box. "I was saving this, you know. For a special moment." William walked back to me and opened the box, revealing the longest string of pearls I'd ever seen. "Three hundred thousand dollars' worth of pearls. Like a rope," he said, his voice raspy as he pulled them out of the box. I eyed the collection. It was beautiful. Stunning. I'd never even seen three hundred thousand dollars, let alone in jewelry.

"Take off your shorts and spread your legs, Miss Cross," he whispered.

I was so desperate to feel something, to connect with my secret stranger despite the pain shared between us, that I instantly obeyed. It was rushed and clumsy. I slid the denim down my legs and then stood with both legs spread as wide as I could make them. William stared at me for a moment before dropping to his knees and looping the pearls around my ankles, loosely tying me to the leg of his desk.

The pearls were cool to the touch and felt delicate wrapped around my trembling legs. The string was so long that he was able to carefully tie it around both legs, then stand up with more slack. "Hands in front of you," he demanded.

I obeyed.

He wrapped them around my wrist twice. I breathed heavily as he then looped the remaining slack between my legs, pulling so that there was tight tension in the string of pearls against my cunt. My thin lace panties provided zero barrier. I gasped, suddenly feeling sensitive.

"Miss Cross," he said while wrapping both arms around me, hugging me close while pulling the string. He worked the bead of pearls back and forth. Back and forth. Faster. "I want you thinking only of me." I tilted my head back and moaned. "I want your eyes on me. I want your hands on me. I want all of you. Everywhere. Always."

He kissed my neck and moved faster. I arched my back, closer, closer, closer. "Yes," I hissed.

"Tell me you belong to me." I went still, despite the building pleasure. My eyes widened, and against William's wishes, I thought of Malice's mouth on my breast and Anthony holding me. William rubbed me faster, the sweet tantric rhythm coaxing pleasure from my body with every ribbed roll of the pearls. He kissed my mouth. Licked my tongue. Bit my bottom lip with his sharp teeth. "Tell me you're mine."

I couldn't say it. I didn't know what the future would bring, but I knew that it was too late to belong to one man.

"Say it, Miss Cross."

I bit my lip. The silence was deafening. I was so close to coming all over his desk, all over these expensive pearls. I was nothing but a collection of blooming pleasure, harsh breaths, and guilt.

Building, building, building.

And then, nothing.

William tore himself away from me. I suddenly felt cold as ice. He reached down and grabbed the rope of pearls and ripped it from my body. The pearls scattered everywhere around his room. They bounced and fled from my body. Everywhere I looked, pearls covered his wood floors, sliding under his cabinets and desks.

William glared at me, anger burning through his brown eyes. "We won't finish this until you can tell me you're mine and only mine, Miss Cross."

I tipped my chin up and glared at him. I was embarrassed, ashamed, horny, and sexually frustrated. "Then we'll never finish, Stranger."

chapter twenty four

"Boss is looking for you," a bald man with arms crossed over his chest said. I stared at him through the crack in my front door. I hadn't been to work in three days and was back at Grams's house. I simply refused. William humiliated me. I had never been so turned on and so denied. It was cruel, and I had met my threshold for bullshit. My job was done. We'd already found out that Hale was the leak. The money was great but at what cost? I felt so fucking cheap and used up. I was just a toy to these men.

"Which boss?" I asked.

"The one that matters."

"They all matter," I replied flippantly. "Tell Malice I quit. Job's done."

The man looked like he wasn't amused by my defiance. "That's not an option."

I glared at him. "What's your name?"

"Garret."

"Garret. You tell Mr. Civella that he can choke on my massive dick. And if he wants me so bad, he can stop hiding like a little pussy and come talk to me himself."

I slammed the door in Garret's face and locked it. Fuck the Civella men. Fuck Eden's Place. Fuck all the nasty things I'd done. I couldn't do it anymore. I wanted a normal afternoon to do normal shit.

I sat down at my old laptop, a trusty steed that had survived years of updates and large podcast audio files. It was slow, but it was mine. I needed to start looking at online colleges in my budget and apply for federal aid. Boring, normal, tedious shit. I loved it.

Except, I didn't love it. I didn't dare look at the application for Texas A&M University, though I already had their admission requirements memorized. They had one of the best forensic science programs in the country. Some of their graduates left to work on elite teams in larger cities. It was a pipe dream, something I'd always wanted but knew wasn't a possibility for me. Grams might be doing well now, but she was on a depressing inevitable road. I refused to abandon her.

There was a community college locally that offered online basics in my budget. I could find a job with more consistent hours and—

A loud knock on my door made me stop in my tracks. Nope. I wasn't opening it. I didn't know many people who could be recognized by the way they knock on a door, but that booming insistent bam, bam, bam was all Malice.

I continued to type on my computer as he banged. I straightened my spine. He couldn't control me. I was done.

The living room window glass shattered, and I jumped out of my seat with a yelp. Sure enough, Garret was breaking through our window. He looked completely annoyed with me as he pushed shards out of the way and climbed into our living room. With my mouth agape, I stared in silent shock as he brushed glass off of his suit jacket and rolled his neck.

He looked at me and smiled. He fucking smiled! As if he knew something I didn't. "You're going to pay to fix that," I said, but naturally, he ignored me. Instead, Garret walked to the front door, unbolted the lock, and twisted the handle.

Malice walked inside with Anthony at his back. "This place is so cute. Kind of looks like it could be a set for a nineties crime documentary," Anthony exclaimed while clapping his hands together. "I mean, the nostalgia! Wow! Is that a photo of you in the third grade? Braces. Love it."

"Hey, Anthony," I said, purposefully ignoring Malice, who was glowering at me. Both men couldn't have looked more different. Malice was in his signature suit, Anthony wore jeans and a faded tee.

"You skipped work," Malice growled.

"I quit," I replied. "Didn't you get my letter of resignation? I left it on William's desk after he taunted my clit with almost over a quarter million dollars' worth of luxury pearls."

"I heard about that," Anthony piped in. "How was it?" My eyes widened. Anthony was seriously unbothered about my relationship with his brothers? It was the other two giving me a hardcore case of whiplash.

"It was great," I replied, my tone dull.

Malice clenched his jaw. "Why are you quitting? I shouldn't have to remind you what's at stake here."

"Right. You're going to kill me? Blackmail me? Fuck me into submission? I'm over the threats, and the way I see it, I have just as much on you as you have on me."

Anthony let out a low whistle. "Oh, baby, I wouldn't have done that…"

Malice took off his jacket, flashing me the weapon strapped to his side. "You're coming back to stay at our house. You can either sleep in my bed or in Anthony's death dungeon."

"Ooh, a sleepover! We just had a body delivered, so it'll be a party! I also saved Hale's dick if you want to stab it a couple times."

My brows raised. "No," I snapped.

Malice nodded, not like he was agreeing with me, but like he was trying to calm himself down. "What do you care? I haven't spoken to you since…" My voice trailed off.

"Since the two of you fucked?" Anthony finished for me, his expression softening. "Technically, you spoke at the fly-swatting situation, but you weren't really there, Killer."

"That's what this is about? You're pissed because I didn't hold you after fucking you? You want to feel special—loved—wanted? From the looks of it, you get plenty of attention from my siblings. One of them is bitching to me because he seems to think that he claimed you first. The other one is whining all day because you're not home. And Vicky? She's threatening to come home if I don't take care of you."

Anthony interjected. "You make whining sound like a curse word. Just because I'm in touch with my emotions and am capable of vocalizing my needs doesn't make me a damn whiner; I just politely asked you to fix this and bring Juliet home."

I sighed. "That's not my home, Anthony."

He scoffed. "You just don't know it yet, but I'm your

home. It's okay, I'll grow on you."

"This is a waste of my time," Malice said while pinching the bridge of his nose.

Without warning, Malice stomped over to me and threw me over his shoulder. I let out a loud yelp, and his strong hand gripped my ass. "You're coming home. Once you're in the gang, there's no getting out. I don't like having to worry about you while you're here, and it's a lot easier to keep an eye on you when you're under my roof."

I punched his back. "You just want to control me."

The sunshine beat on my back, and I let out a scream, not that anyone would help me. Malice had this uncanny ability to make people scatter and slam their eyes shut. "Anthony, go grab her laptop," Malice shouted.

"You mean that dinosaur on her kitchen table? Sure."

Malice set me down, and I glared at him. "Fuck you," I shouted. He lifted his hand up as if ready to backhand me, and I flinched. My sudden terror made him stop. We had a quick stare down for the briefest of moments before he spoke again. "Anthony wants you home," he finally whispered.

Malice suddenly seemed...helpless. He wasn't this big, bad mobster in that moment. He was a vulnerable brother determined to do anything to make up for their terrible past. "Is that why you won't talk to me anymore?" I asked.

"Anthony doesn't usually…"

"I know. But maybe you aren't giving him enough credit. He waltzed right into your room after we…"

"Fucked?" he offered.

"It didn't faze him."

"Anthony was staking his claim," Malice replied.

"No. William was staking his claim when he humiliated me at Eden's Place. You were staking your claim when Hale tried to assault me. Anthony was just…" I thought about what I wanted to say for a moment before continuing. "Anthony was just being there for me. He takes after Vicky in that regard."

Malice cleared his throat. "It's been a while since Anthony has been there for anyone living. I'm trying to navigate it while running our business and protecting my family. Somehow, you've been added to the list of people I now have to protect, and it makes me feel out of control when you pull bullshit stunts like this."

"It's not bullshit."

"It's totally bullshit," Anthony called at my back. He was not only carrying my dinosaur laptop, but he'd also pulled all the pictures off the wall of me from high school and was balancing them in his arms. "I want these. I'm taking them."

I shook my head. "I'm not comfortable there. All I can think about is the man I killed and Hale and all the fucking guards patrolling the grounds. I just need some normalcy, okay?"

"Normal is boring," Anthony sang.

"Killers don't get normal," Malice echoed.

"Fine. But when Grams is back, I'm moving back home. I'm serious. She can't live alone, Anthony. I love spending time with you—"

"So you admit you love me," he cut me off.

"That's not what I said."

He tsked. "So you love me. Continue."

"But Grams needs my help. This is temporary. We can be friends, and you're welcome here anytime you want. But you can't force me to go along with whatever you say. I'm not scared of you anymore," I lied.

Anthony huffed, Malice looked like he wanted to give me a reason to fear him. "Put her in the trunk," Anthony said in a bored tone.

"Wh-what?" Malice didn't even stumble. He clicked his keys, and the trunk to his town car popped open. "I'm not getting in that fucking trunk." I eyed it. "There's a tarp in it. Is this a body trunk? Hell no."

Malice picked me up and effortlessly tossed me into the trunk as if I were a sack of potatoes. I scurried, trying my best to get out of there. Anthony blocked my view. Bending over, he stared at me with his head cocked to the side. "Sometimes, a little fear is good for the soul."

And then, he slammed the trunk shut.

—

I felt claustrophobic. Every inhale was hot and labored. It was like they purposefully hit every bump possible. I bumped my head on the roof of the car and found myself growing angrier and angrier as we drove.

I also felt this overwhelming sense of betrayal. Anthony was supposed to be on my side. Despite his goals for putting me in the trunk, I didn't fear him like I should. I pitied him. Why did he feel like he had to go to such extremes? Why was he so scared to lose me?

After what felt like an hour of stop-and-go traffic, they finally parked the car. Beads of sweat dripped down my neck, and I craved a tall drink of ice water. I waited. And waited. And...waited.

"Let me the fuck out, Anthony!" I screeched. I was going to claw his eyes out when I got out of here. Someone slammed their palm on the trunk. "Fuck you!" I yelled once more.

Minutes passed. It could have been hours, but I wasn't sure. The space seemed to get smaller and smaller. My breathing turned quick and shallow. What if I ran out of air? What if I stopped breathing? What if they left me here to bake in the summer heat? Who would take care of Grams?

And then the trunk opened. "You disappoint me, Juliet," Anthony said.

"And you piss me right the fuck off," I growled before scrambling to get out of the trunk. I was incredibly sore and felt dizzy from the heat.

"Aw, don't hate me. I have a surprise for you," Anthony replied as Malice walked up to me, holding out a water bottle. I reached to grab it from his hands, but he moved it out of my reach, opting to unscrew the top and take slow steady gulps until the bottle was nearly empty. Then, only then, did he hand it to me.

"Dick," I growled before tossing it back with a hiss. Not enough. It wasn't nearly enough.

Once I was done with the water, I took a look around. We were in a residential neighborhood that had seen better days. The wooden homes with chipped paint had overgrown shrubs in their yards and kids toys lining the drives. "Where are we?"

"Guess," Anthony replied while bouncing on the balls of his feet. Malice looked at his watch.

I stared at the house we were parked in front of. It did look familiar. "Wait...," I whispered while walking up the drive. "Is this the Kansas City Butcher's house?" I squealed, as if Anthony had dropped me off at a Harry Styles concert and not the house of a mass murderer.

"The one and only," Anthony replied.

Malice eyed me like I was crazy.

"Can we go inside?"

"Yes. I figured we could take some photos, too, for your podcast landing page," Anthony replied before pulling out a high quality camera.

"This is fucking epic!" I yelled. I almost waltzed up to Anthony and Malice to wrap them up in a hug, but then I remembered that they tossed me in a trunk and drove me here, and decided I was still very, very angry with these assholes.

"Shall we, m'lady?" Anthony asked while holding out his hand.

I squinted at him. "Let's do this thing," I mumbled before waltzing alone inside. Malice chuckled under his breath.

The home had been sitting vacant for many years, because it was covered in dust. Anthony hummed while opening the windows so we could see while I walked around. "I'll get the camera set up!" he yelled while fumbling with the settings. Malice followed after me.

"So this interests you?" he asked tentatively.

I answered his question with one of my own. "You want to actually get to know me?"

He tried not to smile. "Keep your enemies close and all that." Malice then cleared his throat. "Anthony told me about your mother and the significance of Gwendola Lane. You never got any lead at all?"

I looked down at the linoleum floor and shook my head. "Never."

"You sure she wasn't a deadbeat?" Malice asked. It was

such a typical bullshit question. The police had asked it. The news had accused her of it when we went to them to get her missing persons case some exposure.

"She loved me," I whispered.

"Love is a weakness," Malice whispered while running a finger along some faded yellow wallpaper that was peeling.

"I disagree. You act like you're speaking from experience," I replied.

"More as a spectator. I watched my parents' love for one another get themselves killed. My mother was his greatest weakness, and my father had plenty of enemies. It was almost too easy how quickly they took her down. My father was shot while sobbing over her body. He didn't know how to protect his own, was too blinded by care to do what needed to be done."

I looked in the kitchen at Anthony, who was taking photos of the countertops and floors.

"You care about your siblings," I noted. "Are they your weakness?"

Malice gritted his teeth and stared at me, pure venom in his expression. "I have no weakness. I take care of my own—"

"Except when you don't," I interrupted. It was a low blow, but Malice needed a harsh reality check. "You aren't invincible."

"I saved him though. I can save all of them. I can protect

all of them."

I slowly reached out and brushed my knuckle over the back of his hand. "You're proving my point, then," I whispered. "Love isn't your weakness. It's made you stronger. More cunning. Adaptable. Brutal. Determined."

"Oh my God! Is this a blood splatter?!" Anthony exclaimed, breaking the severity of the moment. I smiled. "Nope, spaghetti," he later added in a dejected tone.

"Go enjoy your creepy murder exploration with Anthony," Malice finally said after a long moment. "I'm going to wait in the car."

I watched his back as he exited the room. Anthony snapped a photo of me. "Beautiful," he whispered while staring at the digital screen.

CORALEE JUNE

chapter twenty five

I slept in Malice's room last night. I felt awkward and out of place, but he had work to do, so I was alone. It was better than sleeping in Anthony's death dungeon. I had considered it, but when I went to scope it out there, I wasn't sure what horrified me more: the three bodies sitting in refrigerators or the fact that Anthony's mattress was about two inches thick. No judgment, but I absolutely refused to sleep in the same room where I killed a man, on a bed that looked like it was made for prisoners.

Plus, the whole reason I left was to feel normal again;

sleeping in the death dungeon where it all began wasn't going to do me any favors. At least he had a fitted sheet and wasn't sleeping on a bare, stained mattress. When I left, Anthony made a comment about having one of the rooms upstairs remodeled so that we could, and I quote, "cuddle."

Despite feeling exhausted, I woke up and got dressed for the day. I had the entire weekend off from Eden's Place. Malice made clear that I would eventually need to go back to work, but he understood my need for a break. He even smiled a bit when he suggested taking the weekend off, as if it thrilled him to piss off his brother. I hadn't seen William since the pearls incident. I couldn't determine if I wanted to see him or if the space between us gave me mental clarity. Loving William back would be the easy answer. He cared about me. He knew me. But I didn't want to face the demands I didn't have an answer for.

After getting dressed in high-waisted shorts and an oversized T-shirt, I French braided my brown hair and put some mascara and concealer on. My cheeks were rosy because of the constant stream of thoughts flowing through my mind. Malice had been vulnerable with me yesterday. Anthony was both intrusive and romantic. Having them both together and their undivided attention on me was equally thrilling and terrifying. I wasn't expecting to have as much fun as I did at the Kansas City Butcher's house. We spent a good hour taking pictures and jotting down notes for my podcast. Anthony even wanted to be a guest host. And all the while, Malice watched us with his inquisitive eyes. He didn't wait in the car like he said he would. He openly observed us, like he could figure me out. There was something about his gaze that made me feel warm. I felt like he could break me apart with one glance.

I slowly made my way down to the kitchen for some lunch. The guards were buzzing with activity, walking around and speaking into their radios with giddy expressions. Once in the kitchen, I found some cold cuts and bread for a sandwich and sat down to eat.

A guard, who I didn't know, joined me in the kitchen and pressed his back to the wall, silently watching me. I was always watched. "Is something going on?" I asked him, not really expecting an answer.

"Boss will be here to see you soon," he replied in a bored tone. I spun around to look at him. Ah, Garret. The asshole that smashed my Grams's window.

"You owe me a window," I said, my mouth full of my sandwich. Garret was a good little soldier, but he didn't give me the creeps like Hale did, so I didn't mind having him for a shadow.

"It's already been fixed," he replied.

I took a bite of my sandwich and slowly chewed, surprised with his answer. I was eager to see which boss wanted to see me and why, and when Malice marched into the kitchen, my skin buzzed with awareness. He had an excited grin on his face. It was a look I hadn't seen on him.

"Hurry up and eat, we have somewhere to go," he said before grabbing a water bottle from the fridge, unscrewing the top, and taking a few gulps. I watched his Adam's apple bob up and down as he drank the crisp, cool water.

"Where are we going?" I asked.

Malice didn't answer me, he simply stared at me over his water bottle before setting it down. "Hurry. We don't have time." Again with the hurry?

"Time for what?"

Malice circled the kitchen island in his suit, those designer dress shoes of his clicking against the tile as he marched closer to me. "Remember what I said when you first started working for me?"

I swallowed. I remembered with vivid clarity what he'd said. It still haunted me.

"One day, I could call and say I need you to burn down a building. The next, I could need you in an evening gown and on my arm at an event. I could need you to keep Vicky obedient. I could need you to hurt my brother. Sometimes, you'll know why you're somewhere. Sometimes you won't. You'll be my little pet, showing up whenever and however I need you to."

"Yes," I choked out, dread filling me almost instantly.

"Boss," the guard interrupted. "Want me to get the team

ready?" he asked.

"No. I'm doing this alone."

Garret seemed shocked by this. It was the first time I'd actually seen much of a reaction from the stone-cold soldier. "Alone?"

"Alone," Malice echoed.

If Malice was so determined to do this alone, then why did I have to come along? "Boss, the intel we got said there would be at the very least six men there," the guard added. He stumbled over his words, as if he was scared to speak. Six men? Where the fuck were we going?

"Then tell Anthony that I'm bringing back six fucking bodies," Malice snapped before grabbing my arm and gently lifting me up from my seat on the bar stool.

"Are we going on a killing spree? A treasure hunt? Maybe dinner and a movie?" I asked, stalling.

He paused at the front door and swept his eyes all over me. "All three," he replied with a wink.

Was Malice...flirting with me?

We walked to the car in silence. I probably should have felt scared. That would have been the normal response, but my pulse slowed by the time we got to his car—a blacked out and unrecognizable Mercedes Benz with temporary plates that looked more permanent than anything else. I sat in the passenger seat and watched as one of his men brought him a large gun. I couldn't tell you what it was, but the black metal and large barrel looked intimidating and powerful. He took off his suit jacket and tossed it to another man, revealing two smaller guns and a long knife strapped to his body. His belt was nothing but ammunition.

Wherever we were going, Malice looked prepared for war.

He sat down in the front seat and turned on the car, the engine a calm purr compared to the roaring energy rolling off of my companion for the day. "Should I have brought a bulletproof vest?" I asked, prodding for information.

Malice pulled out of the long, winding drive. "I have one for you in the trunk," he answered, his tone direct.

"Do I need a gun?" I asked.

"Would you know how to use one?"

"Nope."

"Then nope."

Malice sped down the Kansas City streets, with one hand on the steering wheel and the other placed precariously on my thigh. His strong fingers wrapped around my body and inched up, up, up.

"Where are we going?" I squeaked. "If we're going to kill people, don't you think I should be prepared?"

Malice squeezed my leg and turned onto the highway. "We're going to take back something that was stolen from me almost three years ago."

"From who?"

"Cora Albertine," Malice replied.

"Cora? As in the Cora trying to kill you? The Cora that had Hale leave a bomb in your yard?"

Malice revved his engine and started passing vehicles, zipping in and out of traffic with ease. "The very one."

"What did she steal? Why are we getting it back now? Why are you bringing me? I don't like this—"

"Stop worrying. Cora is currently in a meeting with one of my suppliers, trying to steal my territory out from under me. She won't get it, but she doesn't know that. The dumb bitch brought an army with her because she thinks it's a trap, but she's too greedy to pass up the opportunity." He paused to drive on the shoulder to get around a slow moving Cadillac. "I have a man on the inside who informed me where I could find my property and the safe code to get it out. We're going to walk into her home and take it back."

I swallowed. "You make it sound easy," I croaked.

"It will be. I'm going to show her what it feels like to have someone in her space, and I won't even have to use the full extent of my resources to get it, either. She's going to look back and see that I'm a one-man army, and she shouldn't fuck with me."

I stared out the window, feeling an unnatural thrill coursing through me. For some reason, there was something exhilarating about knowing what we were about to do. Maybe Malice had fucked me up in the head. "And what will I do?" I asked.

He eyed me. "Stay at my side."

My eyebrows rose.

Fuck.

—

Cora's compound wasn't as luxurious as Malice's mansion. It had a metal gate wrapped around the warehouse and was built outside of town. It looked like a run-down military base, and I couldn't help but compare her setup to the sophistication of the Kansas City mob. Seeing it up close made me think that she was nothing more than a roach in the Civella kitchen.

"This is where Cora lives?" I asked as we pulled up. Malice didn't even bother parking away from the building. It was like he wanted them to know that he was there. He put on a ski mask with a skull sketch on the face and handed me a matching one.

"Yes. Stay close to me."

We got out of the car and both put on a bulletproof vest. As I zipped it up, my fingers trembled from the adrenaline. What the hell was I doing? My sense of self-preservation was losing to my curiosity.

"Ready?" he asked, almost bored.

"Don't get me killed, Malice."

He paused to stare at me, his green eyes peeking through the black mask. His muffled response was gruff but stern. "Nothing will ever happen to you. Ever." I didn't understand how he could shift from being so overprotective to willingly putting me in harm's way, but maybe he had something to prove.

I nodded, mostly because I was too choked up to respond.

At the front gate, a man with a gun slung over his chest slid open the rusted metal door and greeted Malice. "Boss," he said. I made the connection that this was the man Malice had on the inside. "There's now eight men on campus. The necklace is in the safe in Cora's office. Code is here," he said while handing Malice a scrap of paper.

Malice looked down at it, then crumbled the paper in his fist. "You did good. Now get out. I'll meet you with your money at the safehouse."

The guy nodded and fast walked over to a parked motorcycle in the front courtyard. Eight men? And we were doing this for a necklace?

Malice lifted his chin, rolled his shoulders back, and strolled through the front door like he owned the place, with me practically plastered to his back. I wanted to be as close as possible to the crazy bastard should anything go down. The second we were past the front gate, my eyes scanned the yard. For as far as I could see, the space was clear, but I knew that was only temporary. It was like the calm before the storm.

Cora's compound looked even more run-down on the inside. It was a dirty dust wasteland with stained metal walls covered in rust and broken nails peeking out from each sheet. A few cars were parked inside the wall, and the large warehouse in front of us had a hole in the roof. "Wait," Malice said while holding his arm out. I paused and held my breath. Fuck fuck fuck. What the fuck was I doing? Why was I here?

Malice spun around and lifted his ski mask so that it revealed his soft lips. He lifted his steady hand and rolled up my mask to my nose. "We should commemorate the moment," he said with a smile.

"What moment?" I was high on adrenaline but also terrified. And maybe perhaps sort of kind of a little turned on.

"This is our first date, Little Fighter," he rasped before pulling me in for a passionate kiss right there in the middle of Cora's compound. He wrapped the arm not holding his massive gun around my waist and ran his tongue over my bottom lip. It felt like the sort of kiss that went on forever and ever. My body melted into his embrace. I gasped when his teeth sunk into my lip. Sucking and tasting, Malice consumed me.

A gunshot cut through the passionate moment. I pulled away and realized it was Malice who had fired his gun. His arm was outstretched and aimed at a man now bleeding out on the ground. Had he shot him while kissing me? "Fun's over," he whispered. I licked my lips before pulling my mask back down. He laughed, the sound crazed.

Another man rounded the corner, gun raised and aimed at us. Malice efficiently shot him once. Twice. Three times. Each powerful bullet lodged in his chest. "Follow me," he instructed. Another bullet whirred through the air. I squeaked when a third man shot from above us.

Malice started jogging to the front door that led to the interior building and held it open for me. "Ladies first."

Such the motherfucking gentleman. "You're insane," I whispered before walking in.

I shouldn't have gone first. Right there was a man with a pistol aimed right at my skull. Malice, the efficient protector, wrapped both his arms around my middle, aimed, and fired before my attacker even had a moment to process what was happening. He fell backward, landing in a splatter of blood on the hard concrete floor.

"You just used me as a human shield!" I squealed. Malice, who was still wrapped around my body with his smoking guns, leaned in and scraped his teeth along my neck, drawing blood with their sharp tips. I gasped and he pressed his hard cock against my ass. "I want a real date after this."

Malice chuckled before pushing me forward into the room. I felt like a hostage and a human shield. "I don't do real dates, Little Fighter."

I dug my heels in and spun around to face him. "Right. William is the romantic," I taunted him.

Malice fired off his gun. I didn't even have to turn around to know that another man was chasing us down. I heard the body hit the floor. Malice looked down at me. I wanted to tear the ski mask away and get a good look at his face. "I want to fuck you so bad," he groaned.

The feeling was mutual. "Let's get your goddamn necklace, then."

Malice grabbed my hand with his free hand. By my count, we still had four men to fight off. I was breathing hard, marching across the bloodstained warehouse without a sense of where we were. I just prayed that Cora and her team didn't show up while we were still here.

We were walking up a metal staircase when the lights went out. I resisted the urge to scream. The only thing worse than being in this crazy situation was not being able to see who was coming, not that I could defend myself if I could. "Malice?" I asked.

"Shh…"

I didn't dare move. My feet made too much noise on the metal steps.

All I heard was the loud thumping of my blood through my veins.

Thump thump.

Thump thump.

A bullet sliced through the air, and a man's gurgled screams echoed throughout the compound. Malice turned on the flashlight attached to his rifle and shined it at our attacker. "How the hell did you see him?" I asked.

"Move." We marched up the steps. Almost unable to breathe, I was so scared. "Keep going, Little Fighter. Show me how strong you are."

In a moment of brave stupidity, I snapped at him. "You are unbelievably ridiculous," I argued. "I don't get you. One second you're smothering everyone with your overprotectiveness, the next you're bringing me to a shootout."

At the top of the steps, Malice pushed me against the metal wall, nearly knocking the air out of me. "I'm just proving your point."

I was exasperated. "And what point would that be?"

"You make me stronger. I'm not afraid to bring you here, because you make me feel like the strongest man in the room. I'm untouchable. Invincible. Ask me why?"

I swallowed. His lips were so close to mine. I wanted to tear our masks off and devour his mouth. "Why?"

"Because I would burn the world to the ground before letting anything happen to you. I'd kill anyone, anything, that put you in danger."

I pressed my forehead to his. This sounded like a

declaration, but I was so overwhelmed I didn't know how to process it. "Let's go," he whispered before threading his fingers through mine. We walked down the hall undisturbed and stopped at the end of the hall where we were blocked by a locked door.

"Don't suppose you have a key?" I asked.

Malice kicked it down with his boot and ran inside, gun raised. Silence and emptiness met us.

It was hard to make everything out because of the pitch black room, but Cora's office was unimpressive. It had a single desk, two chairs, and metal filing cabinets lining the wall. Not a bit of this space was intimidating or even memorable. Once again, it made me wonder how she was competing with Malice's men. She was like the Wish.com version of a Mafia boss. Second best. Maybe even third best.

"Come stand with me, Little Fighter," Malice said while pulling open a cabinet hanging on her wall. He didn't have to ask me twice.

Behind the cabinet was a mounted safe in the wall. Malice pulled the crumbled paper from his pocket and quickly typed in the numbers. Two. Five. Eight. Nine. It beeped and opened easily. Almost too easily.

"Back away from the safe," an accented voice demanded. Malice and I turned to look at the door where the remaining two men were standing, guns raised and aimed at us. One of the men was tall, and the other was about my height. Malice's flashlight didn't do much to show their features, but I could hear their heavy mouth breathing.

"Boss is going to be so excited. We caught Nicholas Civella, dude!" the tall one exclaimed. "Joey is going to regret making a run for it."

Malice cleared his throat. "That's Malice to you," he growled before swiftly aiming at them and sending bullet after bullet into their chest. He held onto the trigger and unloaded everything he had, and I watched as the bodies became butchered messes of flesh, gore, and regret.

I crouched low and hugged my knees to my chest. Malice didn't stop. Even when the men were long gone, he kept shooting. Blood splattered everywhere, coating Cora's office in red. The flashlight illuminated the flying crimson fireworks, and I felt hot, wet droplets land on my skin. Soaking through my shirt, my shorts. Slicking the floor.

Malice stopped and loaded a new magazine into his rifle. "Stand up, Little Fighter. We don't cower," he demanded. My legs trembled, but I did as he said. Some sick part of me wondered what was wrong with me. Why did this brutal murder have me wanting to kiss him, ride him, lick the blood from his skin?

Malice pulled a small velvet box from the safe and let out a sigh of relief. "It's here, it's really here," he said, awe littering his tone.

I looked over at what he was holding, curious what inspired so much bloodshed. It was a simple necklace with a gold chain and a single, tiny diamond on it. I was no expert on fine jewelry, but it didn't look worth very much.

"Spin around and pick up your braids," Malice whispered while taking it out of the box.

"What? Oh no, you don't have to—"

"Do it," he demanded.

I spun around and lifted two braids for him. His fingers brushed along my bloodied skin, making goose bumps break out along my body. I felt the delicate chain wrap around my neck and his hot breath feathering down my spine. "This necklace belonged to my mother," he whispered softly.

My heart suddenly panged for him. The sentimental weight and power of this gesture hit me full force, and I felt raw emotions crawl up my throat. "Malice..."

"It looks beautiful on you," he whispered. I doubted he could actually see the necklace in the dark room, but I could hear the relief in his tone. Getting this piece of his parents back was important to him.

I turned around once it was firmly clasped and wrapped my arms around his neck. Malice collapsed into my embrace and let all the strength escape his body. He allowed himself to be vulnerable for the briefest of moments. Tight. I pulled him tight against me.

"Let's go, Little Fighter," he whispered.

I pulled away and touched my bloodied finger to the necklace. "Okay," I replied. And something told me I'd follow this man anywhere.

CORALEE JUNE

chapter twenty six

A layer of dried blood clung to my skin. On the way back from Cora's compound, I experienced an adrenaline rush unlike any I'd ever experienced before. Malice silently navigated the Kansas City streets with his fingers threaded through mine, and when we got to his mansion, the weight of what we'd done settled heavily on me.

"Cora hired the man who killed my parents," Malice admitted before pulling a joint from his pocket and lighting it up. It looked like he was a prisoner of war resting after battle, covered in a layer of blood. Inhaling slowly and exhaling slowly, I watched him. "He stole Ma's necklace the day he killed them. Brought it to Cora like it was some sort of prize."

I looked down at the tiny diamond sparkling in the afternoon sun. So much blood. "I'm so sorry," I whispered, not knowing what else to say.

"Dad bought it for her back when he had nothing," he continued before taking a long drag of his joint. He held the smoke in his chest for a lingering moment before blowing out a huge plume of smoke. "A hundred dollar necklace and a promise to build an empire. He took over this Mafia, you know. There was another family in power before he came along. He always told me how easy it was to lose your footing if you weren't careful enough." He eyed me, his entire demeanor slumping from his high. He looked relaxed and calm. "I want you to keep it. I've got my own promise for you, Little Fighter."

I held my breath, waiting for him to respond.

"And what promise would that be?" Anthony interrupted. I looked up at the driveway. "Promise to keep her safe?"

Anthony had his hands in his pockets as he walked over to us. He looked casually lethal, his expression hard and his strut leisurely. He stopped in front of me and glared at the necklace wrapped around my neck. "I'm assuming that's not your blood," he grumbled before licking his thumb and reaching out to wipe my cheek.

"I'm safe," I replied softly.

"Safe is relative," Anthony whispered.

Malice stared between us, waiting, watching.

"Hey, Juliet?" Anthony then said in a timid whisper. "Remember when we went fly trapping?" I nodded. I expected him to expand on that, but he never did. Instead, Anthony wrapped his hand around my wrist and gently tugged me toward the door.

"Where are you taking her?" Malice asked, his tone cruel.

Anthony tipped his head back and let out a manic laugh. I felt trapped between the two dangerous brothers, unsure what to do. I wanted to go with Anthony but also wanted to hear what promise Malice was making me. Why did this have to be so complicated?

"You know how this works," Anthony said. "I'm so glad that you finally started to feel something after all these years. I was worried the only emotions you were capable of were guilt and anger. It's a good look on you." Anthony was usually so playful. I wasn't expecting him to be so snarky with his brother.

Malice blinked, then took another slow drag of his joint.

"But we both know that you owe me. I like Juliet. She's

kind, funny, and she doesn't make me feel like I'm damaged or crazy or on the edge of my seat. You're welcome to try your version of love with her. I'm not above sharing. I'm half a man these days, anyway."

"Anthony," I murmured. He wasn't half of anything. I saw him as this whole, beautiful, tragic thing. Brave. Strong. Compassionate.

"We both know who is in charge here," Malice said.

Once again, Anthony laughed, as if it were the most hilarious thing he'd ever heard. "You're the boss, but you're a slave to your guilt. Go ahead and cling to what little control you have, because it's the only thing that'll keep you sane. Get used to this dynamic now, because I'm not backing down."

And with those parting words, Anthony guided me into the Civella home. He paused in the foyer and let out a shaky exhale. "I know the dungeon freaks you out, Killer. But it's my safe spot, and I need to calm down. Can we go there? Please?"

I swallowed. "Okay." If there was anyone who I could face my fears with, it was Anthony.

—

The small bathroom filled with steam. It was weird being back here. The last time I was in this room, I was washing my sins down the drain. Now, I was ridding myself of Malice's bloody promise. "May I?" Anthony asked, his voice a rasp. He reached for the edge of my shirt and lightly lifted it. I nodded my head with consent, thrilled that he was touching me. Having Anthony so close felt like coming home. I was too scared to speak. What if I ruined this?

"I was worried about you," Anthony said while lifting the thin, stained shirt over my head and tossing it on the ground. "Almost got in my car and drove to Cora's compound to beat Nick's ass."

I chewed on my lip. "I didn't mean to scare you."

Anthony reached around me, as if wrapping me in a hug, and unclasped my bra. He shuddered the moment the straps fell down my shoulders and my breasts were free. He pressed tighter against me, and I felt him inhale and exhale against my body.

"I'm not sure if I know what scared really means anymore."

He pulled away and dropped to his knees. I watched in fascination as he unbuttoned my shorts and eased them over my hips. "Why?" I croaked.

"I guess when you've been through hell, everything else feels easy. I'm not mad that Nick risked you today. I'm mad that he trusted you to handle it. I'm tired of my family treating me like I'm broken."

"You're not broken, Anthony," I said while stepping out of my shorts. He reached up for my underwear and slowly, slowly eased them down, gasping at the sight of my pussy.

"Nick took you to the devil's playroom because you trusted him to take care of you. I might enjoy the privilege his guilt grants me, but one day, I hope he trusts himself with my safety too. I love my family, Juliet."

Anthony leaned close and blessed my inner thigh with a tragic kiss. He sucked on my supple skin while reaching around to dig his fingers into the meaty globes of my ass. I tilted my head back and basked in his teasing. He moved closer to the apex of my thighs and breathed me in.

"Get in the shower," he demanded before pulling away. I was sad that our moment was over, but I didn't want to pressure him. He stood up and stared at the ground as I moved to stand under the steamy stream of water.

I waited. And waited.

Anthony flipped off the lights, bathing the room in pitch black. I held my breath as I heard him move the curtain aside. He stepped into the small shower with me, his presence warm and comforting. I gasped when he wrapped his arms around me and nuzzled my neck. "It's easier for me..." He paused. "When I can't see."

"Just feel me, Anthony."

I slowly ran my fingers over his abs, his collarbone, his biceps. He let me explore the hard grooves of his body. I avoided his back and the scars I knew that were there, even though I wanted to kiss away the pain with my trembling lips.

Without warning, Anthony spun me around and hugged my back to his torso. I felt too aware of his hard cock poised against my ass. He kissed my shoulder. My spine. He ran his hands along my arms and reached around my waist and between my legs. I let out a moan when his fingers found my sweet spot of pleasure.

"You're too warm," he whispered. "Too alive." His tone sounded pained. I didn't know what he wanted from me, but at that moment, I would have given him anything.

He teased my clit with the pad of his finger, circling around it with rhythmic circles. I braced both palms against the tiled wall as the hot water rained down on us. "Fuck," I cursed. Anthony felt too good for words. In the dark, in this intimate moment, I relished in every sensation.

Then, without warning, Anthony turned the water icy cold. It was a shock to the system, and I jerked out of the way, confused by what he was doing. "What is going on?" I asked.

"When he was done with me, he'd put me in a refrigerator with the others," Anthony admitted.

I tried to move out of the icy stream, but I couldn't. "Who are the others, Anthony?" I asked, my teeth starting to chatter.

"The cold ones. The dead," he admitted before slamming me against the wall and kissing me hard. I pressed tight against his body for warmth. I didn't understand what he was saying and wanted answers.

"He'd touch me. Torture me," Anthony said between kisses. I couldn't tell if it was tears or water running down his face. "Then he'd toss me in with all his other victims. I thought I was dead. I should have been dead."

I started to cry. I couldn't imagine all the pain this poor man went through. I cupped both his cheeks, forgetting how cold I felt. He seemed completely comfortable. "I was naked," he admitted. "I used her like a blanket. They comforted me. All their dead limbs. Their lifeless eyes. I don't know how to be with anyone alive anymore."

Anthony Civella thrived with the dead because they were the only ones there for him during his darkest moment. I pictured this bloodied man being tossed into a pile of victims. It was horrifying. With this realization, I let the water turn my skin to ice. I calmed my chattering teeth. I went stiff. I became what Anthony needed. "Let me die a little for you," I whispered.

He picked me up and carried me out of the shower and out of the bathroom. He placed me on a metal table. He kissed my skin. He ran his hands up and down my body. He got on top of me. He pried my legs open and sunk deep inside of me. It was this detached experience. I felt disconnected. Him. Him. Him. All I could focus on was Anthony Civella and his demons.

As more time passed, I settled into the warmth created

by our moving bodies. I found the surface of my pleasure. I crawled to the forefront of my mind. My body was used for his selfish purposes. It didn't feel sick or twisted or wrong. I didn't feel used. It felt like progress, a step toward taking back his power. When he kissed me, I kissed him back. I moaned. I participated. I enjoyed.

I showed him how alive I was with every response, every hitch in my breath. Every moan, twitch, clench, and sob.

"Yes," I cried out as he moved faster. The metal table was loud, and every jolt of his body created this crashing, screeching sound. Anthony seemed so strong to me right then. He was the most powerful person I'd ever met. He conquered my body and his nightmares.

"I'm never letting you go," he said. "You're mine, Killer."

CORALEE JUNE

chapter twenty seven

I faced my fears and fell asleep in the death dungeon. It wasn't comfortable, lying on Anthony's thin mattress. But he slept soundly, his muscular arms wrapped around my body. I spent most of the night staring at his face. I refused to pity him; a man like Anthony, who had overcome so much, deserved nothing but awe.

The next morning when we woke up, he wrapped me in his soft blanket and kissed my bare shoulder. We didn't talk about what happened the night before. Maybe avoiding it was unhealthy. But I felt closer to him now. I understood his traumatic past better, and I was able to navigate his unique needs, too.

Palm to palm, we held hands and walked upstairs.

Malice was in his bedroom with the door open, and when he saw us, he slammed it shut.

I got ready for the day feeling anxious about what was to come. It was such a strange contradiction to feel as though I belonged to each of these men while knowing at the same time that I didn't. I'd passed the point of no return and crossed that thin gray line of right and wrong, not thinking about my friendship with Vicky, not worrying about how it would affect their sibling relationship. I found pieces of myself within each unique relationship.

Anthony brought out my vulnerable side. My trauma. My broken innocence. He felt the safest to me because we bonded over our shared damage. He was the most open with me, and I saw parts of myself in the way he interacted with the world. He didn't make me feel crazy for still holding hope about my mother. He was my fly swatter. My harbinger of death.

William was my complex analytical side. Like me, he observed the world. He processed. He unpacked a situation and faded into the background. Restrained and secretive, I related to his martyrdom and the way he viewed the world. I wasn't sure if we had a future together. Of all the brothers, he felt the most betrayed by my inability to choose. I hadn't even seen him since the moment in his office. Breaking those pearls felt like breaking our relationship. I wasn't sure we would ever repair it.

And Malice, dark, dangerous Malice. He brought out my inner destructiveness, my power, my deepest, darkest curiosities. Every bit of my filthy soul, he dragged to the light. He personified my most thrilling nightmares. He coaxed passion from every pore in my body. Malice was the wildest parts of my spirit. He was the hardest to love, but the most rewarding too.

And I did love him. I loved all of them. It was a whirlwind. Quick, reckless, and doomed from the start. There was no way that this could work, but I'd enjoy it while it lasted.

After we ate breakfast, Anthony went to the dungeon to work, and I relaxed for a few hours while avoiding the other inhabitants of the house. I needed a moment to marinate in my feelings for a bit. Yesterday was equally thrilling and traumatic. Malice and I would eventually have to finish our conversation, and at some point, I'd need to find William and see if there was still any hope for us.

After working up my courage, I went downstairs and decided that if I ran into Malice, I'd ask him about his promise. I still wore the necklace we'd battled for. The sentimental jewelry felt like a weight around my neck. A secret.

I was making my way to the kitchen when the front

door opened and in stormed none other than Vicky and William.

It took a moment for me to process that she was here and that I had to now come to terms with breaking best friend code. We'd spoken some after my trip to Gwendola Lane but never about my relationship with her brothers. I knew that I needed to face the consequences of my actions. She was my friend first, but that didn't mean I was prepared to do that right this second.

"Vicky!" I said awkwardly. "You're home!"

I walked up to her with my arms stretched out ready for a hug. She had a fresh golden-brown tan and wore a black mini dress with wedges. The sunglasses on her face made it impossible to see her eyes, but her mouth was fixed into a firm line. She didn't return my hug. She stood there stiff as a board.

"I missed you," I whispered, emotion clawing up my throat.

"Did you, Juliet? Did you really?" she asked as I pulled away. I turned to look at William, who was raking his eyes up and down my body, as if assessing it.

"Where is Nick?" she asked while staring at my neck. "And take my necklace off right now. You have no right to be wearing that."

How did she know about the necklace?

I reached up to press my finger against the delicate

chain, my heart thudding with anxiety. "Vicky. Can we talk?"

"Where is my brother, Juliet?"

I looked to William. Was this his doing?

"You're back," Malice said from the top of the winding staircase. He was in slacks and a button-up shirt, both hands thrust in his pockets, as if he had been casually standing there. "I was wondering where you'd disappeared to today, William. Did you decide it was time for our sister to come home? I'm not used to you having the balls to defy my wishes. Someone should take a photo of the moment."

"You're insane," Vicky said. "Is this your way of punishing me? Tricking my only friend into thinking you like her?"

Malice strutted down the stairs, and with each step, a sliver of doubt started to creep in. Was this a game to him? Was I just revenge? He wrapped his arm around my waist and pulled me close. The contact made me sigh in relief. William clenched his fist. Vicky's face turned an angry shade of red. "Don't ever disrespect Juliet like that in my presence again," he said in a stoic voice before bending over to kiss my temple. I squeezed my eyes shut. This was not how I wanted to handle this.

"You took her to Cora's compound," William interrupted. "You risked her life, and for what? Is this another game? Another way to get a reaction out of me?"

"This is insane. You're insane, Nick. Juliet isn't like us," Vicky added.

I cleared my throat. "Maybe I'm more like you than you think."

"That's not a good thing, Juliet," she screeched. "You're killing people and working at a sex club. What happened to you? You've literally become all the things I hate about our world. William told me everything. He said you spent the night with Anthony last night, too. I thought we discussed this," she shouted.

"I didn't realize William was keeping tabs on me," I replied before glaring at him. It wasn't his right to tell her this.

Malice laughed. "Then you must be blind. The man watches everything you do."

"Fuck off," William shouted.

"I get sent halfway around the world, and you're here fucking my brothers. I thought we were friends."

"We are friends, Vicky," I said with a sigh. "I should have talked to you, but I didn't know what to say. I'm still processing it all myself."

"Processing what?" Anthony asked while walking into the foyer. He was barefoot and wearing only a pair of jeans. His hair was wet, as if he'd just showered, and the moment his eyes landed on Vicky, a broad grin broke out on his face. "You're home."

Unlike with me, Vicky actually hugged her brother, but the way her arms wrapped around him made it seem like he was this broken china doll, as if she was trying to catch all his broken pieces in her arms. "I've got so much to tell you," Anthony said while pulling away. He turned to look at me, then strutted to my other side not occupied by Malice.

"I think I already know," Vicky replied venomously.

"Oh great, we can skip past the awkward 'I'm probably going to put a baby in your best friend' conversation then," he said with a shrug. "By the way, I think I have a breeder kink."

"Absolutely not," Malice said before pinching the bridge of his nose.

Vicky threw her hands up in exasperation. "I have never been so betrayed—"

"You're better than this, Juliet. I thought I knew you," William added.

I breathed in deeply, closed my eyes, and tried to find my footing in all this. Vicky had a right to feel the way she did. William, however, did not.

"William," I said, "you don't have any claim to me just because you essentially stalked me for three years. I considered you a stranger all that time, and I'm not some object you can possess. I'm not a toy. You don't own me. And I'm not mad that you brought Vicky here, but hiding behind my best friend and thinking we would somehow magically go back to the way we were, isn't how this works. We could have talked about it. But instead, you humiliated me in your office and stormed off. You hid. You watched me and said nothing."

"Nick was supposed to get bored of you," William growled. "It wasn't supposed to be like this."

"And he very well could decide tomorrow that he's bored of me. Anthony, too."

"Not happening," Anthony sang.

Malice, however, remained silent.

"I'm not responsible for your feelings. I'm not required to love you on your terms. I'll respect you. I'll care for you. But this is too far. Call me when you want to talk like an adult."

"I shouldn't have to share you. I had you first!" he screamed.

Vicky looked at him with disgust. "I had her first," she scoffed. "She was my friend first, and all of you just stole her. Like you do with everything in my life. I can't have friends. I can't go to college. I can't have a career, or dreams, or a boyfriend, or any sort of normalcy. Juliet was my one thing. And you all ruined it."

I pulled away from Malice and Anthony with the intent to comfort her. "Vicky. It doesn't have to be ruined."

"But it is," she cried, tears streaming down her face.

MALICE

"How can you be my friend and be okay with this? All of this." She looked around, and I wished that I could see this world through her eyes. Maybe I just wasn't jaded enough. Maybe I hadn't seen enough death. Maybe I was too similar to Malice to ever fully realize the sort of pain she experienced. One thing I'd learned was that I thrived in the dark. Vicky was forced into it.

"Vicky, I just want to talk."

"No. Get out," she said. "Give me my mother's necklace and leave. Don't come back."

Tears started to stream down my cheeks. I felt that familiar wave of abandonment crawl up my throat. I couldn't handle this. "Vicky. We can work it out—"

"Now, Juliet. I don't ever want to see you again."

"That's not your call to make," Malice, who had been mostly observing the back-and-forth, said. I closed my eyes and let out a sob while reaching up to touch the clasp. "Little Fighter," he whispered in my ear, "don't take off the necklace. Why don't you go to my room and rest, yes? I'll be there shortly."

"She can come to the death dungeon," Anthony piped in.

"It's my turn," Malice replied, his tone leaving no room for discussion.

Vicky let out a dark laugh. "So that's what's going to happen? You're just a fuck doll getting passed around by my brothers now? I didn't realize you were such a pathetic slut!" I opened my eyes in time to see spit flying from her mouth at her cruel slur.

Malice clenched his fist. I wanted to run far away from this place. Maybe she was right. Maybe something was wrong with me. What kind of person was okay with this dynamic? "Vicky," Malice said, her name like a curse on his tongue. "You are my sister, so that allows you certain privileges and allowances that others wouldn't get. This is your one warning. If you ever talk to Juliet like that again, you will not like the consequences."

"You don't have to do that, Malice—" I whispered, but he squeezed my hand, wordlessly telling me to be quiet.

"Juliet is my guest. That necklace is my gift to her. She will stay here indefinitely. I want everyone here to understand something. I'm not going to get tired of her tomorrow. Or the next day. Or the day after that. You know how stringently I protect the people I care about, so know that I won't hesitate to remove anyone in her life who threatens her happiness."

I glanced at Anthony, who had a shit-eating grin on his face. "Cute. Is this your way of pissing on her leg, because I'm not—"

Malice interrupted him. "If you have a relationship with Juliet, it's because I allow it." Malice turned to look at William. "Go ahead and challenge me on this, I'll happily win. And, Vicky? Welcome home. Don't fuck up, or I'll send you away again, and this time there will be no coming back."

Vicky shook her head in disbelief. "You're seriously choosing her over me?"

Malice laughed while rubbing the scruff of his jaw with his palm. "Yes, Vicky. I am. If you have a problem with that, then you can bitch about it to the brother who hides behind you to get what he wants. What was it, William, three years before you made a move?" Malice stroked his chin as if thinking on it. "I'm not surprised. You rarely fight for anything in your life."

And with those parting words, Malice marched me to his room and slammed the door.

CORALEE JUNE

chapter twenty eight
vicky

I watched the world pass outside my window, my fury no less than when I'd left my childhood home an hour ago. I couldn't stay in that house. Every second I spent there just made me rage. Knowing my ex-best friend was in Nick's bedroom made me sick to my stomach. She was a traitor. An idiot. I couldn't believe I ever trusted her.

I tried talking to my other brothers, hoping to get someone with some goddamn sense, but Anthony was... different. It wasn't right. Just because he could finally fuck something without crying didn't mean that he wasn't still a total psychopath. I loved the guy. We were closer than the others, but I knew how twisted he was—how damaged. Juliet was insane if she thought he could change. It was like lying in bed with a wild animal.

Normally, I'd chat with William. He was always on my side. When he called me and told me all the shit that was going on, he had the private jet pick me up within six hours. I thought I'd have an ally here, but William was moping around like someone kicked his goddamn puppy. Things were easier when he wasn't allowed to talk to Juliet. I always knew he had a crush on her, which is why we agreed on the rule. He always listened to me. Why did everything have to fucking change?

"Are you sure this is where you are going, Miss?" the taxi driver said while pulling up to the address I'd given him. The old man in a Brewers hat looked skeptical of the building, and I couldn't blame him.

I looked up at the dismal compound with an arched brow. "Positive." I dug into my purse and handed him cash.

"I'll keep the car running for five minutes in case you change your mind," he said while peering at me in the rearview mirror.

I smirked. "Don't bother."

My stilettos sunk into the dirt as I got out of the car, and I stared up at the guards with a flirtatious grin. I was taking control of my own life today.

Malice, fucking Malice. The man that ran his empire with an iron fist was not my brother. He's always hated me, always tried to keep me away. He liked to pretend his crazy methods were to protect me, but I knew better. Nick wanted me out of the picture. I didn't know what I did to piss him off, but we'd never been close. I always wanted to live my life, and he always wanted to sweep me under the rug.

I couldn't date like normal, make friends, travel, go to college. I wanted to party. I wanted to shop without a fucking security detail. I didn't want to go places and be feared for my last name. Every goddamn thing I did was such a production. We lived in a mansion surrounded by guards. I couldn't even diddle my clit without someone knowing about it.

I was forced to do whatever Nicholas wanted me to do. He snapped his fingers, and I was shipped off to Italy. I didn't want to stick around and figure out what crazy shit he would do next.

Juliet was the last straw. She just didn't get it. This wasn't some game. This wasn't a fucking weekend in Vegas, either. How dare she betray me like this? Juliet was my one thing—my person. My everything. I loved her like a sister, and she went behind my back and fucked my brothers.

I was livid. Furious. It started as this slow rolling anger

that burned brighter and brighter.

They stole the last straw. One thing. I wanted one thing to myself, and they ruined it.

I waltzed up to the guard. I knew it was wrong to be here, but I had to trust in the enemy of my enemy. Cora was weak, but given the right intel—the right resources—she's had proven methods. The scrappy bitch had a growing army, and I needed help if I was going to tear down my brothers.

Working with her went against everything I knew, but it was the only way. She'd been responsible for Anthony's kidnapping and my parents' death, but maybe I'd been putting the blame on the wrong person all this time. It was my father's ambition that got us into this mess. It was Malice who kept expanding and making enemies. If he were gone, I could live a normal life.

Cora can have her paper empire, I wanted to be free.

The guard spit in the dirt at my feet. Disgusting. "What do you want?"

I smiled at the dirty-looking man. "I'm here to see Cora. Tell her Vicky Civella wants to make a deal."

chapter twenty nine

I sat cross-legged on the edge of Malice's bed, wearing his button-up shirt and staring at the bowl of fruit in my lap. "Aren't you hungry?" Malice asked. He was sitting in a lounge chair, shirtless and checking emails on his iPad.

I chewed on my lip. Last night, Malice had to go to a warehouse to check on a shipment, so I ended up sleeping alone. Despite needing answers from him, it was nice to have time to organize my thoughts. I was sad about Vicky, angry with William, and worried about Anthony.

"I'm hungry," I admitted while looking at his bare chest and his washboard abs. The black ink swirling all over his skin made me want to run my tongue all down his torso. He caught me staring and smirked.

Malice slowly set down his iPad and stalked over to me, his pants hanging low on his hips. I stared into his moody eyes and felt the full weight of his attention on me. He picked up the bowl and moved it to his dresser, then sat on the edge of the bed. "Sit," he demanded while patting his lap. I blushed, still new to the affection, and crawled onto his lap, straddling his thighs and facing him head on. "How are you?" he asked while grabbing my hips.

I ran my hands through his blond hair, stalling. "I'm okay," I lied.

He dug his fingers into my hips and pulled me until I was grinding against his hard cock. "Don't lie to me."

"I don't want to fight with Vicky," I admitted. "And I'm mad at William."

Malice looked deep into my eyes. "Yes, I suppose William is quite the disappointment. I was hoping you'd be the one to change him."

I leaned back slightly in surprise. "What do you mean?"

Malice tenderly pulled me closer, forcing me to grind against his delicious cock. The sensation had me biting my lip. "William hides behind money. He's always shown his strength behind stocks and his intelligence. Don't get me wrong, he's brutal when he needs to be, but he's never challenged me. Sometimes I wonder if we would be closer if he would just stand up for himself instead of letting the world fuck him over."

"You actually want him to challenge you?"

"I think it would bring us closer. Right now, he's letting his frustration fester. One of these days, my brother is going to explode and ruin us all. I knew almost immediately that he loved you. I got close to you to try and challenge him some. I hoped that, at one point, he would stand up and stake his claim. But still, he disappoints me."

I had never felt more embarrassed in my life. It was like getting punched in the gut. I was so overwhelmed with a multitude of emotions that my lungs felt tight. Malice didn't care about me. He was just using me. I slowly inched off his lap and put space between us. "I see," I whispered. "Do you think he'll ever challenge you?" I asked.

Malice shrugged. "I thought he loved you enough to at least try, but..."

My heart split.

The necklace wrapped around my throat started to feel like it was choking me.

"The first time we kissed," I whispered. "You waited until he could see."

"I did."

"And yesterday, you put me in danger so that William

would get pissed off," I said. I could feel the tears forming in my eyes, and I begged them to dry up. I wouldn't let Malice see me cry. I could be strong.

Malice let out a sigh. "He didn't even talk to me about it. Instead, he went to get Vicky and let her fight his battles. At some point, my brother is going to have to man up."

This conversation did three things simultaneously.

First, I realized that Malice didn't actually care for me.

Second, I realized that William didn't love me enough to fight for me.

And third, I learned that I needed to leave before my heart was shattered any more than it already was.

Vicky was right. I was nothing to these men. How could I have been so stupid? I threw away my best friend, my morals, my humanity for them. I killed for them. I died a little for them, too.

His phone pinged, drawing his attention away from me. I took a deep breath as I watched Malice check his phone. In that brief moment, my heart turned to stone. Nothing. I would feel nothing. I would treat him like the man I killed. Small box. Smaller box. Locked away forever. "Hey, can we finish this later? I need to go check on something at one of my warehouses. Are you okay?" Malice asked.

I willed my expression to be blank. "Yeah. I'm just going to research some colleges and call Grams."

Malice's brow arched. "We can talk about you going to

college later."

Of course, how could I forget? Malice didn't want me, but I'd never be free, either.

Malice quickly put on his shirt and got dressed. I disconnected from the moment, forcing my mind to empty of all the pain, embarrassment, and self-loathing. I was a monster. I was pathetic. I was so desperate for love that I let this man use me. And worst of all, I knew it. I ignored all the signs and my intuition for what? I was doomed to a life of loneliness, of abandonment. Block by block, I felt my confidence shatter. I had this crazy vision of a future where I belonged, and it was nothing more than a joke.

"I'll see you later," Malice said while buckling his belt. He kissed me on the cheek softly. I didn't understand why he bothered with the tender display of affection. Maybe he liked knowing that he could still take whatever he wanted from me.

What had he said?

I play with toys until they break, and then I play with them harder.

Malice would probably fuck me right now just to prove he could.

"Bye," I replied.

I watched Malice walk out the door, and the moment he was gone, I instantly took off the necklace and sobbed.

—

"Where are you going?" Anthony asked as I walked to the front door. I let out a little sigh and paused to face him. The only genuine person in this house was Anthony. I knew without a shadow of doubt that he had no ulterior motives when it came to me. He cared.

I hoped he couldn't see how red my eyes were from crying. "I convinced Vicky to meet me at a coffee shop down the street. I was going to bring her a peace offering." And I was going to tell her goodbye.

Leaving this town had become my primary goal. Grams was still safely with Aunt Agnes in Palm Springs. I had to come clean to her about what I'd been up to and find a safe place for us away from it all.

I lifted a velvet box to show him. "What's in the box?" he asked.

I cleared my throat. "The necklace."

He winced. "Does Nick know? He gets very cranky when his thoughtful gifts are re-gifted."

I looked down at the ground. "Malice told me that he was just with me to get to William," I admitted. "He didn't actually... He didn't want..." I licked my lips and shook my head free of all the thoughts plaguing me. Put it in a box, Killer.

"I think you should talk to him," Anthony said. "At least before you give that away." He nodded at the necklace.

"I'll talk to him, eventually," I replied. I needed to quit

my job at Eden's Place and end our deal. I'd done my job already. Hale was dead. Grams needed that medicine, but I'd have to find another way to get it. Hell, I'd suck Dr. Hoffstead's wrinkled dick if I had to. "I know where I stand now, and I don't see the point in staying anymore. I've already ruined my relationship with Vicky. William hates me. Malice won't really have a use for me much longer."

Anthony wrapped his arms around me and held me close. "I need you," he whispered, pain coating his tone like thick lead-based paint.

"I need you too," I admitted. I didn't know how Anthony and I could be anything. He would always remind me of his brothers and sister. If I kept seeing him, then I'd be here, surrounded by people who hated me. Eventually, I'd have to talk to him too. Eventually, for my own mental health, I'd have to leave him. And it was devastating to me that I couldn't even have the one man who loved me back.

"How about I walk you to the coffee shop? I need to talk to my sister, too. Maybe if we can fix this with her, we can work on fixing things with William and Nick, okay?" Anthony offered.

There was no fixing this, but maybe if I could mend Anthony's relationship with Vicky, he would at least have someone when I was gone. "That would be really nice," I replied with a tight smile.

Anthony stared at me, his eyes sweeping over every

nuance in my expression. "I'm worried about you," he said. "Want me to call Nick?"

"Please no," I rushed out. "Let's just talk to Vicky, okay? I want you guys to be okay."

"I want you to be okay," Anthony said before pulling out his cell. No. No, I couldn't handle this just yet. He dialed a number and, after a few breaths, spoke. "Hey. I think you need to come home."

I closed my eyes and started walking out the door. I couldn't do this right now. Anthony walked behind me, holding the phone up to his ear and talking to Nick. "Anthony, please, let's just go," I pleaded while walking down to the front gate. The guard there let us through with a wave.

"What's this about you using Juliet to get to William? She's really upset," Anthony continued. I wanted to tear the phone out of his hands and stomp it into the ground. The only thing I had left was my pride. I could pretend that this was just sex and sweep my emotions under the rug. But if Malice knew he'd hurt me, then even that would be ripped from me. "You seriously need more self-awareness, asshole," Anthony said. Anthony moved the phone from his ear. "He wants to talk to you."

I stopped on the sidewalk and stared up at the sky, willing it to swallow me whole. Fuck it. Wiping an erratic tear, I let all the pain burst out of me. "Tell him that I am sincerely sorry that I wasn't inspiring enough for William. I ruined everything, didn't I? My friendship with Vicky. My freedom. My soul." My veins were bulging in my neck. I was shaking so hard from the adrenaline and pain. "I'm so fucking stupid. I was falling for this man, and I wasn't even allowed to call him by name. Malice? I wanted to love a man named Malice? He told me—he fucking told me!" I stomped my foot. "The signs were there. I was falling for him, you know? I thought this was something. Maybe he would pick me and stay." I continued to stare at the sky. I didn't want to see Anthony's pitied expression. "That's what happens to broken, lonely little girls who grow up with nothing. They cling to the first sign of love and run with it, not giving a single fuck for all the red flags." I clenched my fists and held them up to my chin. "I killed for this man!"

Anthony's eyes were wide as I had a full-on breakdown on the sidewalk. "Juliet. Let's go back. Nick is on his way—"

"I don't want to talk to him," I croaked. "For once in my life, I'm going to do the leaving. This is why I don't let people in." I could hear that familiar buzzing start to build up in my brain. The flies were back. I wanted to sit on Gwendola Lane.

"Juliet!" Anthony yelled, his voice panicked. "Juliet! RUN!"

A screeching van pulled up to the sidewalk, and six large men jumped out of the sliding door, grabbing me.

I didn't even have time to process it. Their strong arms wrapped around my body, and a bag was cinched over my head, drowning the afternoon sun in darkness. I was thrown into the van. Anthony's screams filled my ears, and I started to kick, punch and yell as loud as I could. Another body was tossed beside me. Someone grabbed my wrists and zip-tied them. No matter how much I squirmed, they held me down.

"Juliet!" Anthony screamed.

Spit gathered on my lips as I cried out.

And then something hard kicked me in the skull.

And the flies took over my mind.

chapter thirty

The first thing I noticed was the smell. The room was rancid. It was the kind of stench that made me gag. Rotten flesh. Feces. Moth balls. Spoiled eggs mixed with a foul garlic smell. It was completely unique and utterly disgusting.

There was one single light hanging overhead, the harsh beam burning my tired eyes.

I squeezed my lids shut, then opened them again before dry heaving. The smell was just too much. "That's right, Killer, wake up. Let me see those big beautiful brown eyes of yours."

I blinked twice and groaned. With my vision blurred and my head throbbing in pain, it took me a moment to assess where I was. It was a dark warehouse. Specs of dust coated my tongue. I was sitting in a metal chair with my hands tied behind my back. A line of dried blood was on my cheek, and my scalp felt white hot and wet.

"Look how pretty you look," Anthony said with a grin. "Sitting there with blood on your face and your lungs going up and down, up and down." Anthony was sitting directly in front of me in a chair of his own, hands tied behind his back and a smile on his face.

"Anthony," I croaked. "What is that—"

"Shhh," he coaxed me. "Don't be loud. You'll wake them up."

"Who?"

Anthony swallowed and nodded to the floor. I looked down and choked on a scream. Disfigured bodies, swollen and in varying stages of decay, surrounded us. Limbs, curdled blood, and milky eyes stared back at me. I gasped, but the sudden inhale forced the pungent smell to fill my nose, and a thick, rolling wave of nausea traveled up my throat. I dry heaved over and over again; the only reason vomit wasn't splashing on the ground was because I had literally nothing in my stomach.

"I sang them a lullaby while waiting for you to wake

up," Anthony said while looking at them. "You'll get used to the smell."

Once I could choke out my words, I spoke. "Anthony? Do you know where we are?" I tried breathing through my mouth, but it was a stench you could taste.

"I believe it's a warehouse. Might be one of ours, even. I'm not sure. Don't worry though, Killer. My friends will protect us from Cora's nasty tricks," he said while nodding at the ground where the decayed bodies were.

Holy fuck. Cora got us. How could we be so reckless? Of course she would want retribution for Malice and me storming her compound and stealing her necklace.

"Nick will be here soon, I suppose. This sort of situation gives him a hard-on. Damsel in distress and his poor, stupid brother too fucked up in the head to save himself." Anthony laughed. "He'll run in, guns blazing, with his dick hanging out for you to stroke, I bet you five orgasms."

I wanted to believe that Malice would get us out of here, but I couldn't rely on him. "Anthony. Have you seen anyone?" I asked. "Or are we alone?"

"Well, that's rude. My friends are sitting right there, Juliet," he said with a snort. "Say hello to Hank, he's a little shy."

Anthony was navigating his own trauma, and I couldn't rely on him to get us out of here. "Anthony. Did you see anything? Do you think Malice will know where we are?"

"My brother always knows where I am. He put a tracker in me. Wanna see where? I'll have to take my pants off." He started laughing like a school boy, and I wanted to cry.

Fuck. Okay. I could figure this out. I tried to scrape my chair across the floor. Maybe if I could get to the other side of the room... "That's too loud, Juliet. Just relax. Nick will save us!"

"Anthony, I need you to really try and focus. We have to find a way out of here. Malice doesn't know where we are, and quite frankly, I'm not sure if he's coming. Okay? All we have is ourselves right now, and if we don't get out of here, we'll start to look like your friends, okay?"

"Your faith in me is astounding," a smooth voice said. A voice I knew well. A voice that had broken me and saved me now multiple times. I shifted in my seat and tried to find my dangerous hero.

In the shadows, Malice walked up like this was nothing. A rifle was strapped to his chest, and he had a helmet on. Behind him were a dozen men, all ready for a gun fight and strapped to hell.

"That was really fast, Nick, probably a record somewhere," Anthony said. "I'd like to introduce you to my friends. Meet Trevor."

I breathed a sigh of relief. "You're here," I whispered. Malice looked at Anthony and me before strutting to my chair and cutting the rope that bound my hands together.

"How did you find us?"

"Anthony has a tracker in his ass," he said deadpan. "Are you hurt?" He started running his large hands over my body, checking for breaks and cuts.

"My head feels like it was split in two, but I'm fine."

He reached up and gently pressed on my temple. "You're gonna need to see a doctor," he said.

"Is she okay?" another voice called out. William.

Malice rolled his eyes and shook his head. "She is none of your concern. Make yourself useful and untie your brother. Feel like the fucking hero for once, yeah?"

I stood up, not sure if it was appropriate to hug Malice for saving me but deciding to wrap my arms around myself instead. I looked over his shoulder and stared at William. He wore slacks, a button-up shirt, and a bulletproof vest. As he untied his brother, he stared at me. Our eyes were locked in a meaningful trance, and the raw emotion shared in that brief moment was enough to knock me on my knees.

Anthony grinned at his brothers. "Did you meet my friends? Can we take them with us?" William tore his eyes from me to look at the disfigured bodies on the floor and scowled.

"How did you get in here?" I asked Malice.

"We just walked in. No one was patrolling the perimeter. There is no one inside the building, either. No one alive, that is." He looked down and kicked one of the vacant bodies.

"It's probably a trap, right?" Anthony asked before wiggling and wrapping his arms around William. The brothers awkwardly hugged for a moment.

"It's definitely a trap," Malice said before cocking his gun and glaring at me. "Fan out. Prepare for an ambush."

"You shouldn't have come," I said.

Malice pressed his tongue to his cheek and shook his head in exasperation. "The fact that you think I wouldn't burn down every fucking inch of this city to save you is ridiculous," he growled. "When we get home, I'm going to fuck you on every surface of my house. I'm going to make you come on my tongue again, and again, and again until you have some fucking sense."

I pressed my thighs together, but my heart raged. Now wasn't the time or place to argue.

William's voice boomed. "We don't have time for this. Can we please focus?"

Malice rolled his eyes and kissed me hard on the mouth. It was brief but powerful. He crushed my body to his and pressed his palm into the curve of my back. We were surrounded by his army, dead bodies, and were about to be ambushed, but he kissed me thoroughly. Deeply. And when he pulled away, Anthony let out a low whistle.

"Boss! You should see this!" one of his guards, Garret,

said. I suddenly realized how inappropriate this moment was for the setting and the audience, not that Malice ever cared about what was appropriate.

"I don't want to see anything. Let's get the fuck out of here before shit goes down. Stay alert!" Malice growled.

"It's Vicky, boss."

Malice stopped and turned to face what Garret was pointing at. William, Malice, Anthony, and I stepped over the pile of dead bodies and walked toward the glow of a flat screen television on the far wall. The closer we got, the easier it was to make out the blurred face paused on the screen.

"Hit play," Anthony demanded, all his earlier silliness now gone from his tone.

Garret pressed a button on the remote. My heart pounded. What did this mean? Vicky was wearing all black and had bright pink lipstick on. She was popping her gum like this was nothing more than a gossip session on Jersey Shore. "Hello, family," Vicky said. "If you're watching this, you're going to die soon. You can run, but it would be useless. Cora assured me that you wouldn't have enough time."

I wrapped my hand around William's arm and pulled. I didn't need to hear anything else. "Let's leave," I insisted. "Let's run."

"Vicky, Vicky, Vicky," Anthony whispered while

tapping the screen. "What did you do?"

Vicky continued to speak. "Nick used to tell me that in this world, sometimes you have collateral damage in the pursuit of power."

"Get out now!" Malice yelled to the guards. Some of them had already left. The sounds of pounding feet now filled the warehouse. "Anthony, come on," Malice urged, but he wouldn't budge. He stood there, transfixed by the screen.

Vicky's voice continued. "This family has been a ticking time bomb. You just keep taking, Nick. You took my freedom..."

Anthony had tears streaming down his cheeks. "Take her and get out of here, I'll take Anthony," Malice said to William. Within seconds, I was tossed over William's shoulder and he was jogging toward an exit.

Vicky's voice continued. "You took my hopes and dreams..."

Everything seemed to move in slow motion. William huffed. "I'll get you out of here, I promise," he yelled as we made it to the door. I heard the last of Vicky's speech just as we made it outside.

"...And you took my best friend, Nick. You're not going to take anything else from me. I'm done."

It was pitch black outside, and William continued to run with me slung over his shoulder. "William, stop!" I screamed. "Where are Anthony and Malice?" I asked while beating his back.

And then? Then the explosion happened.

Hot flames lit up the sky as metal groaned and power blasted into William and me, sending both of us into the hard ground. Debris soared past us, and a piercing ringing sound filled my ears. I rolled back and forth in agony and went to scream, but no sound escaped my open mouth. William was crawling on the dirt toward the flames.

I dug my fingers into the ground as I tried to orient myself. The blast was too strong. Too powerful. Every last nerve ending in my body was buzzing like the wings of flies.

No one could have survived that.

William scurried to his feet and placed both palms to his ears. I tried to tell him to back away from the flames, but he mouthed something at me. I stared in confusion as he held a palm up, as if motioning for me to wait, before he started running toward the blazing fire.

I writhed in so much pain, the ringing in my head was too loud. Time passed, but then it didn't. The flies were swarming me, comforting me, telling me to go to that dark place where I was safe with the unknowns. I silently sobbed as heat kissed my cheeks. Another blast. Sirens in the distance.

Bzz.

Bzz.

"Juliet!" Anthony yelled. How did he get here? My head hurt so bad. He pulled me close to his chest and held onto me. His face was bloodied, and his finger was sliced open, but he was okay.

Plumes of smoke surrounded us. I choked on the suffocating air and searched for shadows.

The ringing was still drowning my senses. The flies buzzed peacefully.

The last thing I saw before blacking out was a towering man, cradling someone in his arms and staggering toward me.

chapter thirty one

I pressed my cheek against my soft pillow and moaned. My throat was dry, and my bones were stiff and sore. The ringing in my ears was gone, but it still felt like I was holding my head under water. Every sound was muffled. Head throbbing, I slowly sat up and looked at the nightstand beside me, thankful to find two pain pills and a large glass of water. I reached for the medicine and took it, eager for the pain to go away.

I felt disoriented and confused but also relieved. The skin between my lips and my nose was covered in oil that smelled like lavender, a calming scent completely unlike the disgusting decay I was forced to experience at the warehouse.

I wasn't wearing the same outfit as before. Someone had put me in pink, silky shorts and a thin tank top. There was a bandage on my temple, and my hair had been brushed and braided. It was obvious that I had slept through being changed and washed, but I couldn't remember anything after the blast.

The blast.

The explosion.

Where were the others, had they survived?

Not even the flies buzzed at that thought.

I needed to call Grams. It freaked me out to think I could have died and she would have never known what had happened to me.

I didn't recognize the bedroom I was in. Gray walls, brown hardwood floors, ornate furniture that was both bulky and designer. It was warm and luxurious. I sat up and looked around, pulling the soft duvet all the way up to my chin. A noise at the bedroom door drew my attention, and I watched as the knob twisted and William walked through the threshold.

"You're awake," he said in a scratchy voice.

I rubbed my eyes and took in the sight of him. He wore gray sweatpants that hung low on his hips and no shirt. There was a white bandage wrapped around his left forearm and a cut above his eye. He looked relatively okay compared to the intense blast. "Where is everyone?" I asked. Are they alive? I wanted to ask but was too afraid to.

"Anthony took a sleeping pill and passed out in Nick's bed. He didn't want to sleep in his dungeon today." I vaguely remembered Anthony holding me after the explosion, but was still relieved to hear that he was okay.

"And Malice?"

"Nick is out looking for Vicky. We had a GPS device on her, but it seems she removed it."

I shook my head. All my emotions hit me at once. "How could she do this to us?" I asked, my voice saturated with grief. "We could have died." I was thankful to only have a few scratches and a head wound, it could have been so much worse.

William looked stuck between wanting to comfort me and keeping his distance. I supposed we still had a lot of unfinished business between us, but even with all the regret, I needed him. His strong, stoic presence. His quiet comfort. His confidence. I wanted someone to hold me and tell me that everything was going to be okay.

After a slow exhale, he walked to my side of the bed and sat next to me on the edge of the mattress. "The blast knocked Nick out. When I ran back, Anthony was trying to pick him up. They were right by the door."

I pressed the back of my hand to my mouth and stifled a sob. "Oh my God."

William ran his hand through his hair and averted his eyes. "The most fucked up part of it was that I debated leaving him," William admitted. "I was willing to let my jealousy kill my brother. He was just lying there. The flames were about two seconds from wrapping him in a hug, and I...I hesitated."

It took a lot of honesty and trust for William to share this with me. I chewed on the inside of my cheek for a brief moment before speaking. "But you still saved him, William." I cautiously placed my hand on his thigh. "That's what matters the most."

We all had dark thoughts, intrusive impulses, and greedy desires. It's what we did with them that made a person.

He turned to look at me. "What matters is that you're safe. I was so scared when I heard that you were taken. All I kept thinking was that we never got our chance. I never apologized. We never made up."

I inhaled that lavender scent before leaning forward. "I'm glad you're safe, too. We still have a lot to talk about, though. I care about you, William, but you hurt me."

William crawled on the mattress and moved until he was lying next to me. I lay back and twisted so that we were face-to-face. He stroked my cheek and stared deeply into my eyes. I was always comfortable with my secret stranger. Maybe that's why I never felt weird sharing my soul with him listening. I always knew on a soul-deep level that I could trust him.

"I've always had to share, I've always been second. He was the heir, I was the spare. I couldn't handle the idea of him actually wanting you. I thought you'd be like everyone else, just a toy for him to play with and toss away," he admitted.

I still needed to talk to Malice, his very brief declaration in the warehouse was reassuring, but I still felt like we were on ice that was about to crack. I wasn't sure if I was a toy or something more.

"William, you never fought for me. All that time..."

"I know. I know," he rushed out. "I should have tried harder. You were just this high school girl fighting to take care of her grandmother, and I was the extra brother to a deadly empire. I didn't think I deserved you. I saw how happy you made Vicky, and I didn't want to mess that up for her. But after yesterday..."

"It was scary. We almost lost everything," I whispered.

He stroked my arm. "You know what stopped me from leaving Nick to burn alive out there?"

"What?"

"You. I didn't want to hurt you. It would have been easy to let him die. I could have become the boss. It would have been one less person to share you with. But it would have destroyed you. I love you more than I want to take over. I want you to be happy, Juliet. I'd rather have pieces of you than nothing at all."

I sighed. It was a sweet sentiment, but William would have to constantly fight his impulse to keep me to himself. "Thank you for saving him." I truly was thankful to William for saving Malice. I probably wouldn't have survived if something were to have happened to any of them.

A crack in the curtains left a sliver of morning light to land on his face, illuminating William's loving eyes and the hope in his gaze. "I love you, Juliet. I'm going to fight for you—with you."

He scooted closer to me, and my pounding head started to fade into a dull ache. "I don't even know the girl you're fighting for anymore. I just feel like I'm constantly losing myself, William," I admitted. "I killed. I fell for three men. Betrayed my best friend. If I hadn't...maybe Vicky wouldn't have..."

William pressed his forehead to mine and breathed me in. "You are not responsible for Vicky's decisions."

Soft tears slowly rolled down my cheeks. "She was my best friend. Like my sister. I thought we were forever, you know? Ride or die. And..."

The hardest thing about this was the realization that our friendship was really over. There was no coming back from this. We were both selfish, on different roads leading to different places. I threw away our friendship for love, and she was willing to throw my life away for freedom. It was a cutting sort of pain. We'd never go back to the way we were. We'd never joke again. If I ever saw her again, I wouldn't be able to separate the pain from the good times. It was devastating and final.

"Vicky made her choice," William whispered.

"And I made mine," I added.

William pulled away a bit and stared lovingly at me. "Do you think you could choose to forgive me, Juliet? Do you think we could ever try again?"

My secret stranger had been in my life for three years. I couldn't imagine moving forward and staying on bad terms. We all had to grow. I was tied to these men for life. But still... "I don't think I can stop loving them, William," I said, pain in my tone.

"I know," he replied before leaning forward and kissing me. His lips were soft and warm.

"Do you think you could love me?" I asked. "Not the girl you thought you knew. The real me. I'm not the same girl that spilled all her secrets to Vicky at Dick's. I've changed."

"You want to know what kind of woman you are?" he asked before grabbing my fingers and kissing the tips of them. "You are the girl that saw Anthony's demons and still believed he was capable of love. You connected with him. You didn't shame him or judge him." William kissed the top of my hand and continued. "You're the girl that tamed a demon. Nick is the most selfish bastard I know, and something about you calmed him some. You made him feel like the hero, and he needed that."

He moved to kiss the inside of my wrist.

"And you?"

"You made me want to fight for what I want," he whispered. "And I've never wanted anything more than I want you."

William pulled me in and crashed his lips to mine. His kiss was like melting butter on a skillet. I felt every muscle go limp, my reservations disappeared. My heart opened up like a blooming flower, ready to let him in, ready to forgive. I kissed him like a woman who almost died. Like someone infinitely aware of how precious each second, each millisecond, was. Savoring wasn't enough. Moaning and grinding against his hard body wasn't either.

I rolled over on top of him and bent over to taste his tongue. He gripped me, like he was scared I was going to leave. I pulled back to kiss his jaw, to lick his neck.

He pinched the thin material of my tank top at the hem and inched it up. Higher, higher. I stopped running my hands through his hair to pull it over my head. William gasped at the sight of me; that same sliver of morning light cast a glow over my topless body, and he leaned up to kiss the lines of shadow along my breasts. I dipped my fingers past the waistband of his sweats and grinded against him.

I was wild with want, he was wild with me.

Holding my hips, William gently moved me off of him and pressed my back into the mattress. Using his teeth, he dragged my tiny shorts off my curvy body. I looked down at him, my mouth parted, my eyes heavy with lust. "Your body is a precious gift, Miss Cross," he whispered once I was completely bared to him.

He kissed my ankles, my calves. He licked the inside of my thighs. He sucked on the sensitive skin of my ribcage. He tasted me. He teased and kneaded my flesh. He didn't stop until every bit of my awareness was completely attuned to him.

Slowly, he took off his sweats and kicked them off the bed. His hard cock jerked in his palm, and I watched him stroke himself a couple times while staring at me. Veins, thick and pulsing, stuck out on his forearm as he kneeled before me. Every ripple of his abs was tense and flexed. The skull tattoo on his neck throbbed. I saw every beat of his heart, and I wanted to match mine to his.

"You have such a pretty pink pussy," he admired. It was my first instinct to slam my thighs shut in embarrassment, but the way William was looking at me made me pause.

"Feel me, William. Let's finish this," I begged.

He hooked his arms at the bend of my knees and pulled

me closer to him. I felt him bump against my entrance with his thick cock, and he raised my left leg over his shoulder. "I love you, Miss Cross," he said before sliding inside of me. My eyes widened at the thick invasion. He moved slowly at first, never once tearing his heavy gaze from mine. "Don't stop looking at me," he demanded.

I jolted from pleasure when he reached to circle my clit with his thumb.

Faster and faster. He was so deep I felt him hitting that sweet spot within me. He fucked me hard and without restraint. I made a choking sound, something raw and feral. Our skin slapped as my slick juices coated both of our sexes, making each move slippery and fast. He wasn't gentle or kind. It wasn't slow love-making. It was angry, passionate.

William was fighting for me with our bodies.

I came with a loud scream. My pulse was roaring, and every bit of my body tensed up before going limp. As I came down from the high of my orgasm, he came too. I watched as he tipped back his head, parted his mouth and silently screamed with every spurt of his hot cum. When he pulled out, it seeped out of me and soaked the sheets.

We both collapsed in heaving heaps on the mattress, our naked bodies coated with sweat.

I felt whole.

William got up and grabbed a wet washcloth. "What

are you doing?"

"Taking care of my girl," he whispered before wiping me down. I was admittedly a bit tender when he ran the washcloth along my slit. "Let me fix your braid," he whispered before throwing back on his sweats and sitting me up. Wrapping his legs around me, he fit perfectly at my back, and I sat there as he rebraided my hair.

"So beautiful," he murmured. I knew at that moment that William would always take care of me.

"I love you," I whispered. I felt braver saying it when he was at my back.

He stalled.

I jumped when his lips found my shoulder. "I love you too, Miss Cross."

It occurred to me just then that I hadn't been abandoned this time. I had three men who walked through hell and back to be with me. Both literally and figuratively. That night was the last time I heard the flies.

CORALEE JUNE

chapter thirty two

I woke up to the feeling of being watched. I could sense someone hovering over me, breathing down my neck. I slowly opened one eye and was greeted with Anthony's playful face exactly one inch from mine. "Good morning, Killer. Nick wants to have a meeting."

The sheets on our bed had fallen some and were wrapped around my waist. I lifted my arm up to stroke Anthony's cheek. "Are you okay?"

Anthony pulled back slightly and stared at the ground. "Nick wants to see us in the conference room now." He was avoiding my question. Being captured and thrown into a warehouse full of dead bodies was probably triggering for him. I wanted to hug him and discuss the demons plaguing his mind, but instead of pressuring him to talk about it with me, I took his lead and nodded instead.

"Tell Nick he can wait," William grumbled beside me. He snuggled close to me and wrapped his arm around my waist. I felt his lips on the back of my neck, and a shiver traveled down my spine at how comfortable he was—how comfortable I was, too.

Anthony shrugged and smiled at me. If he was jealous of William and me, he didn't show it. "Fine. I'll tell Nick, and you can deal with the consequences. You know he's in a grumpy mood and is looking for any reason to beat the shit out of someone. Saving his life at the warehouse got you some grace last night…" Anthony paused to snicker at me. "But he's losing his patience."

William groaned. "I'm tired."

Anthony leaned forward again and cocked his head to the side. "Tired, huh? Was it all the sex you had? How was it? Did you know that Juliet has a ticklish spot right behind her—"

"Okay," I interrupted. "Boundaries, Anthony."

"Boundaries? What are those?" he teased.

I shifted on the mattress and giggled. "Come on, William, let's go meet with Malice and figure out what the hell is going on."

William sat up in bed and scrubbed his fingernails along his scalp. Turning to look at Anthony, he scowled at his brother before saying, "I thought I locked the door."

Anthony found a shirt on the ground and tossed it at me. "You did," he replied easily. "But I picked the lock. I wanted to see Juliet."

Luckily, William and I had taken a shower last night and collapsed in bed naked. It was a fun night, but we didn't get much sleep. "You couldn't wait?" William grumbled.

"Nope," Anthony replied.

I slipped on my shorts from before and got out of bed to give Anthony a hug. The moment he wrapped his arms around me, the world faded a bit. I could feel some of his vulnerabilities in the way he held me close. It was like he was afraid to let go. His lips hovered over the shell of my ear, and he whispered to me the answer I had been looking for before. "I'm better now that I can hold you."

Anthony followed me into the bathroom and watched me brush my teeth. William took his sweet ass time getting out of bed and getting ready. He slowly gathered his clothes, brushed his teeth, and got dressed. Anthony and I watched him with our arms crossed over our chests.

"He's going to be so grumpy," Anthony warned.

William shrugged. "I don't care."

Anthony nudged me. "You and that platinum pussy

turned William into a little rebel. I love it." Anthony then snapped his fingers. "Dammit, I should've gotten a bowl of popcorn."

I was used to Anthony's lightheartedness and joking during moments of high stress. However, he was laying it on thick. I knew that he was struggling with Vicky's betrayal just as much as I was, if not more. We all had to talk about what happened last night. We were lucky to be alive, but the fight was far from over.

"Alright," William began, "let's go."

We made our way to the conference room, with Anthony making little jokes as we went. He had a ton of energy and looked for any excuse to touch me as we moved. I was happy to provide him with whatever comfort I could.

In the conference room, Malice sat at the head of the table. He had both of his forearms resting against the edge, with his fingers laced together. The angry look on his face made a sense of dread pool in my gut.

But also, seeing him angry thrilled me.

I had given up on questioning why Malice had such a conflicting effect on me. He was exciting and passionate but also terrifying. He brought out the darkest parts of me, and I reveled in it. "You took long enough," he complained. We were off to a great start.

Anthony clapped his hands and found a seat in the middle of the table. William moved to pull out a chair for me, but Malice stopped him. "Sit in my lap, Little Fighter." His demand made my skin warm.

William challenged me with a hard stare. I knew that he wanted me to sit with him, but if we were ever going to navigate the dynamics of our relationship, I would have to set boundaries. I hadn't seen Malice since the explosion, and I needed to be close to him too.

"I'm going to sit with him," I whispered.

William didn't respond.

Slowly, I walked over to Malice, taking in his appearance with fresh eyes. There was a small cut on the corner of his lip and a light bruise on his jaw. His hair was messy from what I assumed was a late night of searching for Vicky, and his clothes were unbuttoned and slightly wrinkled. Up close, he still smelled like smoke, as if it were embedded in his skin, permanently altering him forever.

Though Malice had his arms covered, I still scanned the expanse of his body. I looked for burns or bruises and cuts. "Sit in my lap," he demanded while scooting back. I moved to sit on his thighs, but he twisted me around so that we were facing one another. I straddled his legs and blushed. It was an intimate position that forced us to look each other in the eye. I knew that everything Malice did was intentional, and he had a purpose for forcing me to sit on him this way in front of William and Anthony.

"First order of business," he said while keeping his eyes

locked on me. "Vicky is gone. Her tracking device has been disabled. I had an informant notify me that she was long gone."

Part of me was sad to hear this, but part of me was relieved, too. I wanted Vicky to be safe despite all the pain she had caused. I saw what Malice did to rats. Loyalty was his number one requirement for being a member of his Mafia—for being a member of this family. Vicky had a death sentence hanging over her head for what she had done to us, and even though I struggled to understand why she was so willing to end my life, I didn't want the same for her.

"So what do we do?" Anthony asked, his voice sounding vulnerable. I twisted on Malice's lap to look at him, but Malice reached up to grab my chin, forcing my attention back to him.

"We send a message that if Vicky comes back, she's dead," Malice said, his tone yielding no room for argument.

"She's our sister, Nick," Anthony said.

"And she tried having us killed. She would have been successful if Cora wasn't completely incompetent. She was so worried about having the last word with her stupid fucking video that they didn't time things well. We barely survived."

"Vicky has always had a flair for the dramatic," William noted.

"She's lucky I'm not hunting her down. A traitor is still a traitor, blood be damned." Once more, I tried to turn and see Anthony's reaction to all of this, but Malice gripped me harder. "How do you feel about that decision, Juliet?"

"I don't want her to die," I admitted. "I love her still and hope she stays away." Malice nodded.

"What about Cora?" William interrupted.

Malice didn't look at his brother. "I'm working on it. She's been breathing my goddamn air for far too long. It's time for her to die." Malice's words sent a shockwave of power and silence through the room. "No more fucking around. I want a million dollar bounty placed on her head. I don't care who kills her or how anymore, she's done."

"You always said you wanted to do it, though," Anthony argued.

Malice looked at me. "I've got more important things to worry about right now," he said softly.

"I support that," William replied. "Let's kill the bitch."

"Well alright then. I'm in," Anthony echoed.

"Great. Put the hit out," Malice replied, as if killing her was an easy decision to make. "Next order of business," he said through gritted teeth. "I think we had a bit of a misunderstanding, Little Fighter. Tell me about it."

I straightened my spine defiantly. I knew we'd have to talk about this eventually, but I wasn't prepared to do it in front of an audience. "You made it sound like I was just someone you were using to get to William," I explained. "It hurt."

Behind me, someone shifted in their seat, making a squeaking sound that cut through the tension of the room. "Tell me why it hurt," Malice demanded.

"I thought we were more than that," I admitted.

Malice stood up and lifted me onto the conference table, not once removing his eyes from mine. "More how, Little Fighter?" he prodded. I hated how he was pulling the truth from my teeth, I didn't want to sound or feel foolish admitting the feelings I had for him.

"I thought we were..." He tipped his head to the side, as if to hear me better. "I thought we were possibly together... for real."

"I see. Do you remember the conversation we had when negotiating your salary?"

He reached for the hem of my shirt and lifted it slightly. With a blush, I snapped my hands down, trying to push him away. "S-stop," I protested.

"Answer my question," Malice growled.

"Yep, definitely should have brought popcorn," Anthony added. This conversation was difficult enough, I hated that William and Anthony had front row seats to the entire spectacle.

"Yes, I remember," I forced out as he ripped the fabric of my shirt and tore it from my body. Immediately, I wrapped my arms around my bare breasts and gasped.

"What did I say about knowing your worth?" Malice asked before pressing his palm to my chest and forcing me to lie down on the cool conference room table.

"You told me not to undervalue myself."

Malice tore my soft shorts off my body, baring me to the entire room. "Let me make myself perfectly clear," Malice said. "You are the most precious person in my life now. More valuable than any single possession I own. More valuable than family, than my work, than my own needs and desires. I don't fucking make declarations of love, but when I say I own you…" He paused to unbuckle his pants and pull out his hard, pierced cock. "I mean it."

Malice slammed into me, jolting the table. I let out a scream of pleasure, and he gripped my hips, fucking me raw and unyielding. I moaned and writhed on the table, forgetting where we were and who was watching.

But not for long.

"Sit your fucking ass down. I want you to see this, William," Malice yelled, veins bulging as he reached for my nipple and pinched it. I looked up slightly and saw out of the corner of my vision that William had his hand on the doorknob and was ready to leave. "If you walk out of here, then you are nothing but a fucking coward. I let you have a taste last night because I owed you, but if you want Juliet, then you have to prove it."

I cried out as Malice pulled out, the sudden absence of him making me feel empty. He pulled me forward and flipped me on my stomach with one strong sweep of his arms. I pressed both palms into the wood, and he positioned himself at my entrance and slipped inside once more.

"You have the most perfect pussy," he moaned. "So tight. I love the way it wraps around my cock. Look at you, getting my table wet. I'm going to run my empire on this table and think only of you."

I shuddered when he reared back and slapped my ass. It was a shocking sort of pain that made my eyes fill with hot tears. I lifted up and locked eyes with William. He looked horrified by what was happening, but also frozen to the spot.

I licked my lips and mouthed the only thing I knew that would help. "I love you."

After a few breaths, he moved back to his seat and sat down to watch the spectacle.

I took every inch of Malice and turned my head to see Anthony, who was leaning close to me, trying to get as close as possible. Sweat dripped down my brow, and that building pleasure started to rise inside of me. Anthony licked his lips and adjusted his pants before reaching out to touch me.

"No!" Malice yelled before jerking me off the table and forcing me to stand on shaky legs in front of him. I wanted him inside of me again. Malice wrapped his arms around me and started flicking, pinching, and rolling my clit while he glared over my shoulder at his brothers. "Juliet is mine. If you touch her, it's on my terms. If you have her, it's because I'm gracious enough to share. Every kiss, every fuck, every word that comes out of her mouth, every thought in her beautiful mind is mine. If you want even a sliver of her time or affection, you understand that right here, right now."

I moaned and sobbed, the pleasure was too much. He was working me fast and hard. My legs trembled, and he was the only thing keeping me upright.

"I understand," Anthony said immediately. Through the haze of my pleasure, I looked to him. His eyes were heavy with lust. Though the table was hiding most of him, I could see that he was moving his hand over his lap, the jerky strokes were impossible to miss.

Malice spun me around and kissed me. It was this intense, open-mouthed deviant sort of kiss. Sloppy and coated with slobber and my tears. He wrapped his hand around my neck and squeezed in a threatening way. With my body pressed to his and the smell of smoke settling between us, I got high on the overwhelming sensations. He kissed me for a long while; it was devotion, it was damning.

When he pulled away, my pulse was roaring so loudly that I almost didn't hear William speak.

"I understand," he whispered, soft and defeated.

I didn't turn around to face him. William needed the full effect of his decision. I loved all of them, but I belonged to Malice. He lifted me up and walked me over to the wall. With my legs wrapped around his waist, Malice slid inside of me and started fucking me right there, his impressive strength keeping us both upright as he slammed in and out of me.

"Fuck!" he screamed. "Take that cock. I can't wait to see my cum seeping out of your pussy."

I slammed my head back on the wall and dug my nails into the back of his neck. Harder, faster. I panted and whimpered on every thrust. Yes, yes, yes...

I came like a bullet out of a gun. Powerful, deadly. Both of us were screaming, panting, tensing, relaxing. Every nerve was spent. He heaved in and out, going still on a thrust and holding onto me for dear life, with his mouth pressed against mine and my hands threaded through his hair. It was rough and passionate. I felt completely owned by him.

"Mine," Malice whispered once the aftershocks had disappeared.

I looked at him, my head clear for the first time since I met him. "Yours," I agreed.

chapter thirty three

one week later...

Malice: When are you telling her?

I rolled my eyes at the text message. Grams had been home all of two hours, and Malice was already bothering me about moving in. I wasn't quite ready to let go of my bedroom here. I was dating all three of them, but it was new. Grams didn't know half of what I'd been up to, and it was time to come clean about at least some of it. I loved the sleepovers, but I liked having my own space away from them, too. Malice had this overbearing personality, and I didn't want to completely lose myself to his ownership or Anthony's needs or William's affections. At least not yet.

Juliet: I'm not moving in.

"Who is texting you this late?" Grams asked. Her skin was sun-kissed, and she looked more vibrant than I'd seen her in ages. From the moment I picked her up at the airport, she talked about her trip and hadn't stopped even now.

"Ma-Nick," I replied. Grams didn't know him by his deadly alter ego.

She stopped unpacking her suitcase to grin at me. "Nick? Every time I called while I was gone, you were with him. Are you dating now?"

It was now or never, I supposed. "I'm actually dating him and his two brothers," I blurted out.

Grams rolled her eyes. "You don't have to make jokes, I was only asking because I haven't seen you in an entire month."

I let out a shaky exhale. "I was being serious. I'm dating all three of them. William, Anthony, and Nick."

Grams nodded her head like she was hearing me, but squinted her eyes like she couldn't make sense of what I was saying. "Three men?"

"Three."

"Do they know this?"

"Yes."

"And are they okay with it?"

"Nope," I replied, sticking with honesty.

Grams grabbed one of her bras in the bottom of the suitcase and tossed it at me. "Hussy! I told you to live a little, and you went and l-lived," she exclaimed with a giggle before sitting down on the edge of her bed.

"Three men. You're still taking your birth control, right?"

I rounded the bed to give her a stern look. "I'm not ready to be a mother," I confirmed.

She patted her heart and smiled. "Good. So, tell me about them," she pressed on.

Well, this was going to be hard. "Well...they're... they're..."

A knock on the door stopped me from having to tell Grams that my three boyfriends were murdering Mafia men. "I'll get that," I rushed out.

"This conversation isn't over," Grams scolded.

I jogged down the hall, my short summer dress swishing at my thighs as I moved. After peering through the peephole, I grinned and opened the door.

"What are you wearing, Anthony?" I asked, scanning him up and down. Clinging to his lean frame was a perfectly tailored black suit. His hair was combed, and he had a dozen red roses in his clenched fist.

"I have to make a good first impression, Killer," he said in a way that made me think it was supposed to be obvious.

I looked back over my shoulder. Grams was still in her room unpacking. "I'm not sure now is a good time. She had a long day of traveling and—"

"Grams!" Anthony exclaimed. "I'm home!" He pushed past me, pausing to kiss me on the cheek before strutting inside like he owned the place.

Grams exited her bedroom with a confused look on her face. "Do I know you?" she croaked while patting her hair.

"Not yet, but we're practically family," Anthony replied with a wicked grin. Once they were toe to toe, Anthony handed Grams the bouquet of flowers and bowed. "I couldn't decide between getting you a cat or this cool retro record player I found online. I was trying to find something old ladies like, but William told me that flowers were more appropriate."

After a very long, excruciating pause, Grams let out a snort. "I've always wanted a cat...," she joked.

"I knew it!" Anthony exclaimed. "I can't wait to rub this in William's face." Anthony fist pumped the air, making my Grams flinch in surprise. "Wait right here. I have a back-up cat waiting in the car in case the flowers didn't work." My eyes widened, and Grams looked stuck between laughing as if he was joking or checking his forehead for a fever. "Be right back!"

MALICE

Anthony turned on his heel and sprinted back out the front door. "Juliet," Grams hissed. "Who in the h-hell is th-that?"

I peered outside. Anthony was trying to wrangle a kitten from the back seat of his BMW. "That's Anthony," I replied. Fuck, I loved him.

"Is he alright?"

"Most of the time," I answered honestly.

Grams shook her head in disbelief. I continued to stare out the front door. Anthony had a kennel, a large bag of cat food, a litter box and some toys. "Do you love him?" she asked, this time her tone gentler.

"Yes," I whispered, zero hesitation in my voice.

Grams shrugged. "Well, I guess I love him too. Go help the poor boy bring all that in." I giggled, then smiled affectionately at her. Grams really did make it easy. She opened her heart without reservation and loved me so much that it extended to anyone that I loved. "What the fuck am I going to do with a cat?" she mumbled under her breath as I walked out the front door.

—

"I cannot believe you asked Grams if you could spend the night."

"I wanted to be here in case Jeffrey needed anything," he protested. Jeffrey was Grams's new cat. Surprisingly, she had instantly become attached to the little black fur ball and was completely delighted by Anthony's gift.

"And now we're both crammed on a twin mattress," I grumbled. Anthony petted my hair and stroked my back. I was lying on his chest with my legs between his.

"I could sleep like this every night," he whispered before bending down to kiss the top of my head. Physical affection was getting easier for him. I had been worried that Vicky's betrayal would set him back, but if anything, it made him touchier. Anytime we were together, he'd grab my hand or wrap his arms around my waist and hold me close.

I traced my finger over his chest. "Anthony?"

"Yeah, Killer?"

"Thank you for coming today. I'm still not sure how I'm going to tell Grams about everything. It almost feels selfish to involve her. Once she knows, she can't ever not know. And what will she think about my job? Malice keeps pressuring me to move in and—"

Anthony pressed the tip of his finger to my lips. "For starters, Nick can be patient. He wants you home because he cares about you and it freaks him out that you're away unprotected."

I rolled my eyes. "I literally saw three cars full of guards parked outside, Anthony."

He ignored me. "Anyway...something tells me that you could be completely honest with your grandmother and she'd still love you, gory details and all."

"I just don't want to scare her."

"Then don't. Be honest, with flare." He waved his hand to accentuate the point.

"Can you give me an example?"

"Instead of saying your boyfriend is in the Mafia, say he's an entrepreneur," he said, eyebrows raised. "Eh? It works, right?"

"Right," I replied, unconvinced.

"Instead of saying you work at a sex club, say you're a hostess at a nightclub that specializes in evening entertainment."

I was not going to do that, but I was enjoying his spin on things regardless.

"Instead of saying my best friend tried to kill me?" I asked, my tone bitter.

Anthony let out a low sigh. "Say your best friend felt so trapped in her circumstances that she did something horrible to escape." Anthony had a faraway look in his eyes. We'd talked some about Vicky since the explosion, but he didn't want to open up. Like me, he missed his sister but felt conflicted about it. "And instead of saying you're dating a fucked up man who talks to the dead and has debilitating nightmares..." His voice turned haunted.

I threaded my hands through his, then finished his statement. "I'm dating a man who can make me smile no matter the situation. Someone who is thoughtful, kind, selfless, and strong. I'm in love with someone who makes me very happy, despite all the crazy shit happening."

Anthony shifted, then sat up. "I don't want to mess this up. I'm not always"—he paused to tap his temple—"here, you know?"

I grabbed his hand and pressed it to my heart. "You're always here, though," I whispered. His eyes watered for a moment, and I felt like this was a defining moment for us. Time slowed, my pulse roared in my ears.

I cared for Anthony and loved every version of him. "So let me get this straight," he began. "I'm always...in your tit?" I looked down and realized that he was holding my tit with his massive hand. Pervert. I shoved his hand away and tackled him into the mattress with a giggle.

"We should probably fuck now, I mean we just shared a sentimental moment and everything," he teased while tugging at the hem of my faded shirt.

I swatted him away. "Grams is asleep in the next room," I argued.

"So?"

"So, this bed squeaks!"

"We can fuck on the floor, we've never done that before. Or in the closet. That sounds kind of kinky."

"It's not happening, Anthony!" I replied before playfully shoving him.

Anthony grabbed my arms and eased me off of him.

Then, he stood up and lifted me out of the bed. "I know what you're thinking right now," he whispered while cradling me to his chest and sneaking me out of my bedroom. He padded down the hall and to the front door. The floorboards creaked, and I knew without a shadow of a doubt that Grams was going to wake up.

"Anthony!" I hissed.

"You're thinking, damn, my boyfriend is strong. Well, let me tell you, that's from all the dead bodies I bury. It should really be a workout regimen." Anthony carried me all the way to his BMW, unlocked the door, and tossed me in the backseat. "Back seat of my car is, in fact, on my sex bucket list," he said while rubbing his palms together and settling next to me.

"You have a list?" I asked.

He immediately started rattling off places, some of them so bizarre that I wasn't sure if he was joking or not. "Cemetery, funeral home, a crypt, a Catholic church, Area 51, Target dressing room, the park, a pond, the pool, the White House, a bounce house, a—"

I pressed my hand over his mouth and leaned in. "Can I kiss you, Anthony?" I asked.

He stared at my mouth for a long moment, and I moved my hand. "Can I have you forever, Killer?" he asked back softly.

I kissed him.

CORALEE JUNE

chapter thirty four

I woke up alone in my twin-sized bed but could hear Anthony laughing with Grams down the hall in the kitchen. The early morning sun was creeping through the cracks in my blinds, and my neck was sore from sleeping at a weird angle all night. Anthony took up the entire bed. If we were going to keep doing sleepovers, then I needed a full-sized mattress.

Grams laughed. "Are you making my granddaughter dick-shaped pancakes, Anthony?"

Of course he was. I shot out of bed and let out a huff.

That definitely sounded like something he would do. "I've never made pancakes before, the possibilities are endless!"

After getting dressed, brushing my teeth, and throwing my messy brown hair up in a bun, I made my way to the kitchen and found both of them wearing aprons and flipping pancakes.

Bowls, flour, sugar, and other baking items were scattered over the countertops, and the roses Anthony got Grams last night were in a vase on our kitchen table. The room smelled like freshly brewed coffee and syrup. Grams and I loved to make breakfast together. It was one of our many little traditions.

"Good morning!" Anthony said while swaying from side to side. He looked happier than I'd seen him in days. Grams had that effect on people. He put one sassy hand on his hip and winked at me. "I'm making pancakes!"

"I see that," I replied.

Grams grabbed a handful of chocolate chips and tossed them in the batter. "Morning, baby," she said distractedly. My heart swelled at the sight of them together. It felt so normal. Like they'd been doing this for years.

"More chocolate?" Anthony asked before putting his hand to his chest in mock horror. "William hates sweets."

"Is William coming over?" I asked.

Grams looked over her shoulder at me and arched her brow. "And Nicholas. I thought it would be nice for all of us to eat together."

I crossed my arms over my chest. "So nosy," I hissed.

"I d-do my best," she teased back.

The doorbell rang, which put a halt to our familial banter. Grams and I hadn't had time to discuss my unique relationship status yet, but as usual, she was rolling with the punches. I should have known that she and Anthony would have coordinated a nice little breakfast for all of us. I just prayed that it wasn't awkward.

"Go get the door, baby. I have to keep an eye on Anthony to make sure he doesn't burn another pancake," Grams said before swatting the top of his hand. "No more penises, Anthony, so help me!"

I watched them fuss for a few seconds before turning to answer the door. I wondered briefly if I needed to change clothes as I walked down the hall, but decided it didn't need to be a formal event. I opened the door with a shy smile. William and Malice were standing on our porch, both wearing suits, both clutching bouquets of flowers, both looking handsome as hell.

"Fancy seeing you here," I said. William crossed the threshold to kiss me on the cheek. It was warm and pleasant. I wrapped my arms around him and nuzzled his neck. "I'm glad you're here."

William kissed the top of my head and pulled away. "I heard about the cat," he grumbled. "I told him not to."

"Anthony rarely listens. She loved the gesture, though. You'll never live it down," I teased. "She loves Jeffrey."

"How am I going to top that, huh? I was researching luxury cat tree condos this morning," he joked back.

I kissed him on the mouth and groaned at his minty taste. Malice cleared his throat. I didn't break the kiss, though. He could wait a minute. Part of me thrilled in breaking his rules a little bit; it made Malice want to stake his claim, and I benefited from his jealousy more than anything.

"Enough," Malice growled.

William pulled away and rolled his eyes. "I want to take you to dinner tonight," he said, ignoring his brother. The two of them lived in a precarious battle, stuck between challenging one another and accepting the alpha dynamic Malice established.

"It's a date," I replied.

"William?!" Grams said. I hadn't even heard her approach. "I know you."

What? I looked between Grams and William, suddenly feeling very confused. "Do you know each other?"

"I can explain," William said.

"This man sits with me at the bus stop on Wednesdays," Grams said. "You know, for bingo night. Our schedules always aligned, and we'd sit together."

"Sneaky bastard," Malice mumbled under his breath.

William didn't even look ashamed, just embarrassed more than anything. "It wasn't creepy or anything," he rushed out. "You had just mentioned to Vicky one time that you were worried about her riding the bus alone but didn't want to take away her independence. So I started meeting her there. I hope that's okay."

I smiled. My secret stranger was full of thoughtful secrets. He was always looking out for me. "You mean to tell me that the girl you've been in love with all these years is my granddaughter?" Grams asked.

William cleared his throat. "The bus ride is an hour long. We've had a lot of time to chat," he explained.

I stared at him with stark disbelief. "You've really been secretly hanging out with my Grams all this time?" I asked. "That's so thoughtful."

William smiled sheepishly at Grams before stepping closer to me. "I would do anything for you," he whispered.

My heart swelled for this man. I didn't think it was possible to love him more than I already did, but this just furthered my resolve to fight for all of them.

"Nicholas, it's so good to see you again," Grams said, putting our moment on pause.

"It's lovely to see you too, Ruthie." His voice was thick, and I wondered if he struggled with being slapped in the face with my history with William. All of us would have to learn how to navigate this jealousy. It would take time to find a groove, but I had faith that we would.

Grams linked her arm with William's. "Come help me cook. We can discuss this double life you've been living."

I watched the two of them walk toward the kitchen, and once they were out of sight, Malice approached me. "Sleep well, Little Fighter?" he asked before tucking a stray hair behind my cheek. I leaned into his touch and closed my eyes. My heart was already picking up.

"No," I groaned. "Anthony stole the covers, and my bed wasn't really big enough for the two of us."

"I could fix that problem," Malice taunted. "Your bed at the mansion is plenty big enough."

"But the mansion doesn't have Grams," I argued.

"I could fix that, too. Have a little guest house built for her."

I reached up to grab the lapels of his suit jacket and pulled him in. Hovering my lips over his mouth, I spoke. "No, Malice."

He looked down his nose at my lips and exhaled. "Call me Nick," he whispered.

I wasn't expecting the tears that spilled from my eyes, but I suddenly became overwhelmed with emotions. "Nick?" I asked, testing the name on my tongue. It felt both wrong to call him that and oh, so right.

"Nick," he replied sternly. He let out a slow exhale. "And okay. I won't pressure you about it anymore."

My brows rose. I wasn't expecting him to give up that easily. "Really?"

He looked around, as if making sure no one could hear him. It was an oddly vulnerable move. "I want you to be happy," he whispered. "I'll take you on dates—"

"You said you don't do dates," I interrupted.

"Well, for you, I fucking will. I want you to live where you want to live, be who you want to be. If you want to go to college, I'll follow you."

"Nick..." His name made a shiver travel down my spine. I didn't know what to say.

He averted his eyes. "Vicky felt trapped by me, and I don't want you to feel that way too," he admitted. "As much as you're mine, I'm yours." I blushed and swooned and felt my heart sink a little deeper for this dangerous man. I never thought I'd hear him say such sentimental things. "One more thing..." Nick dug into his pocket and pulled out a small, familiar box and an opened envelope. "This arrived at the house for you. I already read it. I wanted to make sure..."

I grabbed the envelope first and quickly pulled out the note inside.

Juliet,

I'm not sure what to say. I wanted freedom. You wanted them. Take care of yourself.

Vicky

"She gave back the necklace," Nick said while taking it out of the box and draping it around my neck. We stood face-to-face as he clasped it. "I had it inspected. It's safe to wear." When he was done putting it on, I reached up and brushed my hand along the chain.

"Why would she send it back?" I asked.

"Guilt, theatrics, redemption. Who knows?"

A heavy weight settled on my chest. I wanted answers. This letter felt lackluster and anticlimactic after everything we'd been through. I wish that Vicky would have given us the chance to make it better. I couldn't help but look back on our friendship and question everything. Was she always this selfish? Was she always this self-absorbed? Like many mysteries in my life, I'd never know.

"It feels wrong," I admitted. "Vicky was my only friend for three years. I'm sad but also detached about it. She almost killed me, then abandoned me. I thought we were more than that. Maybe we weren't. I'm alive and with you…"

"You don't have to cry just because you think you're supposed to be sad that she's gone, Little Fighter."

"I just want to be done with her," I replied before crushing the letter I'm my fist and tossing it on the floor. In a box, then a smaller box…lock it away.

"Come on," Nick said before raising his voice. "Ruthie! I'm ready for pancakes."

Nick placed his hand at my back, spinning me around and guiding me toward the kitchen.

Inside, Grams was giggling and cooking with William and Anthony. "Come give me a hug and roll up your sleeves. Anthony is making quite the mess of things."

"Yes, ma'am," Nick said. "Just one more thing." We paused in the entryway of the kitchen, and he bent down to kiss me on the cheek. From the corner of my eye, I saw Grams clutch her chest and swoon.

I watched as William and Anthony fought over the spatula, and Nick set the table. Grams walked over to me. "I like them enough, I suppose," Grams said before nudging me playfully.

"So you approve?" I asked. Every single man stopped what they were doing to listen to her answer.

"I do," she whispered back.

"But I'm the favorite, just so everyone is clear," Anthony said with a silly shimmy before taking a plate stacked high with pancakes and setting it on the table. "Time to eat. The penis pancakes are strictly for Juliet."

"I don't have favorites," Grams replied before winking at William. I really wanted to know more about their little bus stop dates. She was obviously very close to him.

"But if you did have favorites, it would most definitely

be me," Anthony argued.

"Yeah right," William muttered.

"You're just mad that I'm Grams's favorite because I got her a cat."

Grams giggled to herself and shuffled to her seat. Since we only had three chairs, Nick leaned against the countertop with his plate in hand, Anthony sat next to Grams, and I awkwardly sat in William's lap. He politely cut up my penis-shaped pancake and fed me little bites. It was weird, but Grams didn't mind. If anything, she seemed happy.

I had never felt as loved as I did in that moment. I was surrounded by people who cared about me. For so long, it had been Grams and I, but now we had a small army. It wasn't an easy road, but it was ours. Grams and I had spent many nights sitting at this table and staring at Mom's empty seat, wondering where she was or what she was up to. I never really felt whole. The unanswered questions used to plague me, but now I felt like I was taking the first step to moving forward with my life.

You never really moved on from the loss of someone you love. You just learned how to cope with their absence. And these men were filling a void in my life that I didn't even know I had.

I looked at Anthony, my soulmate. William, my stranger, and Nick, my savior. In finding them, life became less about the unanswered questions and more about living my truth.

Author's Note:

Thank you so much for reading Malice. If you enjoyed it, I hope you'll leave a review. If you hated it, I hope you still leave a review.

I know some of you might be upset that we never find out what happened to Juliet's mother. Unfortunately, that is the reality for family members of most missing persons. Juliet's journey in this book was to let go of the unanswered questions and heal. I think the Civella brothers helped her in that regard.

I used several Kansas City area locations as inspirations, but they are not meant to be accurate in this fictional world. The Kansas City Butcher's home was demolished over twenty years ago, but it made for a cool scene in the book. I also wanted to mention that the name Nicholas Civella was inspired by a once powerful mob boss; however, this is a work of fiction. Names, characters, businesses, events and incidents are the products of my imagination. Any resemblance to actual persons, living or dead, or actual events is purely coincidental.

I truly had to fight for every single word in the book.

I started writing Malice early this year when my grandmother passed away. She was my best friend and my biggest cheerleader. The idea for this book started with her. It started with grief and pain and anger.

Due to Covid restrictions, we were unable to have a funeral for her, but maybe if I can share with you all a bit of who she was, it'll help with this massive hole left in my heart. Some of you might think it's strange to commemorate her in a book like Malice. Maybe it is. But Memaw appreciated the best and worst parts of me. She loved, she didn't judge.

The first book I ever wrote was called Little Blue Car. It was a short picture book about my grandmother's Buick and how I'd see it all around town. At my recitals. At my softball games. At the school pick-up line. At my favorite ice cream shop. In front of my house. At Girl Scout meetings. At the park. On vacations.

My Memaw was so proud of that book. She printed it off, handed it out, and emailed it to everyone she could. It wasn't until I got older that I realized the story wasn't about a beat-up Buick. It was about the love of a grandmother.

There are very few childhood memories that don't feature my Memaw. We lived down the street—close enough for me to ride my bike to her house for dinner. She was funny. She was witty. She was my best friend.

Memaw fiercely loved her children, grandchildren, and great-grandchildren. She was kind. She was generous. She made the best pumpkin pie and blushed when my husband gave her flowers for Valentine's Day. She collected cow figurines and tea pots and friends and hugs. She was an incredible proofreader and taught me how to have a proper tea party. She also taught me how to be grateful and treat everyone with kindness.

We loved to get Big Macs after school. We used to walk laps at the park by her house and feed the ducks stale bread.

She loved baked stuffed lobster. She loved having her family all together. She loved traveling the world and collecting magnets from every place she'd been. Her fridge was completely filled from her travels.

Memaw was a worrier. She was the kind of woman to call before a thunderstorm to check on you. She was also the kind of grandmother to put five dollars in your gas tank when you visited. She loved thank-you cards and would spank your ass if you didn't write one.

She was hilarious. She once chased a hovercraft balloon for six blocks on a windy day because she'd paid $19.99 for it. I still to this day wonder what her neighbors thought when they saw my seventy-five-year-old grandmother running through the streets, yelling, "Catch the hovercraft!!!"

Memaw grew up in what our family lovingly calls "The Old Place." It was a tiny cabin surrounded by lavender roses that were planted by her grandmother. She used to brag to anyone who would listen that she was Grandpa Kitchen's favorite growing up. Her childhood was spent working on the farm and whispering to the ghost of her Aunt Pearl, who supposedly haunted the place. She was a Depression-era baby who could stretch a dollar, and her parents ran moonshine on their property during Prohibition.

She was a military spouse and lived in Germany with her family until her husband—the love of her life and a pilot—tragically passed away. She volunteered at Walter Reed Hospital and not only went to The Ed Sullivan Show numerous times, but she also received a couple of invitations to dinner at the White House.

Memaw was adventurous and used to race her blue Austin-Healey on the 410 in DC on her way home from work. She loved all animals and had a goat farm that brought her a lot of joy. She was convinced that her grandfather could talk to animals and that the ability was passed down in our family. She was very proud of her family.

She used to tell us that when she died, she didn't want us to be sad. She didn't want us to cry. She wanted us to sit around a big table and tell funny stories about her life.

I'm so thankful for a lifetime of seeing that Little Blue Car everywhere I went.

I'm so thankful for a Memaw that loved me as much as she did.

CORALEE JUNE

Acknowledgements:

This book would not have been possible without the support and love of Christina Santos and Christine Estevez. I could not do what I do without them.

I would like to especially thank Katie Friend, Meggan Reed, HarleyQuinn Zaler, Savannah Richey, Lauren Campbell, Mercedez Potts, and Claire Jones for beta reading. Thank you for the late night messages, encouragement, and calls. I am so thankful for each of you and truly appreciate all the hours you put into reading my messy manuscripts.

I am grateful to all of those whom I have had the pleasure of working with during this book. I'd like to especially recognize my editor, Helayna Trask. She always takes the time to dive into the worlds I create and make sure they are perfect for you all. I would also like to thank all the dedicated members of The Zone and Cora's Crew.

I would like to also thank Angel Hall, Tenika Spells, Jade Ford, Heather Olson, and Caitlyn Childress for their support and inspiration during this book. You helped me cultivate details that brought this story to life, and I sincerely thank you for that.

CoraLee June

MALICE

Made in the USA
Middletown, DE
01 October 2021